It's a Wonderful Wife

JANET CHAPMAN

JOVE BOOKS, NEW YORK

JOVE

An imprint of Penguin Random House LLC
375 Hudson Street, New York, New York 10014

IT'S A WONDERFUL WIFE

A Jove Book / published by arrangement with the author

ISBN: 978-0-515-15515-0

PUBLISHING HISTORY
Jove mass-market edition / September 2015

PRINTED IN THE UNITED STATES OF AMERICA

10   9   8   7   6   5   4   3   2   1

Cover illustration by Jim Griffin.
Cover design by George Long.
Text design by Laura K. Corless.

Penguin
Random
House

ONE

❧

Jesse stole a quick glance at the dash of his pickup in hopes the navigation device knew where it was, because he sure as hell didn't. Forget that he hadn't met any cars since turning onto the winding, narrow road half an hour ago; the power lines had stopped at the last house he'd passed some eight miles back. He checked his right-hand outside mirror only to see the tires on the camper were barely staying on the asphalt, and wondered what had made him think leaving Route One while hauling a forty-foot-long fifth-wheel had been a good idea.

At least he had a place to sleep if he didn't reach civilization by nightfall. He'd be going to bed hungry, though, because he had planned to stock his cupboards in Castle Cove tomorrow morning before loading the camper on a barge for its short voyage to Hundred Acre

Isle. But the farther down the desolate road he drove, the more it looked like he might have to reschedule, all because he hadn't been able to wait two days to get a look at the house he was having designed.

Not that Stanley Kerr, of Glace & Kerr Architecture, was expecting him today. But rather than reassuring Jesse that everything was right on schedule, the vague drawings of a very modern kitchen Stanley had emailed him three weeks ago had only fueled his impatience. So instead of getting the camper settled on the island and backtracking over an hour on Friday, he'd decided to cut across to Whistler's Landing this afternoon on the chance the architectural model he'd commissioned had arrived a couple of days early. But even if it hadn't, he could at least see the preliminary plans the model builders would have used, and maybe talk Stanley into giving him a copy. That way he could spend the week studying the layout while imagining he was sitting on his new porch overlooking the Gulf of Maine—which he'd be doing this time next year if everything *stayed* on schedule—and decide on any changes he might want to make.

Jesse had purchased the island that sat three nautical miles offshore of Castle Cove the very day he'd set foot on it late last summer. He'd then spent the next six months traveling from New York to Maine to look at houses and interview homeowners before settling on an architect he was confident could give him the state-of-the-art yet unpretentious home he wanted. Hundred Acre Isle was to be his sanctuary from the corporate world, the place his children would run free every summer, his . . . Rosebriar. But where his grandfather's sprawling estate north of New York City had been Abram Sinclair's deliberately pretentious testament to his love for Grammy Rose, Jesse had decided to build *before* finding the woman of his dreams.

That is, assuming such a paragon even existed.

Because despite his grandfather's best efforts, Jesse had become an expert at dodging all the marriage-minded women the scheming old wolf had constantly thrown in his path. But seeing how wedded bliss appeared to agree with his two older brothers, he'd started worrying he might in fact be missing out. And since both Sam and Ben had found the women of their dreams in Maine . . . well, maybe the state could pony up one more Sinclair bride.

Not that he intended to marry the first beauty to catch his eye simply so he'd stop rattling around Rosebriar all alone but for a way-too-familial staff. Yet he really couldn't see himself settling in for the long haul with any of the self-absorbed and high-maintenance women he was in the habit of dating, any more than he could see his current interest, Miss Pamela Bowden, spending her summers chasing a passel of kids around an isolated island. Which meant he really needed to start dating *mother*-minded women if he hoped to have children close in age to their cousins, seeing how his two older brothers already had a three-year head start on him. In fact, Sam was expecting his second little bundle of joy in October.

Getting two of his grandsons to the altar from his grave had been quite a coup for Bram, considering all three men had been experts at dodging women. But Sam had married Willa within six weeks of following her home to Keelstone Cove—which, ironically, had been exactly six weeks after Bram's death—and Ben had given Emma less than two weeks to plan her wedding not a month after showing up at her sporting camps in the western mountains of Maine.

But then, Sinclair men did have a reputation for moving quickly once they made up their minds about something—in matters of the heart as well as business, apparently.

Jesse crested yet another blind knoll and immediately slowed to a crawl when he spotted the car parked just off the pavement, its two right tires nearly touching the water of an encroaching bog. And even though flames were shooting above the raised hood of the late-model luxury sedan, he didn't dare brake to a stop for fear of being rear-ended if someone should crest the knoll behind him.

It was just as he swerved to the other side of the road to get past the car that he spotted the woman up ahead, who had stopped walking and turned at the sound of his engine. She was carrying a large white box, there were no fewer than a dozen brightly colored balloons tied to the bulging purse hiked up on her shoulder, and he couldn't help noticing her expression go from hopeful to disappointed. Obviously seeing he wasn't a local, she started walking again, apparently unconcerned that her car was on fire.

Jesse continued past her, edged to the side of the road as far as he dared, and brought his rig to a stop on the crest of another knoll so it could be seen by anyone traveling from either direction. He set the park brake as an extra precaution, shut off the engine and got out, and walked down the length of the camper. "Have you called 911?"

he asked, only to watch the swirling balloons knock her wide-brimmed hat askew when she stopped a good twenty yards from him.

"No," she said, shifting what appeared to be a pastry box to one arm and righting her hat. "I was afraid they'd get here before the car was totaled."

Jesse stilled in the act of pulling out his cell phone. "You *want* it to burn?"

"Right down to its four crappy tires," she shot back, her curt nod making her hat slip sideways again. Only this time instead of righting it, she pulled it off and sent it sailing into the woods. She glanced back at the car, which now had black smoke billowing out all four open windows, and shrugged. "It's not close enough to any trees to start a forest fire," she said as she started walking again. "I'll call it in when I get to town."

"How far would that be?" Jesse asked, moving into the road when he realized she intended to walk right past him. "I'll give you a ride."

She stopped again. "Thank you, but I'll walk. It's only about a mile."

That flawless complexion, pale-to-its-roots curly blonde hair, and those intelligent, arresting blue eyes made Jesse realize he knew her. "Miss Glace," he said, unable to believe he hadn't recognized her immediately, considering how often she'd invaded his dreams over the last three months. "I'm Jesse Sinclair," he explained at her startled look. "Your fiancé is designing my house. On Hundred Acre Isle?" he added to jog her memory, since he obviously hadn't left as memorable an impression on her. "You sat in on my meeting with Stanley back in

February"—to take notes, he'd thought, since she'd brought a notebook and pencil. But though she hadn't said another word beyond a warm "Nice to meet you" at being introduced to him as Cadi Glace—Stanley's fiancée and the daughter of his deceased partner, Owen Glace— Jesse had certainly been aware of her as he'd spent the next two hours explaining to Stanley exactly what he wanted in a house.

"Pooh Bear," she suddenly blurted.

"Excuse me?"

Her gaze dropped to the box she was holding, but not quickly enough to hide the soft blush creeping into her creamy white cheeks. "I mean . . ." She looked up, exposing an irreverent smile. "Winnie the Pooh? He lived in Hundred Acre Wood with Piglet and Eeyore and Tigger?" she added when he frowned. Her smile turned warm. "The few times Stanley took me to your island to check out building sites, it was all I could do not to run around looking for pots of honey hidden in hollow logs." She shrugged her free shoulder. "I developed the habit years ago of imagining my father's clients as whatever fictional characters I thought matched the homes they wanted designed."

And she'd decided he was a roly-poly, *slow-witted* teddy bear?

"Yes. Well," she murmured when he still said nothing, hiking her balloon-anchoring purse higher on her shoulder and heading to his truck. "I guess I will—"

Jesse had her pushed up against the camper before she'd even finished gasping when the car suddenly exploded, surrounding her in a protective embrace just as the percussion reached them with enough force to pop several of the balloons. He stayed pressed against her, waiting to see if anything else might explode, and tried not to notice that Cadi Glace felt even better in the flesh than in his dreams. Casually dressed in slacks, a long-tailed chambray shirt, and flats, she was a bit taller than he remembered, and definitely . . . curvier.

"Well, that took care of that problem," she said, her tentative push making him step back when he realized he was still holding her. She moved away from the camper and shifted her purse to look past the balloons at her burning car. "I guess I will take that ride. Well, damn," she muttered when she spotted the white box sitting on its side in the middle of the road.

Jesse walked over and crouched down to pick it up, seeing through the plastic cover that the round layer cake saying *Happy Birthday, Stanley* was no longer round. He gave the box a quick jostle to re-center the cake and stood up. "I'm sorry. It's not as pretty but should still be edible." He held it toward her. "Feel free to blame me when Stanley asks what happened."

She took the box and headed for his truck again. "Please don't apologize for graciously choosing to protect me instead of the cake."

Jesse managed to beat her to the passenger side, but instead of getting in when he opened the door, she opened the back door, set the cake and her large purse on the backseat, then began wrestling the balloons inside— sighing when another one popped as she quickly closed the door to keep them from escaping. "I can't imagine what else can go wrong," he heard her mumble as she climbed onto the running board and slid into the front seat, only to hold up her hand when he tried to speak. "And don't even think of apologizing for my crappy day."

"Wouldn't dream of it," he said dryly, closing her door, then jogging around the front of the truck. But instead of getting in, he looked down the knoll at the car to see it was completely engulfed in flames. Doubting the fire extinguisher in the camper would do much good, Jesse pulled out his cell phone and opened his door. "Can I call it in now? It's definitely totaled."

She leaned forward to glance in her outside mirror. "I suppose you should."

"Where do I tell them it is?"

"A mile outside of Whistler's Landing on Bog Road." She looked at her watch and sighed again. "They're going to make us wait until they get here."

Jesse called 911 and reported the burning car, assured the dispatcher no one was hurt, then got in his truck. "Leaving the scene of an accident is a serious crime."

"That wasn't an accident. It was attempted murder. That crappy car's been out to get me since the day I bought it."

"Naw," he drawled. "I figure the most they could charge it with would be assault."

Those arresting blue eyes snapped to his.

"It did wait until you were a safe distance away before exploding."

Instead of the smile he was looking for, her eyes narrowed with her scowl. "Actually, now that I think about it, many of my troubles today *are* your fault."

"Excuse me?"

"Stanley said he had to spend all evening working on the Sinclair project because you were arriving *this Friday*, so I was forced to move his surprise birthday party to the office," she explained, swatting at a balloon creeping along the ceiling between them. "But when my engine quit and what I thought was steam started billowing out the front grill, I let the car coast down the hill, thinking I could add some water from the bog to the radiator. Only when I lifted the hood and the engine burst into flames, I decided to roll down all the windows, grab the cake and balloons, and start walking."

"You don't have a cell phone? If you didn't want to call the fire department, you could at least have called one of your party guests to come get you."

Of all things, that got him a smile. "I cherish my friends too much to subject them to one of my little snits, and figured I'd be calmed down by the time I reached town."

"Can I ask what you had against the car? It looked to be this year's model."

"It's an old lady's car," she shot back. "And it's been a lemon since the day I drove it off the lot. I told the dealership there was something wrong with the electronics, but they kept insisting that because the car I traded in had been nine years old, I couldn't possibly understand the new car's sophisticated technology. And that I shouldn't," she added, her scowl returning, "worry my pretty little blonde head over it."

Jesse pretended to check his side mirror to hide his

grin. "If they were going to be condescending chauvinists, why didn't you have Stanley talk to the dealership?"

"Because I am perfectly capable of fighting my own battles."

"May I ask why you bought an old lady's car?"

"Because Stanley said the sporty red Mercedes convertible I wanted wasn't practical."

Jesse decided that Cadi Glace in a "little snit" was even more appealing. Not that he should be surprised, having found the woman a beautiful anomaly the first time he'd met her—which, now that he thought about it, was probably why she kept haunting his dreams. There'd been a distinct I-know-a-secret sparkle in those intelligent blue eyes when she'd politely shaken his hand three months ago only to then spend the next two hours as silent as the furniture. But when she'd stood up to say good-bye and dropped her sketchbook, he'd caught a glimpse of two of the pages before she'd snatched it up and quickly closed it, and discovered that instead of taking notes the woman had spent the entire meeting . . . doodling.

Definitely a talented artist. One of the sketches, he now realized, had been of a tipped-over honey pot inside a hollow log. But it was the larger drawing on the opposite page that had vexed him at the time—and still did—as he couldn't imagine why she'd drawn a large, scruffy dog covered in mud and busily chewing on a tattered boot.

He'd give a year's salary to know what had been on the other pages. Hell, considering her little confession of likening clients to fictional characters, he would *buy* Miss Glace that sporty red Mercedes for just five minutes with that notebook.

Jesse heard the tired-sounding wail of an off-key siren not ten seconds before an ancient fire truck came barreling around the curve up ahead, followed by a parade of pickups and cars—as well as two equally ancient men on bicycles pedaling furiously to keep up. "That was quick."

"Not really," she said on another sigh, "since there are probably more police scanners than televisions in town, which everyone listens to with bated breath waiting for something exciting to happen."

TWO

❧

It was nearly an hour later when the parade of vehicles Jesse was now part of reached what he could only describe as a classic Maine fishing village that hadn't quite made it into the twenty-first century. A bit remote for tourist traffic, businesses evidently had to diversify to stay afloat, as Whistler's Landing's financial district consisted of a post office/convenience store/gas station, a diner/lounge/ice-cream parlor, and a gift shop/hardware/feed store. There was a large white building sporting a sign claiming it to be the Grange, the requisite bell-towered church, and a one-bay fire station attached to the town office. The residential section boasted a good two dozen homes crowded up against the rock-bound cove spilling in from the Gulf of Maine, at the center of which was a small working pier to service the three lobster boats bobbing on their moorings.

In truth, Jesse was surprised the town was even on his navigation device.

"There's a large area down behind the office where you can park," his passenger said as Jesse took his turn stopping at the intersection that didn't even have a stop sign. "The driveway circles the building, so you don't have to worry about turning the camper around to get out."

Jesse looked left and right, not exactly sure which way the office was, since he'd come in from the direction of Castle Cove the few times he'd been here—on the slightly wider but no less crooked road he still had to haul the camper across. Oh yeah; he'd definitely let his eagerness to see his house overrule his *usually* sharp mind. "Which way?" he asked.

"Just follow everyone," she said, gesturing to the right, "since they're all going to the party."

So he'd gathered while standing in the peanut gallery watching the volunteer firemen efficiently douse the flames on the definitely totaled car. Miss Glace, however, had elected to remain in his truck while dealing with the sheriff and then receive blow-by-blow updates from the small gathering of female friends crowded around her. She'd also elected to ride into town with him despite those friends offering her a lift—Jesse presumed because she didn't want to battle the balloons again. "Won't everyone descending on Stanley before you get there ruin your surprise?" he asked as he turned right.

"My car could have exploded right in front of the office

and he wouldn't have known, because he always closes the blinds and locks the door and plays opera music loud enough to rattle the windows when he's drafting." Her snit apparently over, she shot him a smile. "Since my father took Stanley on as a partner five years ago, I swear that poor old building has settled another six inches into the ground."

Instead of turning down the driveway when he spotted the peanut gallery reassembling in front of the familiar building, many of them now carrying pans of food, Jesse stopped in the middle of the road. "I'll just drop you off and come back on Friday as planned," he said at her questioning look. "I don't want to crash your party."

"But you're supposed to take the blame for the cake. And why come back in two days when you're here *now*?"

"I'd feel guilty for ruining Stanley's evening, and I can't wait until the party winds down for him to show me the plans, because I'd rather not drive that road to Castle Cove in the dark."

"Then just spend the night in the back driveway."

Jesse shook his head. "The camper is supposed to be loaded onto a barge tomorrow morning, and I still have to stock it with supplies."

And there was that I-know-a-secret smile he remembered, the one responsible for making those large blue eyes sparkle. "I happen to know there are *two* architectural models in there with your name on them," she said in a conspirator's whisper as she nodded toward the office. "One of your house, and the other one showing it sitting on Hundred Acre Isle." She leaned closer. "And I also happen to have a key to the room where he keeps them."

"You'd sneak me in even though Stanley told me he doesn't like showing clients anything until he's certain a design works?" Jesse countered in mock surprise, deciding Cadi Glace in a playful mood was even more appealing. Which had him wondering if there might be something in the Maine air that was responsible for producing such interesting women, since his two sisters-in-law certainly hadn't wasted any time captivating Sam and Ben.

Miss Glace gestured toward the driveway when a horn honked behind them. "It's the least I can do after you graciously protected me from my exploding car." That sparkle intensified. "Trust me, Mr. Pooh, the moment you lay eyes on those models you'll not only see a home that works perfectly but one that belongs tucked up against that southeast-facing bluff."

That surprised him, as he'd always pictured the house sitting on top of the high ridge at the north end of the island, where it would have a three-hundred-sixty-degree view. The horn honked again and Jesse put the truck back in gear. "Well, Ms. Rabbit, you definitely know how to catch a man's interest."

"Rabbit?" she repeated, her smile disappearing.

"If I remember correctly," Jesse said, watching in his right side mirror to make sure the camper didn't run over any partygoers as he turned down the driveway, "didn't Winnie the Pooh have a scheming buddy named Rabbit?"

That sparkle returned. "Ah, yes, Rabbit. If *I* remember correctly, he was the brains of the operation," she said, deadpan, escaping out the door before he even shut off the engine.

Unable to stifle a bark of laughter, Jesse quickly got out and hustled around the front of the truck to find Cadi Glace scowling again as she eyed the remaining balloons pressed up against the window in eager anticipation of being set free. He gently nudged her out of the way, determined to hold on to the elevated position of gracious hero rather than slow-witted bear. "You bring the cake and I'll battle the balloons. I promise not to let them go even if the sea breeze sends us soaring over the trees." He stopped with his hand on the door and slashed her a grin. "Will you come find me if I get carried off?"

She arched a delicate brow. "I guess that would depend on whether or not you have a check in your wallet for the second installment on your design."

Oh yeah; there definitely had to be something in the air around here, as Jesse couldn't remember the last time he'd dared to flirt with a woman who wasn't at least sixty years old.

But then, Cadi Glace was safely engaged.

"I guess you'll have to hunt me down to find out," he said as he opened the door. He lunged at the strings tied to her purse when the balloons shot forward in a mad dash to escape, and this time Jesse heard himself sigh at the sound of two sharp pops when the stiff sea breeze drove them into the corner of the door.

"That room isn't getting unlocked until you take the blame for the cake *and* the balloons," she said, ducking the swarm to reach past him when he straightened.

"What have you got in here?" he asked, holding up the heavy purse when she backed out with the cake. "Rocks? A small red Mercedes sports coupe?"

"I wish," she said, rolling her eyes as she started up the driveway. "I've got two bottles of wine in there." She shot him another smile as he fell into step beside her. "And a small brick of modeling clay, so I can add one final detail to your island before you show up *this Friday*."

"You build the models? Stanley doesn't source those out?"

"Why would he do that when he has me?"

"Because during my search for an architect, I was led to believe fabricating architectural models was a specialized field, and small firms like Glace and Kerr hired that out."

"They usually do," she said dryly, "unless the architect happens to have a young teenage daughter he can teach to build them for free."

"You don't get paid?"

"I finally wised up by age sixteen," she said with a laugh. "So trust me, Mr. Sinclair; I will definitely hunt you down if the balloons carry you off, because a good chunk of that check in your wallet will be going into mine."

Jesse decided he was buying a compressor and bottling up the air on his island to take back to New York. And instead of sending flowers after his next date with Pamela, he would have a bottle of Maine air delivered the day *before*, and see if it didn't get the woman interested in talking about something other than her latest shopping trip to Paris. "Then if I don't want to spend the night stuck in a tree with a bunch of deflated balloons, I probably shouldn't mention that I mailed the check to Stanley last week."

"Come on, Cadi, hurry up," a woman called out, carrying a huge rectangular pot as she walked down the driveway toward them, a wild-haired, sun-weathered gentleman shuffling along beside her. "We need to plug in Elmer's chowder to reheat it. Your car blowing up set us back a good hour, and everyone's starved."

"Them fools wanted to dig out the plastic spoons and eat it right outta the pot," the man said, having to raise his voice over the muted blare of music coming from the building.

Jesse perked up. "Would that be clam chowder?"

"If'n it ain't got clams in it, mister, you ain't eating real chowdah." He started shuffling back up the driveway. "That fancy rig of yours is a tad big to be hauling across Bog Road, don't yah think," Elmer continued—Jesse recognizing him as one of the bicycle-pedaling madmen. "If'n you was coming from Ellsworth, yah coulda just gone another two miles and taken Clancy Lane. It's a mite longer but a helluva lot straighter."

"So I've been told," Jesse murmured. Five times, actually, by members of the peanut gallery as they'd stood watching the flames being doused.

The sea of hungry people parted when the four of them rounded the corner of the building, opening a path to the door. "I hope you realize, Cadi," an elderly woman said, "that your car exploding was a sign you shoulda gotten that fancy Mercedes you wanted."

Miss Glace passed the cake to a nearby empty-handed gentleman. "Don't worry, Doreen, I always take something trying to kill me as a sign."

"Hey, what happened to the cake?" the man asked, scowling down at the box.

"Apparently Mr. Sinclair isn't a fan of chocolate," she said, reaching toward Jesse with a smug smile. "The office key is in my— Darn," she muttered, dropping her hand. "It's hanging off the ignition of my crappy car. Okay, everyone; turn around and no peeking," she instructed, bending over to the sound of several snorts as not one person turned away. She lifted an edge of the welcome mat and straightened holding a key. "Thank you for not starting without me," she continued, sliding the key in the lock and cracking open the door.

But instead of going inside, she looked back at everyone. "I'll go upstairs while you all squeeze into the front office. Try to get settled before he shuts off the music so he won't suspect anything." She took the cake back from the gentleman and frowned in thought, then looked at Jesse. "Except you, Mr. Sinclair. You can stay in the lobby, and I'll get Stanley to come down by telling him you decided you couldn't wait until Friday. Okay, people, it's party time," she said brightly, stepping inside.

Using his choke hold on the remaining balloons to control them while trying not to trip over the strings of the ones that had popped, Jesse rushed in behind her and immediately stepped to the side to avoid being trampled as he recalled the last party he'd attended. He'd bet a year's salary that even though the elegant birthday bash Pamela's socialite parents had thrown her had probably cost more than two Mercedes, he was going to enjoy this party a whole lot more.

Especially the clam *chow-dah*.

It was a good thing the music was loud enough to rattle the windows, because a herd of elephants would have shaken the building less when what Jesse suspected was the entire population of Whistler's Landing raced to the front office. Or rather, quickly shuffled to the office, as he didn't see one person under sixty years old in the group. Her face glowing with anticipation, Miss Glace headed across the lobby, only to momentarily still in surprise as she set the cake on the reception counter. She then continued to a door on the back wall and opened it to reveal a stairway, but halted again and shot him a brilliant smile. "Well, Mr. Sinclair, consider yourself aptly rewarded for today's heroics," she said over the even louder music, gesturing to her left and then heading upstairs.

Spotting something painted deep blue peeking out from behind the counter, Jesse untangled himself from the balloons and set the heavy purse on a nearby chair as he rushed forward—only to also go perfectly still at the sight of the large, detailed model of Hundred Acre Isle. Immediately drawn to the southeast-facing bluff that he knew rose nearly twenty feet above the high tide mark, he could only stare at what was undeniably a state-of-the-art home that appeared to be constructed of concrete, steel, and glass.

He was absolutely stunned. The house was in fact so unpretentious, it was hard to tell where the island ended and the concrete began, as the bluff itself seemed to make up the entire rear wall of the long, gently curving structure. But despite being all but lost in the hundred acres surrounding it, he could clearly see the roof—which cantilevered out over half again its width as it rose to a full two stories at one end—was almost completely covered in low-growing shrubs. And the exposed southeast-facing wall, rising from a stone patio running the full length of the house, was made entirely of glass.

He was going to have to stop betting away his salary, because it was going to take every penny he earned over the rest of his life to pay for all that concrete and glass and what he was afraid might be *stainless* steel trusses, and another lifetime to cover the labor costs. Hell, he could probably have a cargo ship built cheaper.

His chest tightening with some indefinable emotion, Jesse reached out and gently ran a finger along the tiny roofline that rose like a deep ocean wave just about to crest. The house was so much more than he had envisioned—more beautiful, stunning, organic, so . . . perfect.

But how was that possible? How could an unassuming architect hidden in a remote Maine town, with only a two-hour discussion and half a dozen emails asking Jesse to elaborate on something from their meeting, design a home which shouted—no, unpretentiously whispered—that this particular configuration of concrete and steel and glass, sitting on this particular bluff, was the heart and very soul of Jesse Sinclair?

Either Stanley Kerr was a genius or the man had a pact with the devil.

No; not even the devil himself could have—

"What *is* that noise?"

Startled out of his spell, Jesse turned to see an elderly woman frowning up at the ceiling as she stood in the doorway of the front office. "Does anyone else hear that banging and squeaking mixed in with the music?" she asked no one in particular.

"Sounds to me like there's already a party going on up there," a man said as people started spilling back into the lobby.

Jesse looked toward the open door leading upstairs while listening along with everyone else, and finally realized that embedded in the blaring music—which he recognized as Wagner's *Tannhäuser*—was the rhythmic thump and accompanying squeak of . . .

Christ, those were *bedsprings*. His chest tightening again, this time with the realization that Cadi Glace's day was about to go from crappy to devastating, Jesse started toward the stairs only to stop when the music suddenly stopped.

The thumping and squeaking, with labored breathing and soft moans now clearly audible, continued on for several heartbeats before ending abruptly with a startled feminine shriek and male shout of surprise. Jesse looked over to see the peanut gallery frozen in place, every last one of them staring wide-eyed at the ceiling. He started forward again just as a succinct, distinctly male curse echoed down the stairway, but stopped with his foot on the bottom step when the same man growled, "Paula, get me out of these damn cuffs! Jesus, Mark, help her!"

The ceiling shook when what sounded like several people suddenly sprang into action, the footsteps accompanied by male and female voices muttering curses—not one of those voices sounding as though it belonged to Miss Glace.

Jesse was just starting up the stairs again when she suddenly appeared at the top, her face pale but for the two flags of red darkening her cheeks and her expression completely unreadable. Uncertain how involved to get in something that was absolutely none of his business, Jesse backed away when she calmly started down toward him, deciding to stay out of it unless things got physical. Well, if *Stanley* got physical. But if Miss Glace felt like taking a swing at the stupid bastard, Jesse sure as hell wasn't stopping her.

"Cadi!" Stanley shouted, sounding like he was trying to put on his pants while hopping after her. "Dammit, Cadi, don't leave. Let me explain!"

She exited the stairway only to suddenly stop and blink in surprise, as if she'd forgotten everyone was there.

"Cadi, what's going on?" an equally pale-faced woman whispered.

"Who all is up there?" another woman asked. "What did you see?"

Seriously? They hadn't figured it out? No, the men had, Jesse realized when he noticed every last one of them staring down at their feet.

The whole building shook again when a small herd of footsteps came tromping down the stairs. "Cadi!" Stanley shouted as he burst into the room, the arm contorted over his head trying to find the sleeve of his shirt being hampered by the handcuffs dangling from his wrist. Stanley jerked to a barefooted halt when he saw everyone, only to be knocked forward when three . . . no, four . . . no, *five* people in various states of undress came barreling out of the stairway behind him to the collective gasp of the female portion of the peanut gallery.

The townsmen merely remained mute and motionless, but instead of staring at their feet were now eyeing Stanley's party guests—most likely focused on one of the ladies in particular, who was wearing a tight leather corset under a partially buttoned man's shirt. But Jesse would bet *two* years' salary it was the hot pink dildo strapped to her pelvis that really had their attention.

"What are all you people doing here?" Stanley snarled, still wrestling with his shirt while also trying to keep his unfastened jeans from falling down.

The woman who had been carrying the pot of chowder earlier, her face the color of cooked lobster, strode up to the counter and flipped open the pastry box, pulled out the ruined cake, and held it up for him to see. "Gee, Stanley, I can't imagine why your *fiancée* would sneak all your friends in here today of all days."

Speaking of Miss Glace, Jesse scanned the room looking for her.

"Happy birthday, you no-good, cheating pervert!" the woman added in a shout, winding back and hurling the cake at him.

Stanley managed to duck enough that it only hit his shoulder, sending chunks of cake flying toward his fellow perverts as they also ducked to avoid being hit. But Miss Pink Penis, apparently too short to see it coming, took a large piece of cake directly to the face, which sent her stumbling back with a shriek of surprise, her flailing arms taking two of her buddies with her.

And Jesse could only helplessly watch as all three of them slammed into Hundred Acre Isle, upending the chairs it was sitting on and exposing a second, larger-scaled model sitting on the floor beneath it—giving him a quick glimpse of his beautiful house before both models were crushed under the weight of the woman and two men landing on them.

Stanley abandoned his shirt with a muttered curse and turned to help untangle his friends from the mess of splintered wood, plaster, and dried modeling clay. "Are you hurt, Paula? Mark? Jason, your arm is bleeding. Why don't you guys go upstairs, and I'll be up in a minute." He waited until they started up the stairs, the man named Mark with his arm around the sobbing Paula as she pulled tiny trees out of her hair, then rounded on his utterly silent audience. "Jesus, Beatrice, there's no need to get violent."

"Don't you go cussing at me, Stanley Kerr," Beatrice snapped. "You're the one carrying on like a godless heathen with no regard for your sweet, loving fiancée."

"This is between Cadi and me." Stanley angrily gestured behind him. "And if you're so worried about her feelings, think about the fact that you just caused three months of her work to be destroyed. I've never known Cadi to be more excited about a client seeing one of her models, and now she has nothing to show Mr. Sinclair when he gets here Friday."

"Actually, Mr. Sinclair is here now," Jesse said, smiling tightly when Stanley turned to him in horror. "And I don't know if any of you noticed, but Miss Glace is not."

THREE

❧

Jesse turned into the grocery store parking lot in Castle Cove just as the sun was setting. He pulled to the far end of the lot and shut off the engine with a tired sigh, then sat staring out the windshield at the whitecaps frothing beyond the breakwater that protected the small fleet of recreational and working boats crowded inside the small harbor. He couldn't see Hundred Acre Isle from this vantage point, but his contractor had assured him the well and septic system, generator, and gravel pad for the camper were all in place.

And even though he knew his own mood probably wasn't even close to what Cadi Glace must be feeling right about now, he was more than ready to crack open a cold beer and see the ass-end of this crappy day.

Two seconds; all he'd gotten was a two-second glimpse

of the larger-scale model of his beautiful house before it had been crushed beyond recognition. And feeling it really wasn't appropriate to hang around and ask to see the plans, considering everyone—Stanley included—had been worried about Miss Glace, Jesse had waited only long enough to learn she hadn't run down to the pier and jumped in the ocean. Her response to Beatrice's text message asking where she was had said she was fine and wished to be alone. A second text had arrived after Beatrice had asked if she would like a ride home, in which Miss Glace had reiterated she was fine and promised to call tomorrow. A third text had said she was shutting off her phone.

Cadi was a levelheaded woman, Beatrice had assured Jesse as they'd stood on the sidewalk watching the silent exodus of shocked townsfolk, and she wasn't at all worried her friend would do anything crazy. The petite, sixtyish owner of the gift shop/hardware/feed store had also apologized for causing his models to be destroyed and promised she'd apologize to Cadi the moment she saw her. She'd then glared at the upstairs windows and gone on to assure Jesse that everyone in town would help Cadi through this ordeal, just as they had fourteen months ago when the poor girl had walked into the office one morning to find her father slumped over his drafting table, his body long cold.

Yeah, well, her friends might not think she'd do anything crazy, but Jesse figured Miss Glace wouldn't be in any hurry to call 911 if Glace & Kerr Architecture were to suddenly catch fire, either. Hell, considering it had been the scene of two recent heartbreaks, he wouldn't be surprised to hear the woman had set a match to the building, opened all the windows, and walked away just like she had her car.

Damn. Did Stanley keep copies of works in progress at home, or at least backup his computer to a cloud or off-site storage device? For that matter, did he even use a computer for drafting? Wait; maybe Miss Glace had a set of his plans. She'd brought clay with her today, which implied she fabricated the models at home.

The same home she shared with Stanley and would be in no hurry to return to?

Jesse pulled the key out of the ignition, grabbed the folded piece of paper out of the cubby on the dash, and got out of the truck, deciding he must be more tired than he realized to be letting his imagination run wild. A levelheaded woman did not torch a building simply because she'd walked in on her fiancé carrying on like a "godless heathen."

Apparently Whistler's Landing didn't have many opera enthusiasts; not if they thought Stanley was painstakingly drafting detailed house plans whenever he locked the door and played Wagner's decidedly rapturous *Tannhäuser.* And they truly must spend their time listening to police scanners instead of watching television, considering how long it had taken them—well, at least the women—to guess what had been going on upstairs. Although to be fair, it hadn't been until he'd heard all the footsteps that Jesse had realized it was a full-blown orgy.

He walked down the length of the camper, momentarily stopping to inspect the tires, then continued around the back and up the other side, making sure none of the thousand potholes he hadn't been able to avoid had done any damage. Seeing nothing more than a good amount of road dust on the ditch-side tires, he unfolded the paper and scanned the grocery list his cook had handed him before he'd left Rosebriar.

He couldn't help but grin, remembering Sonya packing boxes with dishes and various cooking paraphernalia for the camper while giving him a lecture on eating nutritious meals, which she'd ended by threatening to have Peg—Rosebriar's former cook, who had followed Sam to Keelstone Cove and subsequently opened her own restaurant—drive over an hour down the coast to make sure Jesse's cupboards weren't filled with junk food.

He'd told the motherly woman he hoped Peg brought along a boat.

Jesse frowned when he spotted the unfamiliar handwriting on the bottom of the list, then snorted when he realized who it belonged to. It would appear the ever-interesting Miss Glace had passed her time waiting for the firemen to finish putting her car out of its misery by snooping through his truck, and had added *large pot of honey* to his grocery list.

Not the least bit apologetic for where his mind started heading—he was a man, after all—Jesse wondered how long it might take a woman to get over such a public humiliation, as well as how long before she might consider dating again. Because instead of stealing occasional visits to the island this summer like he'd planned, maybe he'd work on clearing his calendar when he got back to the office. Hell, if Sam and Ben could have the corporate jet shuttle them back and forth for meetings they needed to attend in person, he might as well begin his own ritual of commuting to work at the speed of sound.

And when he returned next month, he should probably pay Miss Glace a visit.

No, he'd better get back here in two weeks, just in case some of the local men also realized those sparkling blue eyes and delightful curves were suddenly available. Yeah; surely two weeks was enough time for an intelligent woman to decide that today's little disaster had probably saved her from a lifetime of crappy days.

As for Stanley Kerr . . . well, he hoped the stupid bastard knew a good model-building firm if he couldn't sweet-talk his *ex*-fiancée into recreating the ones that had been destroyed, because Jesse knew for a fact the check paying for them had already cleared the bank. He stuffed the grocery list in his pocket with another tired sigh, deciding to grab a frozen pizza and cold six-pack of beer and leave the rest of his shopping for the morning. But he stopped in mid-stuff, his fatigue suddenly vanishing when he spotted two deflated balloons dangling from the bottom of the camper door.

Well, this was . . . interesting. In his line of business, sneaking onboard a vessel to get from point A to point B was a serious crime. Hell, it could even be fatal. And despite Abram Sinclair knowing firsthand the risks people were willing to take to get ahead in this world, the international shipping company the old wolf had started nearly five decades ago with nothing more than a thousand dollars and a fondness for taking outrageous risks had purposefully garnered a reputation for not tolerating stowaways.

Shanghaiing a person like they had Willa's brother-in-law three years ago, however, was perfectly acceptable if it happened to be a Sinclair putting the idiot on a slow boat to Italy.

Was Miss Glace right now hiding in the closet, listening to see if he was going to enter the camper or go directly to the store? But Jesse suddenly bolted for the door at the realization there was an equally good chance she was passed out cold from hitting her head on something during any one of the times he'd dodged a monstrous pothole.

He vaulted inside without bothering to lower the steps and immediately tripped over the huge purse sitting just inside the door, his curse lost in the sharp pops of bursting balloons as he fell and nearly slammed his own head into the kitchen island counter. He cursed again when he spotted his stowaway lying faceup on the floor in the narrow space between two of the camper's retracted slide-outs, and he quickly scrambled to his feet.

"Cadi, are you okay?" he asked, dropping to his knees beside her.

"I will be just as soon as this stupid camper stops moving," she said tightly, not opening her eyes as Jesse carefully brushed the curls off her forehead looking for bumps or blood.

Damn; she had to be concussed if she thought the camper was still moving. "Where are you hurt? Did you hit your head?" he asked, gently lifting one of her eyelids.

Both beautiful blue eyes snapped open as she jerked away. "I'm not hurt."

Jesse sat back on his heels. "Then why are you lying on the floor?"

She looked around as if to confirm she indeed was on the floor, then went back to scowling at him. "Because it's impossible to lie on the bed or couch of a moving camper," she said, turning her scowl on the couch beside her. "I know because I kept getting bounced off before I finally smartened up and just stayed on the floor."

"What are you doing here, Cadi?" Jesse asked as he fought a grin, already knowing the answer but curious to hear hers—only to be surprised when he did.

"Isn't it obvious? I'm getting drunk," she said, lifting her hand on the side away from him to expose the empty wine bottle clutched in her fist—which explained the pale pink spots on the front of her shirt. "I don't have a car anymore, so I don't have to worry about drinking and driving. And I *thought* hitching a ride in your camper would be a good way to leave town." She dropped her hand and closed her eyes on a soft groan. "They don't need to keep building bigger and scarier roller coasters; they just have to load people up in a camper and haul them over a hilly, crooked Maine road."

"Did you have any plans beyond reaching Castle Cove?" he drawled, quickly stifling his grin again when her eyes opened and shot to his. "Other than spending the night in jail?"

"In jail for what?"

"Trespassing."

"Trespassing *where*?"

He gestured around them. "The business I'm in has zero tolerance for stowaways."

Those beautiful eyes narrowed. "That's right," she said over the sound of the wine bottle hitting the floor as she rolled over and awkwardly rose to her hands and knees. "You own some big shipping company with your brothers. Tidal-something-something," she muttered, weaving slightly as she grabbed the corner of the slide-out and tried to stand before apparently deciding to simply sit on the floor and lean against the couch.

"It's Tidewater International."

"And you really have poor, desperate stowaways arrested?"

"Only those who don't die from dehydration," he said, turning serious and even angry. "You could have been badly hurt. Why didn't you just hide in my truck until everyone left?"

She dropped her gaze to her lap, a telltale blush rising to her cheeks. "Because I didn't want to see or talk to anyone, including—no, especially—you."

Jesse was instantly contrite for teasing the obviously embarrassed woman. "Why especially me?" he asked gently. "I would think dealing with a stranger would actually be easier. *Especially* if he happens to be a slow-witted bear," he added, wanting to lighten the mood.

She lifted her gaze and smiled sadly. "No one can spend three months building a man's home one wall and window at a time and not get to know him inti . . . intimately," she ended in a whisper, her blush deepening as she looked down again.

"You can't know me very well if you don't even know the name of my business."

She looked up with a frown and waved that away. "What you do to earn your millions isn't even close to who you really are. The model I built wasn't for the

high-powered executive who tried to crush his competition by stealing their boat captains with outrageous
salaries; it was for the man who asked an architect to
design him a home that would instill wonderful childhood
memories in a passel of kids who aren't even born yet."
The smile she suddenly shot him held hints of the interesting Miss Glace—or else that of a woman who'd just
downed an entire bottle of wine. "You know the guy
I'm talking about? *That* Jesse Sinclair?"

Jesse could only stare at her, undecided as to whether
he'd just received a compliment or been insulted. "That
article on Tidewater's personal little war with Starrtech
was written over two years ago. Where in hell did you
even find it?"

"We get the Internet in Whistler's Landing. I also read
several *three*-year-old articles. Did your grandfather really leave his big fancy estate, his even bigger bankbook,
and all his shares of Tidewater to a young woman he'd
known less than two months?" Both eyebrows disappeared into her curls. "The same woman your older
brother married six weeks after the funeral in order to
save her from being forced to sell those shares to your
archenemy for ten cents on the dollar?"

"No," Jesse said, standing up. "Sam married Willa to
save her from herself." He walked to the kitchen and bent
to pick up the purse, only to have it jerked out of his hand
by the strings trapped in the door.

He heard a snicker behind him. "Those ribbons are
stronger than steel. I know because I tugged on them
until one of my purse handles broke."

Jesse crouched down and opened the purse, remembering Willamina Kent's disastrous entrance to a Tidewater board meeting three years ago, when Sam had found her in the lobby holding a pair of handles as the elevator had ascended with her overnight bag still inside.

"Hey, you can't just go through people's belongings without their permission."

Jesse pulled out a small brick of modeling clay and set it on the floor. "It's standard procedure with stowaways." He glanced over to see her glaring at him from her hands and knees again—apparently still waiting for the floor to stop moving so she could stand up—and arched a brow. "But I try to refrain from adding items to their grocery lists." Seeing those creamy white cheeks turn a lovely pink again, he went back to feeling his way through the cluttered, seemingly bottomless purse and pulled out a rolled-up pink canvas hat—not the one she'd thrown in the woods, as he remembered that one being blue. He set it on the floor beside the clay and dove in again. "Oh good," he drawled, pulling out a large, rabbit-ear corkscrew. He set it on the floor beside the clay and hat, then resumed hunting until his fingers closed around his target. "I apologize for assuming you'd snooped through my kitchen looking for a cork—"

Jesse stopped in mid-sentence when he pulled out a second, *empty* wine bottle, holding it up as he silently arched a brow at her again.

"It was a long ride," she muttered, somehow managing to look both guilty and indignant as she flopped back against the couch. "Were you in a contest to see how many potholes you could hit, or did the dealership just hand you a driver's license with that fancy truck?"

For some unfathomable reason, Jesse found Miss Glace in a drunken snit to be the most appealing of all, which sent his mind wandering in a totally inappropriate direction—the fact he couldn't get Wagner's *Tannhäuser* out of his head probably not helping. But hell, it wasn't like he'd kidnapped the woman; she was the one who'd chosen to stow away in the camper of a man she'd spent the last three months getting to know *intimately.*

"So, about your plan for after you reached Castle Cove," he said, standing up and walking back to the living area, his hope of a drink thwarted. He started to sit in the recliner in the opposite slide-out, but changed his mind and sat on the floor to lean against it facing her. "Are you intending to hide out here in town for a few days?"

"I can't," she said, shaking her head. "Wiggles falls into a deep depression if she's left alone for more than twenty-four hours."

"Wiggles?"

"My cat."

"Surely Stanley will go home tonight."

Apparently just hearing the bastard's name was enough to get her scowling again, even as she blinked in obvious confusion. "What's he got to do with—" Her eyes widened. "We don't *live* together. Stanley lives up over the office and I live in my parents' house." She looked utterly scandalized. "And even if our engagement was real, we wouldn't live together without being *married.*"

Now Jesse was confused. "Are you saying you and Stanley aren't really engaged?"

She dropped her gaze and slowly started sliding the diamond ring up and down the fourth finger of her left hand, her bluster evaporating on a deep sigh. "It's only pretend," she admitted softly. "Just like the stone in this ring." She looked up. "We got engaged shortly after my father had his second heart attack over two years ago. Knowing Dad worried about my being alone if he died, Stanley and I hoped that telling him we were engaged might ease some of the stress on his heart."

"And for the fourteen months since his death?" Jesse asked gently.

"Since everyone in town also believed the engagement was real, we decided to go on pretending until we could make it look like we simply fell out of love but could still be friends."

"And it's taking over a year to fall out of fake love?"

"No, it's taking Stanley that long to find a new partner." She snorted. "And for me to work up the nerve to finally leave Whistler's Landing."

"And go where?" Jesse asked in surprise.

"Anywhere," she muttered, stretching to reach the wine bottle, then lifting it to her mouth and tilting her head back in the apparent hope it had magically refilled.

Jesse remembered the other thing she'd said that had caught his attention. "So you wouldn't consider living with a man you're not married to?" he asked when she finally gave up and lowered the bottle. "I realize Whistler's Landing might be frozen in time, but surely you know this is the twenty-first century."

That got him a derisive smile. "You try living in a small town full of people who are two and three generations older than you and not be old-fashioned. My parents tried having children early in their marriage without success, until my mother suddenly found herself pregnant at fifty-one years old." She chuckled. "I got my driver's license the same day she got her first social security check in the mail." But then her smile turned sad. "She died in her sleep when I was twenty. I left college to come home and be with Dad, and finished working on my degree by driving to the University of Maine in Machias three days a week."

"A degree in architecture?"

She shook her head. "I'm not a detail person and would go insane if I had to spend hours hunched over a drafting table trying to decide where every light switch should go."

Jesse arched a brow again. "You don't spend hours hunched over your models?"

"That's different," she said with a shrug. "My dad realized early on that I visualized things three-dimensionally, which is why he decided to teach me to fabricate his models. When I'm building, it's like I'm actually walking around inside the house." She shot him a smile. "Or traipsing all over a forested island."

"So what is your degree in?"

Her smile went back to being derisive. "My original plan was to become a lawyer and set up shop in Ellsworth so I'd be close to my parents. But when Mom died, I switched from pre-law to environmental tourism when Dad suggested we could build a campground at the far end of our property to bring tourists to the area."

"But now you've changed your mind and want to leave?"

"Well, yeah," she said somewhat defensively. "It's not

like anything is keeping me here anymore, and there's a whole world out there to explore." The hint of a sparkle came into her eyes. "Do your overpaid captains leave your boats unlocked when they're tied up to the dock?"

"It's *ships*, not boats," Jesse said, fighting a grin again. "And no, they don't. In fact, there are armed guards on board both in port and at sea. So you'd like to travel?" he asked, remembering his own parents often dropping him and his brothers off at Rosebriar, then hopping on whichever Tidewater ship was heading in the general direction they wanted to go.

Bram and Grammy Rose, however, preferred escaping on their Sengatti sloop.

"I want to at least *try* traveling," she said, "rather than always wonder what I missed."

Jesse found Miss Glace was getting more interesting by the minute, which made him want to probe deeper. "I can understand not living with a man you weren't married to out of respect for your parents, considering their ages, but that doesn't explain your still feeling the same way." A thought suddenly struck him and, seeing how his somewhat drunk stowaway was being so talkative, Jesse decided to simply go ahead and ask. "Are you a virgin?"

Her jaw slackened—either in surprise that he'd asked or disbelief that he even thought she might be—just before she shot him a haughty glare. "I was away at college for two and a half years before I moved back home, and I'll have you know I had *lots* of boyfriends."

"I'm sure you did," he quietly agreed, imagining the college boys had also found those big blue eyes, bouncy blonde curls, and lovely curves appealing.

"I'm not a prude," she insisted, her chin lifting as her cheeks filled with color again, "but I am discriminating. So who's to say what I'll do if—no, *when* I finally fall in real love."

Lord, he bet she hated having such an expressive complexion.

"But I can't very well run around looking for Mr. Right," she continued heatedly, "if I'm supposed to be engaged, now can I?"

"That didn't seem to be a problem for—" Jesse knew he hadn't checked his words in time when he saw her cheeks turn a blistering red just before she dropped her gaze. "I'm sorry. That was uncalled-for." He stood up, feeling like a first-class jerk as he watched her slip off her fake engagement ring. "Do you have friends in Castle Cove you can stay with tonight?"

"No," she whispered, staring at the ring she was now holding. "And I prefer to get a motel room anyway."

Jesse didn't like the idea of her spending the night alone when she might be depressed and possibly just drunk enough to get in trouble. He crouched down beside her again. "Or, since I happen to have a camper that sleeps six, you could stay here." He held up his hand in a Boy Scout's salute when her eyes snapped to his. "My word of honor, Miss Glace; I will be a perfect gentleman." He blew out a heavy, exaggerated sigh. "And although it goes against company policy, I will also feed you."

She rolled to her hands and knees again. "That's going to be kind of hard," she said, grabbing the edge of the couch, "since all you've got in your cupboards are some weird spices and enough powdered Tang to keep a passel of kids hydrated all the way to Mars." She straightened to her knees and scrunched up her nose. "Four-year-olds drink Tang."

Jesse stood up with a snort. "Remind me to find a good hiding place for my checkbook," he said, catching her by the shoulders and setting her on the couch when she nearly fell attempting to stand. "And I'm afraid you may have to take me up on my offer, because I'm pretty sure motels don't rent rooms to inebriated people," he added as he straightened.

"Of course they do," she shot back. "Why else do you think they always build them right next to bars?" Up went that haughty chin again. "And I'm not inebriated. I just haven't gotten my land legs back after that roller-coaster ride from hell."

Jesse turned away so she wouldn't see his grin. "Well, you definitely were sober when you decided to stow away on that roller coaster." He walked to the kitchen and put the corkscrew and clay and hat back in her purse, cracked the camper door enough to free it, then opened a drawer, pulled out a knife, and cut off all the balloon strings—releasing the sole survivor to float up to the ceiling. "So if I go get us a pizza or rotisserie chicken," he said, walking over and setting the purse on the couch beside her, "will you promise to be here when I get back?"

"That would depend on whether or not you promise to also get a bottle of Moscato. Pink. Preferably bubbly." The sparkle suddenly returned. "And feel free to get something for yourself." She cocked her head. "My guess is you'll tolerate wine in social settings, but that you're really more of a Scotch, no ice, kind of guy. Single malt? Aged at least ten years?"

Jesse stilled in surprise. "Single cask," he said quietly, "aged no less than twenty."

"Whatever floats your boat," she said as she started looking around the camper, only to stop long enough to flash him a smile. "Excuse me—your *ship*." She bent over and ran her gaze along the slightly raised floor under the couch. "I really like the idea of these slide-outs," she went on, seemingly to herself, as she straightened to study the slide-out on the opposite side of the camper. "They'd be cool in a house." She looked at him, her eyebrows disappearing into her curls again. "Think of all the wonderful childhood memories a passel of kids would have if they grew up in a home that had moving walls."

The woman was all over the place, her mood rising and falling more often than a real roller coaster, making him wonder if the wine was responsible or if she might have a mild case of attention deficit disorder. Not that it mattered, because either way he was about to send her plummeting downward again. But hell, she was going to find out eventually, and when better than after drinking *two* bottles of wine? "Speaking of homes, I'm hoping you won't work up the nerve to leave Whistler's Landing until after you rebuild my models."

She snapped her gaze to his, her face draining of all color. "What do you mean, rebuild them? You . . . you don't like the house?"

Jesse shoved his hands in his pockets. "I liked the short

glimpse I got of it before both the island and house models were crushed."

"Crushed?" she repeated in a whisper, her eyes widening as she clutched her throat. "They were destroyed? Both of them? How?" she asked when he nodded.

"Beatrice threw the birthday cake at Stanley, but most of it hit his friends standing behind him when he ducked, and three of them stumbled back and fell on the models."

"But only the island was behind the reception counter."

"The house was sitting on the floor beneath it."

She stared at him for several seconds, then simply . . . imploded. "Oh, God," she rasped, covering her face with her hands and bending at the waist until her head touched her knees.

Jesse dropped to a crouch in front of her and laid a hand on her back when he saw her shudder, not exactly sure how to respond. He usually was unmoved by tears, since in his experience they usually only showed up when a woman wasn't getting her way. "I'm sorry," he said, dropping his hand when she lifted her head to look at him, her expressive blue eyes filled with pain. "I can only imagine how much work went into making them."

"I spent four weeks just on the island alone," she said thickly. "Clients rarely ask for presentation models, so the ones I make are usually just rough studies to help them understand the plans. But right after your meeting in February, I asked Stanley to hire a pilot to fly over the island and take aerial shots." She slowly shook her head. "I lost count of all the individual trees and rocks I made, and

I perfectly replicated that stand of pines to the west of the lower bluff."

"I saw the pines," he said softly. "The island model was beautiful."

"And the house," she cried, burying her face in her hands again. "I *loved* that house."

"And I loved what I saw of it. I'm sorry," he repeated when another shudder wracked her. "Would you like me to drive you home tonight, Cadi? It won't take me a minute to unhook the camper."

"I can't go home," she said, straightening on a deep breath and using the sleeve of her shirt to wipe her eyes. "I don't want to see anyone. I don't even want to talk to them. Oh, God," she groaned, lifting her hands to hide her face. "They're all going to be so *nice*."

Jesse was back to not knowing how to respond. "I'm pretty sure that's what people do when someone they care about has . . . had an upset," he said lamely as he stood up and slowly started backing toward the door, only to stop in surprise when she lowered her hands to glare at him—her mood apparently switching directions again.

"I was just finally getting everyone to stop treating me like a fragile piece of china. My father had had two heart attacks; it's not like I didn't see it coming. And now this thing with Stanley," she hissed, gesturing at the lone balloon bumping along the ceiling, "is going to start the coddling all over again."

"Because they care," Jesse repeated.

"Yeah, well, you spend over a year with an entire town giving you sympathetic smiles and patting your shoulder and constantly asking how you're doing. Or having them tell you to be happy because your father's with your mother now. Or worse, having them push you to set a wedding date so you can get busy having babies."

"You don't want children?"

Her glare turned thunderous. "Not with *Stanley*."

Undecided if this particular snit was about her fake fiancé's little perversion or the destroyed models, Jesse simply gave up. He walked to the door, but stopped and looked at her. "Promise you'll be here when I get back, and I promise that after you've eaten enough food to soak up at least some of that wine, we'll decide whether you'll get a motel room or sleep on my couch." When her only answer was silence, Jesse shot her a grin. "But instead of snooping to pass your time, why don't you play with the slide-outs," he said, tapping the panel on the wall beside the door. "And see if you can't figure out how to make some of the walls of my house move when you rebuild the model."

As he had suspected she would, the woman immediately zeroed in on the panel. "I prefer chicken," she said, waving him away as she turned her attention to the slide-out across from her. "And mashed potatoes. And I've changed my mind; bring me a Moxie instead of the wine. Please," she tacked on while pulling her purse onto her lap.

"Moxie? Is that a beer? I really don't think you should be mixing beer with wine."

She went back to glaring at him. "It's *soda*." But then she suddenly smiled, although it looked more sinister than sparkly. "You should also get yourself one if you want a true Maine experience. Oh, and see if the deli has any premade stuffing, will you?"

The woman definitely had an attention problem. "Anything else?" he drawled. "Ice cream? Cookies? Blueberry pie?"

"No thank you. I'm not really into sweets," she said, rummaging around inside the purse. She pulled out a small wire-bound notebook and used it to give him another dismissive wave. "Go on. I'm starved."

"And you promise to be here when I get back?" he thought to clarify when she frowned at the notebook then started searching through her purse again.

Her hand emerged holding a pencil. "I'll be here," she murmured, leafing through the notebook. "Wait," she added when he opened the door. "Does your truck have to be running to power the slide-outs?"

Oh yeah; did he have the lady's number or what? "No, the camper's battery system can handle it," he said to her head of big blonde curls, since she was bent over her notebook already furiously scribbling.

FOUR

⤸⤹

Jesse beat a hasty retreat—having to leap to the ground at the last second when he realized the steps weren't down. He closed the door and lowered the steps on the chance his stowaway was a liar as well as a snoop, then sprinted up across the parking lot and shot through the store's automatic doors just as a man was approaching holding a set of keys.

"We're closing in five minutes," the guy said, his grin more resigned than inviting.

"Then I'll only take four," Jesse offered, grabbing a shopping basket.

"That your rig out there? I'm sorry, but we don't allow overnight parking," he added when Jesse nodded. "There's a campground fifteen miles east on Route One."

"I'll move on if you insist, Mr. Dean," Jesse said,

reading the name tag claiming Ken Dean was the owner/manager. "But it would be convenient for me to be here when you open in the morning, so I can stock my cupboards before I take the camper out to my island."

That certainly perked him up. "You the gentleman from New York who bought Hundred Acre Isle last summer?"

"Yes, I'm Jesse Sinclair."

Ken Dean's entire countenance changed right along with his grin. "You go ahead and take all the time you want, Mr. Sinclair. And I don't have a problem with you spending the night in my lot." Ken fell in beside him when Jesse started toward the back of the store. "Corey Acton's been working out on your island for the last month, getting it ready for your camper. He said you're planning to build a home out there and hired him to do all the site work."

"Since we're going to be neighbors, please call me Jesse," Jesse said, stopping in front of the deli display case. "And yes, I hope to start construction in the next few months."

"If you ever need anything besides groceries, my brother owns the only hardware store in thirty miles. If he doesn't have something in stock, he can get it here in two days."

"Thanks. I will definitely look him up."

"And if your wife needs anything, my sister and brother-in-law own the drugstore right next door," Ken said, nodding toward the side wall. "And their daughter has the beauty salon at the end. I suppose your wife would get her hair cut in the city, but Joanne also offers manicures and pedicures."

"I'll take those last two chickens," Jesse told the deli clerk when he spotted her putting them on a tray as she cleaned out the case. "And a container of stuffing and one of mashed potatoes." Jesse looked at Ken and decided not to correct him on the wife situation, since he really didn't want to become a target for every marriage-minded woman in Castle Cove. "Any suggestion on who I should contact about getting a boat slip and a couple of moorings—one here in the harbor and one out at my island?"

"My uncle is the harbormaster. Oren can fix you up on this end and probably get a mooring set at your island." He gave Jess a calculating look. "You're also going to need a rugged deep-water dock."

Jesse decided his contractor had been passing word around that a deep-*pocket* flatlander was moving to town. "You wouldn't happen to have any relatives in the dock business, would you?" he asked dryly.

"Well now," Ken murmured behind his hand—which was likely hiding his grin. "It so happens my son knows a little something about building docks. In fact, Jason's just about elevated it to an art form."

"That's good," Jesse said with a nod, "because I know a little something about docks myself, since I've overseen the construction of several here in the States and overseas. You wouldn't *happen* to have one of Jason's business cards on you, would you?"

Ken reached in his hind pocket and pulled out his

wallet. "That's right, Corey mentioned you're a high-up executive in a big shipping company, Tide-something-or-other."

"Tidewater International," Jesse said, also deciding not to mention he was in fact one of the majority shareholders.

"Well, Jesse," Ken said, handing him *three* cards, "my youngest son also has a business you might find yourself needing once your house is finished. It appears you're not the only one drawn to our remote coastline in recent years, and many of the summer folks started looking for someone to keep an eye on their homes. Amos is a full-service caretaker; he'll do regular property checks, lawn maintenance, painting, and tree-trimming, and he'll put your floating dock in and out of the water each spring and fall. In fact, he's even planting a vegetable garden for a client and his wife this spring, so they can pick their own salad fixings all summer." He shook his head. "This week the boy's been out hunting up half a dozen laying hens for another couple, because they thought it would be fun to mosey out to the coop for fresh eggs every morning."

Jesse used his thumb to fan the business cards to see the third one. "And Samantha?" he asked, reading that Samantha Wiggins apparently did something with interiors.

"You need a reliable, discreet housekeeper to clean once a week while you're here, my Sammy's the girl for you. She'll also do some baking if you have guests coming, and even cater and serve small dinner parties."

Jesse lifted his grin to Ken Dean. "How many children do you have?"

Ken grinned back. "Five. My oldest son, Kenny Jr., runs this store with me. I have one daughter still in the nest; Abby helps her sister out when she's home from college, and she'll also babysit." He suddenly frowned. "Jason's the only one I couldn't talk into going to college. You got any kids, Jesse?"

"Not yet."

Ken shook his head again. "Well, I can tell you that despite coming from the same gene pool and having the exact same upbringing, every one of them will have their own personality." He went back to grinning. "And opinions. And the older they get the dumber *you* get, because they're certain they know a better way of doing things."

"Mr. Dean to the service desk, pa-lease," a frustrated voice called over the speaker.

Ken's grin broadened. "That would be Oren's granddaughter, Malinda." He started backing away. "If you'll allow me a little fatherly boasting," he said, gesturing at the cards Jesse was holding, "you won't find more reliable, harder working people at a fairer price than those three."

Jesse slipped the cards in his shirt pocket. "Coming from a close-knit, hardworking family myself, I appreciate what it takes to build a business from the ground up. Once I'm settled in and get my bearings, I will likely give them a call."

Ken Dean backed away with a nod, then turned and sprinted toward the front of the store when Malinda paged him again, several drawn out words indicating she was nearing the end of her patience. Jesse loaded his basket with the chickens and fixings, gave the girl behind the counter a warm thank-you, then headed off in search of cold beer and Moxie.

Satisfied he had enough food to sober up his stowaway, Jesse tossed a couple of candy bars onto the conveyor belt as Paul—whose name tag said he was in training—slowly scanned and carefully arranged each item into four bags. Jesse swiped his card and entered his PIN, then patiently waited while the teenager tried to decide which register button he needed to push to conclude the transaction.

"Sorry about that, Jesse," Ken Dean said as he walked up beside Paul and tapped a button that made a sales slip shoot out of the register. "Wednesday evenings are usually slow and a good time for training. You help Mr. Sinclair carry his purchases to his rig, Paul," he added, pulling out the drawer. "Check the lot for any stray carts on your way back in, then we'll sit down together and cash out your drawer." Ken looked at Jesse. "I'll leave my cleaning crew a note saying you have permission to spend the night and for them not to sweep the parking lot." He chuckled. "They usually wait until one in the morning to fire up our old sweeper and make several trips past any campers who ignore the signs for no overnight parking."

"I appreciate the note," Jesse said, grabbing two of the bags. "What time do you open up in the morning?"

"Officially at seven, but I put on a pot of coffee and unlock the doors when I get here at six in case any fishermen need something before they head out."

"I'll see you in the morning, then," Jesse said as he followed Paul.

The boy exited the store, immediately headed to the lone shopping cart in a nearby aisle, and dropped the beer and bags inside. He then grabbed the handle as he set a foot on the bottom rail, pushed off with his other foot, and rode the cart down the parking lot toward the camper.

Jesse couldn't help but grin when he saw the living room slide-out extending three feet beyond the camper. There were four slides total—which he imagined had all been opened and closed several times by now: a large one on this side, two on the other side in the main area and kitchen, and one in the raised bedroom that jutted out over the cargo bed of his pickup.

"Nice rig," Paul said when Jesse caught up with him. The boy took the two bags and beer out of the cart and set them on the ground beside the steps. "You the guy my dad's been building a campsite for out on Hundred Acre Isle? He said you was coming this week."

"You're Corey's son?" Jesse asked in surprise, since Corey Acton had to be in his sixties.

"No, he's my grandfather. My dad runs the bulldozer and excavator while Gramps hauls the gravel." The boy frowned toward the store. "I'm only working here for the next two years because the stupid insurance company told Gramps I can't work for him until I'm eighteen, even though I've been running heavy equipment since I was seven." He stepped closer and lowered his voice. "I went out to your island last weekend while Gramps was gone to Bangor, and Dad let me use the bulldozer to level out the last three loads of gravel on your camper pad." He threw back his shoulders. "You won't be stepping in any puddles when it rains, because I made sure it was pitched so the water will run right off. All the trees we cleared for the pad are sawed into firewood and stacked, we hauled away the stumps and underbrush just like you told Gramps you wanted, and we planted the septic bed with a mix of grass and wildflower seeds."

"I appreciate that."

"Me and Dad spent all day Sunday cleaning up the beach where the barge has been off-loading the equipment and trucks, so to make it look all natural again. All you'll see when you get there is a more permanent landing site at one end and a small road leading up to the pad. We made sure the road curved instead of running straight down the hill, so it won't wash out when it rains." He glanced toward the store when half the parking lot lights suddenly went out, then started backing away, hauling the cart with him. "School gets out next Friday, so if you need anything else done on your island this summer, I'm willing to work any days I'm not working here. I can run a chainsaw and I don't mind hauling brush and stuff like that. You just tell Gramps and he'll tell me." He stopped and shot Jesse a wide grin. "And I won't charge you an arm and a leg, neither, just because you're from away."

"That's good to know," Jesse said with a nod. "I'll definitely keep you in mind."

The boy swung the cart around and set his foot on the bottom rail, gave a wave over his shoulder, then pushed and rode and pushed and rode his way back up the parking lot.

Jesse chuckled, having to admire Castle Cove's obvious bent toward entrepreneurship, which apparently started in the cradle. Oh yeah, he couldn't think of a better place to bring his kids every summer.

Speaking of which, hearing that Cadi only seemed

opposed to having children with Stanley had certainly been a relief. He was also quite heartened to learn she wasn't firmly entrenched in her own safe little corner of the world the way Willa and Emma were, which had compelled Sam and Ben to make Maine their permanent home. That Cadi wanted to travel was probably her most appealing trait at this point, since it should make her open to living at Rosebriar the lion's share of the year.

Well, assuming they got married. But if their grandfather had taught his three grandsons only one thing, it was that when a Sinclair decided he wanted something—be it in his personal life or business—he single-mindedly went after it. And Bram couldn't have driven home that lesson any more outrageously than when he'd left everything he'd worked his whole life to acquire, including his beloved Rosebriar, to a disaster-prone little partridge from Maine.

Jesse opened the door with a snort as he remembered how Bram had even bequeathed Willa one of his grandsons—although the old wolf had magnanimously left the choice of which one up to them. Jesse set his bags inside on the floor, then picked up the beer and other two bags and walked up the stairs with the single-minded intention of finding out if the ever-interesting Miss Glace might indeed be the woman of his dreams—only to find himself standing in a now spacious, starkly silent, apparently *empty* camper.

He closed his eyes and dropped his head in defeat. Had Cadi not believed his promise to act the gentleman tonight, or had she simply taken another downward spiral and—

Jesse snapped his head up when he heard the soft thud of something hitting carpet. He set the beer and bags on the counter, turned and closed the camper door, then quietly walked up the short set of stairs leading to the raised bedroom. He passed the open door to the bathroom, noting the light over the vanity was on, and stopped in the bedroom doorway when he spotted his stowaway curled up on his bed, hugging her purse like a pillow, sound asleep.

Okay then; he was still in business.

He bent down and grabbed the notebook off the carpet, then headed back to the kitchen, snagged the six-pack of beer on his way by, and walked over and set the beer and notebook on the table tucked into one of the slide-outs. He went back and emptied the bags onto the island counter, quietly opened cupboards and drawers looking for eating utensils, then filled a plate with fixings. He ripped several paper towels off the roll hanging under the cupboards, carried his plate and one of the warm chickens over to the table, and pulled out a chair and sat down.

Freeing one of the beers and popping the tab, Jesse actually groaned as he took a long guzzle. He took two more guzzles before shoveling several forkfuls of lukewarm stuffing and potato in his mouth, then picked up the beer again with one hand while he opened the notebook with the other, only to stop the beer halfway to his mouth as he stared down at the pencil sketch on the first page. It wasn't so much the small boy soaring high on a swing suspended from a towering pine that caught him off guard, but rather the name *Sinclair*, written in the upper right-hand corner of the page, under which was written, *Add swing to pine tree on the large house model before Friday.*

He closed the notebook just enough to see the front cover, even though he knew this wasn't the one she'd had at his meeting with Stanley back in February, as it had been twice this size and thinner. He opened it up to lay flat on the table, deciding Cadi must carry this one in her purse to quickly sketch ideas when they came to her. The woman might claim she saw things three-dimensionally, but she certainly didn't have any trouble rendering in two dimensions.

He took a quick swig of beer, then turned the page to find a sketch of . . . Hell, was that the Mad Hatter from *Alice in Wonderland* sitting in a water fountain, holding a bulging-eyed rabbit by the neck? Or maybe . . . well, whichever character he was, the guy definitely looked sinister. Jesse saw the name *Stapleton* at the top, then grinned to see *pompous ass* written beneath it.

He slowly turned pages, noting the different names above the mostly happy, animated characters, some commanding two and even three sketches. Other clients, Jesse figured, whose rough study models Cadi must be working on for Stanley. He stopped when he saw the Sinclair name again, quickly leafed through several more pages to see they all contained similar sketches before going blank, then went back to the beginning of the series.

With the same reverent awe he'd felt as he'd studied his house on the island model, Jesse slowly worked his way through the hastily-drawn sketches; not of his home, he realized, but of what appeared to be several . . . playhouses with moving walls and bookcases that opened to reveal secret alcoves behind them. Except for the last sketch, which showed an entire room rising from the ground, its four walls dotted with large portholes set at different heights.

He leafed back through the series, this time noting that each drawing was populated with simply rendered male and female children varying in ages from toddlers to young teenagers, all wearing huge smiles, all totally engrossed in the moment as they danced, sat quietly reading a book, or dueled with wooden swords.

Jesse lifted his head and rubbed his face on a deep breath, then simply sat staring off at nothing. He'd been ten, Ben fourteen, and Sam sixteen when they'd gone to live with Bram and Grammy Rose after their parents had died in a plane crash. And although its forty rooms, indulgent staff, and sprawling twelve hundred acres had been every kid's dream of a personal adventure land, on that day Rosebriar had gone from being whatever their wild imaginations could conjure up to merely being their home.

And judging from the sketches she'd drawn while he'd been in the grocery store, Jesse decided Cadi hadn't been boasting about spending the last three months getting to know him intimately. Hell, it would appear she knew him better than he knew himself. He hadn't even realized what he'd been looking for when he'd asked Stanley Kerr to design him a home that would instill lasting memories in children rather than impress adults.

Jesse looked down at her sketch of the room magically rising up from what should be solid granite, and wondered if Stanley didn't have Cadi sit in on his meetings with clients so he could tap some of her own obvious creativity.

Had Owen Glace realized his daughter's talent and done the same?

Jesse turned the page and read the notes she'd made.

Exactly how many kids in a passel, anyway?
One clubhouse for girls and one for boys, or a single hideaway with separate wings?
Hidden? Or a towering, impenetrable fortress?

Jesse couldn't stifle a snort. Apparently the woman felt that even after shelling out several lifetimes of salaries on the main house, he should still have enough money left to build his kids an elaborate clubhouse—or two—complete with moving walls and rising rooms.

But then, what does true creativity care about costs? Jesse glanced toward the stairs leading to the bedroom, then pulled the pencil out of the notebook's spine and turned the page.

I'm thinking a passel is at least four kids, not counting cousins.
Definitely two clubhouses, if only to keep the peace.
Boys' should be hidden.
Girls' should definitely be impenetrable, with Dad having the only key once they're teenagers. (Isn't Maine known for its pink granite? That would make a girly fortress.)
Preferably situated at opposite ends of the island— again, to keep the peace.

He studied what he'd written, then added: *No television or electronics except for an intercom to the main house.* He thought for a minute, then tacked on: *Plumbing, though, so they don't have to keep running home to use the bathroom. At least in the girls' towering pink fortress; the boys can whiz in the woods.*

Jesse closed the notebook and slipped the pencil back in the spine, then slid it out of the way. He then spent a full minute wrestling the chicken container open and ten minutes stuffing his face before he felt his eyelids growing heavy. He carried his mess to the kitchen sink, washed his hands, and put everything in the fridge. He grabbed the notebook off the table, quietly walked to the bedroom, then carefully leaned over his softly snoring stowaway and tucked the book beside her.

But seeing her cell phone peeking from a pocket on the purse, he gently pulled it out, then powered it on as he walked to the bathroom. Figuring he wasn't doing anything Miss Snoop wouldn't do if given the chance, Jesse pulled out his own cell phone while hers booted up, then opened his contacts. Relieved but not really surprised that Cadi didn't have password protection, he went into her settings, found her number, and added it to his phone. And to be fair, he added his contact info to her phone so it would show on her screen when he called to see how she was doing in . . . well, a gentleman would probably wait at least two weeks before beginning his pursuit in earnest, but Jesse gave himself four days—five, tops—before he caved in and called.

He returned to the bedroom and slipped the phone

back in her purse, then just stood there grinning down at her. Damn, she looked soft and inviting and . . . vulnerable. The lady might think she'd gotten to know him over the course of building his house one wall and window at a time, but he'd learned quite a bit about her just today—which is also why he wasn't surprised she'd helped herself to his bed. Oh yeah; despite her boast that she'd had *lots* of boyfriends in college, Cadi Glace was an innocent. She was also way too trusting for his peace of mind.

Regretting that he couldn't join the real-life Goldilocks sleeping in his bed, Jesse lifted the corner of the down comforter and carefully folded it over her, then snagged a pillow and went back to the living area. But eyeing the couch and deciding he was too tired to take the plastic off the mattress, he turned to the recliner. He kicked off his shoes and was just about to sit down when he caught sight of movement in the parking lot and stepped to the window in time to see a semi-deflated balloon skimming along the ground. He scanned the ceiling, looking for the sole survivor, but headed for the door with a curse when he realized it had gone missing. He quietly went outside and hurried around to the rear of the camper, then sprinted toward the trees when he saw the balloon tugging against a bush in the soft breeze—muttering another curse when one of his socked feet landed on a small rock and made him limp the last few strides.

He untangled the balloon and straightened, only to still in surprise. "Son of a bitch," he whispered at the sight of Cadi's engagement ring tied to the end of the ribbon. "Son of a bitch," he repeated, closing his fist around the ring.

He had half a mind to cut his losses and fire Stanley Kerr.

But that would mean he'd also be firing Cadi. And although he'd only seen the small version of it on the island model, he didn't want to hire another architect—he wanted *that* home. Jesse coiled the ribbon around each hand and pulled until it snapped, finished popping the balloon and stuffed it in his pocket, then opened his fist to stare down at the ring. To hell with waiting two weeks, or even four days; tomorrow he was sending Miss Glace a large bouquet of flowers, because he was counting today as their first date.

FIVE

❧

Sitting on a bench tucked between a rack of spring pansies and a pallet of charcoal briquettes outside the grocery store, Cadi adjusted the brim of her hat as she watched the parade of fishing boats idling past the breakwater toward the rising sun, and tried to decide when she'd become such a people-pleaser. Long before her mother had died, certainly. Probably even before she'd let her father talk her into building his models. Heck, if she really wanted to pin it down, she would say everything had changed right about the time she'd reached the age of reasoning at around seven or eight years old.

But the foundation had likely been laid in kindergarten, when she'd made the shocking discovery that her parents were old. None of the other kids' parents had had gray hair; only their *grandparents*. And all her friends had had exciting moms and dads who picked them up from school on motorcycles, took them tenting in Acadia National Park and hiking up Cadillac Mountain, and even went swimming with them in the numbingly cold ocean.

She had also climbed Cadillac, but in the backseat of a sensible sedan after spending the night in a charming bed-and-breakfast in Bar Harbor. Her parents had taken her to Sand Beach in Acadia at least twice every summer, but had only allowed her to go in the water up to her knees while they'd hovered at the edge of the waves, and then only after slathering her from forehead to feet with sunscreen. They'd always insisted she wear a wide-brimmed hat, had always packed up within an hour—because everyone knew the sand magnified the sun's strength—and had always taken her to Jordan Pond House for afternoon tea and popovers on the lawn as consolation.

God, she was *still* wearing hats.

Cadi remembered being in the first grade and angrily asking why she couldn't go dig clams with her friends one Saturday. "You're our miracle baby," her mother had said by way of explanation, "and we'd worry about something happening and us not being there to help you."

"Then you come clamming, too, so if I get stuck in the mud, you can pull me out."

Her mom had laughed then. "Oh, honey, I'm afraid *you* would be pulling *me* out. My knees aren't what they used to be, and I wouldn't be able to walk for a week if I went slogging through a clamflat." They'd gone on another "adventure" that Saturday instead, and Cadi had once again explored the wonders of Maine from the backseat of their sensible sedan.

But it hadn't been until three of her friends had each lost a grandparent over the course of her second-grade year that she'd realized she could just as easily lose her parents. She'd also realized they couldn't help being old. So she'd stopped asking to do stuff with her friends and started making sure she never upset her parents, afraid one or both of them might suddenly keel over dead at the dinner table, just like her best friend Susan's grandma.

Yes, that was when she'd started down the slippery slope of pleasing people, which had quickly grown to include friends, teachers, townspeople, college roommates, and even Stanley.

Not coworkers, though, because she'd never held an actual job. Heck, the IRS probably hadn't even known she existed up until fourteen months ago, since her parents had always given her unbridled access to their money, even going so far as to present her with a blue—to match her eyes—leather-clad checkbook on her thirteenth birthday; the enclosed card saying whatever was theirs would always and forever be hers.

Who gave a thirteen-year-old a checkbook, especially one without a register? "You don't worry about that, Cadi," her father had said when she'd asked how big a check she could write. "Whatever amount you fill in will be covered." He'd smiled and patted her hand. "Just try not to bankrupt us, okay?" And then he'd slipped a pad of Glace Architecture checks in where the register should have gone. "But I want you to use these checks whenever you're purchasing materials to build your models, because supplies are a business expense."

Good Lord, two weeks after he'd died she'd had to go

to the bank—to a branch clear over in Ellsworth, she'd been so embarrassed—and have someone show her how to reconcile the monthly statements. It was then she'd vowed that if she ever had children of her own, she would make damn sure they grew up knowing how the world worked.

Her dad had even purchased her cars; the first one when she'd gotten her driver's license and the second when she'd come home from college and had had to commute to Machias three days a week. Which was why she'd taken Stanley with her when she'd decided to buy a new one a couple of months ago, since she'd never even set foot in a dealership before. And being such a people-pleaser, she'd let him talk her into another boring, albeit luxurious, sedan. Which was also why, fourteen months after Owen Glace's death, she was still engaged to a man who was in no hurry to get off his comfortable couch.

Cadi knew the real reason Stanley wasn't looking for a new partner was because of their agreement that when he found one, she was leaving. He didn't even have to buy out her father's half of the business, because Owen had signed it over to him—lock, stock, and building—the day they'd gotten engaged. The problem was that Stanley worried he wouldn't *have* an actual business if she left, to which she'd argued that all he had to do was find the right partner.

But for that to happen, he had to at least *look*.

Cadi twisted the cap off her bottle of Moxie with a heavy sigh, took a sip of the bittersweet soda, then screwed the cap back on with another sigh. Unless she finally started pleasing herself, ten years from now someone was going to find her cold dead body slumped over one of her models, with *sheer boredom* cited on the certificate as the cause of death.

And really, only two things were stopping her from going home this morning, packing a suitcase, and simply driving away—Stanley and Wiggles. Well, three things, since she didn't have a car to drive away in. No, four, as she wanted to see the entire world but had absolutely no idea where to go first.

Okay, so she wouldn't leave today. But she could at least start packing.

Wiggles might actually be the easiest, Cadi decided as she studied the camper at the end of the parking lot. All she had to do was buy a small motorhome and take the little brat with her. She could also get that sporty red convertible and tow it behind them, so she'd have something to zip around in once she got where she was going.

There; problems two and three solved.

Then all she had to do was climb in her camper and drive away, because the direction wasn't nearly as important as seeing Whistler's Landing in her rearview mirror.

So she guessed that solved that problem.

Stanley, however, wasn't quite so solvable, since she loved him like the brother she'd always wanted. The man had been a rock when her father had suffered his first heart attack, and it had been Stanley's idea they pretend to get engaged. He'd also shouldered most of the workload at the office, often drafting into the wee hours of the night to meet the impossible deadlines Owen Glace kept promising all the clients he refused to turn away.

Both she and Stanley had begged him to slow down

and enjoy the fruits of his labor, but apparently her dad's only concern had been to build an even larger nest egg—which Cadi had realized only after she'd learned how to read investment statements. Because despite his already substantial portfolio, the man had spent the last twenty-nine years of his life making sure his daughter could spend the rest of *her* life fulfilling her heart's desires on just the dividends alone.

She still wasn't sure how she felt about his working himself to death on her behalf, since she knew he likely would have *worried* himself to death even sooner if he hadn't been able to go to the office and get lost in his designs—which he loved doing almost as much as he loved her.

But it was time she started loving herself, even if that meant she had to kick Stanley off his comfortable couch with a size-eight sneaker of tough love. The man had an innate talent for laying out the mechanics of a house and drafting amazingly smart plans, and if she could somehow . . . force him to find the right partner, Kerr & Whoever Architecture could outshine her father when it came to designing award-winning homes.

Tough love . . . Tough, creative love . . .

Cadi stopped twisting the soda bottle cap. No, she couldn't.

Or could she?

No, it was just too cruel. Too unlike her.

It would certainly be effective, though. And she could soften the blow by giving Stanley a couple of weeks to realize she was serious. But only if during their ride home this morning he promised to start setting up interviews with potential partners *today*. And if she didn't see the first candidate sitting in his office by . . . oh, by Friday of next week, she would start burning models. No candidate by the following Monday, she'd start burning her sketchbooks.

Okay, that was the plan, and she was sticking to it. She'd give Stanley fair warning, and if he didn't like it . . . well, he'd just have to pull up his big boy pants and discover for himself that he had the creative talent to design award-winning, million-dollar homes.

Because telling him didn't seem to be working.

Cadi heard a sound and lifted her head to see Jesse turning from closing the door on his camper. Even from this distance she could see he was scowling as he scanned the parking lot, making her wonder if he might be a bit of a grump until he had his morning coffee. Or, she thought with a snicker, maybe he simply didn't like having uninvited guests write *Thank You* in pink lipstick on his bathroom mirror before sneaking away. Not that she could imagine a *normal* woman being in any hurry to leave his bed, even as she tried to imagine what it would have been like to have had him in it with her.

God, he was handsome. And not in a polished urban-businessman way, either, as his deceptively casual manner and easy smile did little to disguise an underlying strength only a fool would challenge.

He certainly didn't appear to be lacking in physical strength, either.

Heaven help her, it had been all she could do to pay attention to what he was saying during his meeting with Stanley last February, much less concentrate on her drawings. And she'd gotten all flustered when he'd stood up to leave and focused those sharp, Atlantic-blue eyes on hers as he'd held out his hand to say good-bye. She'd shot out of her chair like an idiot, dropped her sketchpad, then nearly bumped heads with him when they'd both bent to pick it up.

Stanley had noticed, of course, and hadn't stopped teasing her until she'd threatened to make the Covingtons' rough study model look like a gingerbread house.

Cadi felt herself getting flustered all over again as her repeatedly gracious rescuer headed toward her, his stride as commanding as his reputation. Had he honestly thought she hadn't recognized him yesterday when he'd stopped to offer her a ride? God, if it wasn't bad enough she'd spent the last three months imagining herself living in the house she was building *with* the man she was building it for, she'd also spent every night dreaming of him— some of those dreams positively salacious. But even more disconcerting had been her *day*dreams of the two of them on his island, playing hide-and-seek with a passel of kids who just happened to be theirs.

He stopped in front of her, and Cadi lost the shade of her hat brim when she looked up and had to squint into the sun trying to read his expression—although she didn't have any trouble guessing his mood when he spoke.

"Exactly what were you thanking me for before sneaking off without saying good-bye?"

Nope, not a morning person. "For answering the questions in my notebook. You know the one I'm talking about? The private notebook I carry in *my purse*?"

She wasn't sure, but she thought the corner of his

mouth twitched. "The only notebook I know of is the one I found on the floor beside *my bed*."

Yup, that was definitely a twitch.

"How's your head this morning, Cadi?"

"The same as it is every morning—quite happy and raring to go. Why, does yours hurt? Maybe you're addicted to caffeine and need a cup of coffee so you'll be happy, too."

She heard him sigh. "Maybe you're right. Can I bring you back one?" he asked, his gaze moving from the soda she was holding to the box sitting on the bench beside her purse.

"Thank you, but no. I think coffee is as nasty-tasting as it is addicting. Wait," she said when he started toward the door. With the sun hitting him square on when he stopped, she could see he did look a tad tired, making her wonder why he'd slept in the recliner if the camper had enough beds for six people. She shot him a smile, hoping his sense of humor got up early. "I feel I should warn you that the owner thinks I'm your wife. Mr. Dean saw me walking up the parking lot from the camper when he was putting out the pansies, and insisted I come in and get coffee and some of the fresh doughnuts that had just arrived."

Up went an eyebrow. "And you didn't feel the need to correct him?"

"Not once I realized the name Sinclair literally opens doors."

"Well, sure," he drawled, walking back and dropping onto the bench beside her. "Why not also help yourself to my name."

"That's what I thought," she said, widening her smile

because she couldn't tell if he was okay with her little deception or not.

"And when I show up here again *without* my wife?" he asked.

"Oh, I hadn't thought about that. Wait, I know. You can say I ran off with Rosebriar's pool boy."

He twisted slightly to lean back against the bench and crossed his arms over his chest as he appeared to ponder her suggestion, then slowly shook his head. "I think I'll tell them you're home tending your aging aunt. That way I won't have to endure sympathetic smiles and pats on the shoulder from everyone in town for being jilted, which would also make me a target for every single female in twenty miles."

Okay, maybe he was a morning person after all. "Sure, why not. I've been a fake fiancée for two years; I don't have a problem with being a fake wife." She picked up the box and held it out to him. "You can have a doughnut if you want, but the other two are for Stanley."

He halted in mid-reach. "Excuse me?" he said, his good mood vanishing.

Cadi nodded. "I called him an hour ago and apologized for yesterday, and asked if he'd come pick me up. He should be here any minute now."

"You apologized? For *what*?"

"For bringing the entire town to the office without asking him first. You don't think it's rather embarrassing to have all your friends walk in on you having an org— Having group sex?"

"And you don't think— Wait, you knew about Stanley's sexual preferences?"

"Of course. Well, maybe not completely, since he usually meets his friends in Ellsworth. But he said they just showed up yesterday wanting to surprise him for his birthday." She snorted. "Apparently they had the same idea as me when he told them he had to work late."

"So you didn't run away last night because you were humiliated that everyone in town thought your fiancé was cheating on you?"

"I was humiliated for Stanley." She set the box back on the bench. "And because I knew they were going to start treating me like a fragile piece of china all over again." She beamed him a smug smile. "But I've figured out how to solve that problem, as well as the problem of Stanley finding a new partner. I'm going to buy a small motorhome, and in two weeks I'm setting off to see the world before I start looking for Mr. Right. Well, whatever parts of the world I can drive to."

"Alone?" he asked, a distinct edge back in his voice.

"No, with Wiggles. That's why the camper, so she can come with me. Um, maybe you should go in and get yourself a large cup of coffee."

She saw him take a deep breath. "What about my house and island models? If you leave, who's going to rebuild them?"

Cadi looked down at her bottle of soda. She'd gone out of her way to forget that three months of her work—that she'd poured her heart into—had been destroyed. "Stanley can hire a professional model builder."

"I want you to build them."

Oh, God. It was hard not pleasing a person right to their face, which was why Cadi continued to stare at her soda. "Your contract is with Glace and Kerr Architecture, and I'm not really part of the firm."

"Stay long enough to rebuild both models, and I'll double whatever Stanley pays you."

She looked up in horror. "I can't hang around another *three months*." She took a deep breath. "You don't understand," she said calmly. "I have a small problem saying no to people, and if I don't get away from everyone I care about in the next week or two, I may never leave. And I really don't want someone finding me slumped over one of my models ten years from now, having died of sheer boredom before my fortieth birthday." She gave him a warm smile, even though she was shivering inside. But if she couldn't say no to a client—even one she'd come to know quite well and truly liked—how did she hope to stand her ground with Stanley? "A good model firm can have both your island and house done within a month of receiving the final plans, and probably do a better job."

He said nothing, his steady gaze unreadable, and Cadi went from shivering to quaking inside as the silence deepened, which caused her to flinch when he suddenly stood up. "I need coffee," he muttered as he headed off, only to suddenly turn and stride back just as the automatic doors opened, making her flinch again when he lifted her to her feet, pulled her against him with one hand and cupped her head with the other, and kissed her full on the mouth.

And not a quick I'll-see-you-around smooch, either, but a full-blown yet confusingly gentle lip-lock that made all of Cadi's dreams come roaring to life with salacious clarity, even as she tried to decide if she was shocked he was kissing her or dismayed that she didn't have the nerve to kiss him back.

He smelled of soap, tasted of mint, and felt as solid as the granite on his island. Which meant he must really be angry at her for refusing to rebuild his models, because why else would a man kiss a woman who smelled of stale wine, tasted of bittersweet Moxie, and who she knew for a fact looked like a rumpled piece of seaweed, if not hoping to . . . charm her into rebuilding them?

Oh God, she must have been really drunk last night to admit she'd spent the last three months getting to know him *intimately*.

"Er, sorry," a male voice said, followed by an embarrassed chuckle. "I'll come back and water the pansies later."

Cadi's dream came to a roaring end when Jesse lifted his head, although he continued to hold her. "No need, Ken. I was just letting my wife know how much I'm going to miss her."

Cadi disguised her attempt to step away by patting his chest, which only made his arm around her tighten as he glanced back at Ken Dean.

"We got a call this morning that Cadi's aunt isn't feeling well," he continued. With his fingers still threaded through her hair—hey, where was her hat?—he kissed her forehead, then dropped his arms and stepped back. "If you don't mind, honey, I'm not going to hang around and watch you leave with the guy who's driving you to the Trenton airport. Just be sure to give me a call when you get home and let me know how Aunt Angela is doing, okay?"

Fighting the blush creeping into her cheeks, all Cadi could do was mutely nod.

The outrageous liar bent down and picked her hat up from the ground—it must have fallen off when he'd kissed her—and set it on her head. He slowly tucked several curls inside it as he stared down at her with eyes darker than the Atlantic in winter, then suddenly shot her a wink, reached in his shirt pocket as he turned away, and walked over to Mr. Dean. "Well, Ken, I hope you have everything my wife and our cook seem to think we need."

Cadi just barely stifled a snort at his not even missing a beat, using *our* and *we* as though they'd been married for years. God, he'd even come up with a name for her *fake aunt*.

So this was the high-powered executive who ruthlessly went after his competition; the one she'd purposely *not* dreamed about.

Mr. Dean took the list Jesse handed him, read down through it, then gave Cadi a pained grin. "I haven't even heard of several things on here, and I doubt you'll find some of the items I do recognize sold in any store in Maine, except maybe a specialty shop in Portland." He frowned at the list again. "What's cordyceps?"

She had absolutely no idea.

"It's a mushroom," Jesse drawled, "that my loving bride has been adding to my salads ever since someone told her they help boost a man's sperm count."

Cadi didn't know whose face turned redder, hers or Ken Dean's. The store owner cleared his throat. "I, ah, I'm afraid you'll have to bring those back with you from New York."

Where in the heck was Stanley? "Not a problem," Cadi said brightly, deciding it was time to get in the game. "Jesse can text what items you don't have to our cook, and she can overnight them." She batted her eyes at *her husband*. "You eat every mushroom she sends you, Pooh Bear, so we can get started on that passel of kids the moment you get back to Rosebriar."

God, she hoped it was the sun causing that glint in his eyes, because if it wasn't, she'd just made the biggest mistake of her life in trying to one-up a professional competition crusher.

Ken Dean cleared his throat again. "I'll just go get started on this list," he murmured as he turned and nearly ran into the doors before they could open.

It was all Cadi could do not to also turn tail and run when Jesse continued to stare at her, the glint gone and his eyes unreadable again.

Oh yeah, big mistake.

"Are you truly determined to leave in two weeks?"

Not quite sure of his mood, she decided to be honest. "I have to," she said just as softly. She canted her head. "Do you know I've never even been on an airplane? Or a train? Or ridden on a real roller coaster? I want to see a lava flow. Touch a redwood tree. And stand on a glacier. I want . . . I don't want to die without ever having lived."

He went back to simply staring at her, the silence seeming to grow . . . more intimate with each passing second before he suddenly smiled. "If your travels bring you to New York, give me a call. Rosebriar's just over the state line in Connecticut, and I'd enjoy giving you a tour."

Still unsure of his mood, she slowly nodded. "I'd like that."

He silently nodded back, then turned and walked inside the store.

Cadi backed up and plopped down on the bench with a silent groan. For as much as she'd love to see Rosebriar, she knew better than to think she could hold her own against Jesse Sinclair on his home turf. She ran her tongue over her still-tingling lips and tried to remember the last time a man had kissed her. A couple of years, maybe, if she didn't count the pretend kiss Stanley had given her at their fake engagement party? Three years, then? Surely it hadn't been more than four.

No, the last guy she'd dated had been in Machias, before they'd both graduated and he'd taken a job on a research boat in Alaska. She'd gotten her degree . . . what, six years ago?

Cadi covered her face and dropped her head to her knees with a snort. No wonder Jesse had questioned her experience with men last night. Heaven help her, *virgins* were probably more sexually active than she was.

SIX

Damn, this tough love business was hard. Not only was she now officially unengaged, Stanley was barely speaking to her. But Cadi was still proud of herself for not backing down, considering the man had almost driven into the ditch when she'd mentioned burning the models and sketchbooks. And confronting her ex-fiancé was only the beginning, as she still had an entire town—starting with Beatrice—to reeducate, since she still intended to call Whistler's Landing home. But she didn't suppose a person could suddenly stop being a people-pleaser without hurting anyone's feelings, now could they?

"Yes," Cadi told the large, sleek, gray-and-black-spotted cat glaring down at her from the top of the refrigerator, "I'm all done worrying about your precious tail getting in a twist. So I didn't come home last night—deal with it. In fact," she continued as she opened the tiny can of gourmet food and spooned it into a bowl, "you're about to start dealing with a harness and leash, and taking naps in front of a window that has landscapes zooming past. Because," she added as she set the colorful ceramic dish beside its matching water bowl, "in two weeks you and I are heading off on our first of *many* adventures."

She straightened and smiled up at Wiggles staring down at her. "I'm going to buy us a cute little camper, and we'll practice sleeping in it here in the dooryard and take some day trips before we head off for real. And once you get used to your home moving, I bet you'll actually enjoy having a change of scenery." She headed across the kitchen when the phone rang. "I know I certainly will. Hello?" she said after picking up the ancient wall phone's large receiver.

"Cadi, you're home."

"Yes, Bea, I'm home. Stanley dropped me off ten minutes ago."

There was an abrupt silence. "You spent the night with Stanley?" her friend whispered.

"No, I called him this morning and asked if he'd come pick me up in Castle Cove."

Another silence, and then, "You called Stanley to go get you instead of me?"

"I didn't need to have a heart-to-heart talk with you, Bea," Cadi explained gently.

"So everything's okay between you two? Last night was just a . . . misunderstanding?"

"We're okay," Cadi said, again gently, "since we've agreed to end our engagement."

"Oh, sweetie, I'm so sorry."

"There's nothing to be sorry for. Stanley and I both realized we love each other like a brother and sister instead of romantically. Hey, you wouldn't happen to be free today, would you?" Cadi rushed on, wanting to change the subject.

"I can be. You want me to come over? You say you're okay," Beatrice also rushed on, "but only because you've probably blocked out last night's . . . scene, just like you did the morning you found your father. Oh, sweetie, I called your house several times, worried about you being alone all night. How on earth did you get to Castle Cove?"

"Mr. Sinclair saw me walking down the road and was kind enough to give me a ride."

A loud gasp came over the line. "Cadi Abigail Glace. You got in a truck with a virtual stranger—a man from New York City, no less? Your poor mother and father are likely rolling over in their graves. I realize Mr. Sinclair appears nice enough, but what do you really know about him?" She gasped again. "Please tell me you didn't stay in his camper."

Heaven help her, Cadi wasn't sure she'd survive even two weeks. "Of course not. I had him drop me off at a motel. And the reason I asked if you're free," she rushed on again, "is because I need a ride to Ellsworth so I can buy a new car."

Another silence; Bea apparently not ready to leave the subject of last night's sleeping arrangements. "Of course I'll take you, and that will give us plenty of time to talk. When do you want me to pick you up?"

Wonderful; just what she wanted. "How about in an hour?" Cadi looked at the clock on the stove. "Say, around ten? I need to shower first."

"You didn't shower at the motel?"

"Why bother when I'd just be putting dirty clothes back on again? Ten, then?"

"I'll be there."

Cadi hung up with a heavy sigh. So when had she become such a bald-faced liar? Oh, that's right; right around the time she'd become a flaming people-pleaser.

"I'm not replacing that food, so eat before it crusts over or go hungry," she told her pet still perched on the fridge as she headed to the front hall. She stopped in the doorway and looked back. "And just so you know, there's going to be even more changes around here. I'm not the same person who left here yesterday, Wigs. From now on you'll be living with a woman who drives a sports car, who dresses like a twenty-nine-year-old instead of a senior citizen, and who does *not* listen to music on vinyl records. Oh, and Wigs? You're going to have to work on your fear of strangers, because I intend to start dating again—a lot." She shot the cat a smile. "And with any luck, your half of my bed will occasionally be occupied." She hesitated. "But I don't want you to worry that I'm going to turn into a slut or anything, okay? I have no intention of sleeping with every man who catches my eye, and definitely not on my first or second date."

Apparently not the least bit concerned, Wiggles began washing her sleek Bengal tail. Cadi crossed the foyer of the traditional Cape-style home, stopped in the living room doorway, and sighed again. Just like every other room in the house, it was frozen in time; the wallpaper, curtains, furniture, and knickknacks were all about the same age. That was because ten years into their marriage, the house Owen Glace had built his bride as a wedding present had burned down to its foundation, which made everything in *this* house nearly forty years old.

Cadi surveyed the room and decided it all had to go, right down to the ancient wallpaper. She loved her parents with all her heart and missed them terribly, but it was time to emerge—no, *burst free* of the safe, sensible, unchanging cocoon they'd built around her.

She sucked in a shuddering breath when her eyes landed on the grandfather clock they'd purchased to commemorate her birth. Okay, maybe not *everything*. She would keep some things to pass on to the children she hoped to have, to remember grandparents they would only know from pictures and the stories she would tell them. Well, and also from the beautiful homes scattered up and down the coast that she would take them to see, which, as far as she was concerned, were the true heirlooms.

Cadi turned and walked upstairs past the ascending gallery of photos documenting her life; the last photo added being that of her engagement reception right here in this house, of her and Stanley and her ecstatic father standing between them. She turned right when she reached the upper hall and stopped in the doorway of her parents' bedroom, her gaze immediately going to the gold curtains that were *not* the ones she'd bought in Bangor nine years ago.

Those had been a bright, airy yellow. But unable to wait until Christmas morning, she'd given the curtains to her mother the moment she'd arrived home on winter break, then helped her iron and put them up that afternoon. Her mom had gone to bed early that evening, claiming she had a headache and was feeling all tuckered out from spending the week helping Santa wrap a whole sleigh full of gifts. Cadi had been crawling into her own bed a few hours later when her dad had barged in without even knocking, looking frantic and saying he didn't think Sandra was breathing.

It had been quite a shock, since her mom hadn't even been sick, but Cadi knew it was supposed to be a blessing for a person to die in their sleep. Heck, that must make her twice blessed, since her father had died at his drafting table. But she considered it a blessing only for the ones not waking up, as the sudden voids they left were damn hard on those still living.

She'd re-hung the old curtains and thrown the bright yellow ones in the trash, to this day wondering if the exertion of hanging them may have caused her mom's aneurysm to rupture. Beatrice had come over a week later and helped clean out her mother's closet and drawers, then repeated the ritual after Owen's death, her friend gently but firmly helping Cadi decide what mementos to keep and what to donate.

Nearly everything in this room had to go, too. But since she couldn't see herself haggling over prices at a yard sale only to then watch her parents' belongings leaving in the back of a pickup, it appeared the Salvation Army was about to get a huge influx of furniture, curtains, towels and linens, and a small collection of vinyl records.

Cadi walked across the hall, stopped in her bedroom doorway, and tried seeing it through a man's eyes—maybe a certain Atlantic-blue-eyed man in particular—as she recalled watching a talk show six years ago about a grown woman who'd moved back home. She'd come upstairs right after that show and decided that even though she'd been twenty-three at the time, her room had looked like it belonged to a ten-year-old.

So she'd climbed in her sensible sedan the very next day and driven to Bangor—taking her dad with her, of course—and completely refurnished her bedroom. Her father had walked around the car when they'd returned home and hugged her, and said he'd been waiting years—since her mom had died, actually—for her to finally cut loose. He'd also said he hoped she kept it up, so he could have the pleasure of seeing her spend money on herself instead of on everyone else. Because what in tarnation was he supposed to do with another cardigan sweater, or a cell phone that didn't have buttons or even a dial tone?

Cadi had honestly tried. But since her little people-pleasing problem had been so firmly entrenched, she'd soon returned to purchasing only necessities and birthday gifts. She did buy a few things she didn't need or even want, but only because the proceeds from the craft fairs the Grange ladies put on went to a local animal shelter. She'd also given Bea a smartphone for her birthday a couple of years ago so she'd have someone to text other than Stanley, seeing how nearly ninety percent of the population of Whistler's Landing was over sixty years old.

And Jesse Sinclair had wondered about her being old-fashioned. Good Lord, nearly half the population was over *seventy*.

Cadi walked to her bed, threw out her arms as she spun around, and flopped back onto her pink comforter. Her room now looked like it belonged to a sixteen-year-old, all because she hadn't wanted to hurt her father's feelings when he'd gotten excited about the bedroom set he'd found in the furniture store. "Oh, and look," he'd said, "it's named the Princess Collection."

Not even a sixteen-year-old would have chosen a white, traditional, full-sized canopy bed with a matching bureau and sit-down vanity. "It's beautiful," Cadi remembered saying, even as she'd glanced over at the black-lacquered queen bed and matching armoire she'd just spent the last ten minutes picturing in her bedroom.

The bedroom she *had* intended to paint a crisp, modern teal.

She stared up at her pink canopy and remembered imagining herself walking through Jesse Sinclair's ultra-modern home as she'd slowly, painstakingly built his model; the stained mahogany concrete floor burnished to a rich shine, the great room's accent wall painted a deep ocean teal as it rose two stories to an oak ceiling supported by massive steel trusses, the entire house infused with dappled light coming through the floor-to-ceiling windows as the sun peeked in and out of the trees swaying in the constant ocean breeze.

She just hoped whoever Jesse eventually chose to have his passel of kids with liked concrete and steel and lots and lots of glass. The lucky lady better like her own company, too, since she'd be spending her summers almost completely cut off from the rest of the world. But then Cadi sat up with a snort, figuring no woman in her right mind would complain about being stuck on an island with a handsome, sexy husband. Heck, there was a good chance all four of their kids would be conceived on Hundred Acre Isle.

"I bet you'll get to go with him on overseas business trips, too," Cadi muttered to the nondescript woman as she stood up and pulled her shirt over her head without bothering to unbutton it. She unfastened her slacks, then pushed them down and stepped free. "But probably what I envy about you the most is your obvious sophistication," she added as she headed to her en suite bathroom, knowing Jesse would marry a woman who wasn't only beautiful but who could socialize with business clients from all over the world. "You'll also have to know how to put on fancy parties at Rosebriar for his pet charities," she continued out loud, "entertain his wealthy friends with witty banter, and talk to their wives about the latest fashions."

Well, that certainly put her dreams in perspective, didn't it, since she doubted potluck church suppers counted as sophisticated . . . anything. And the most experience she'd had with people from away had been foreign students in college, and then she'd been too shy to talk to them.

Nope, she definitely didn't have any business picturing herself spending summers on Hundred Acre Isle, much less living at Rosebriar the rest of the year.

But that didn't mean she had to *stay* old-fashioned and unsophisticated.

The reason wealthy clients chose Glace & Kerr Architecture instead of a big-city firm was because they wanted homes just like the ones dotting the coast from Kittery to Eastport: large, opulent structures with weathered cedar shingles, meandering screened-in porches, and huge granite fireplaces. That's why she'd barely been able to contain her excitement when Jesse had said he wanted a modern house. But seeing the terror in Stanley's eyes, since he'd started with Owen Glace right out of college to find himself working almost exclusively on traditional homes, Cadi had given him a thumbs-up and mouthed the word *yeah*, then started drawing in her sketchbook. Hearing that Mr. Sinclair was a top executive at an international shipping company, she'd instantly thought . . . Waves. Steel ships. Concrete docks. And large expanses of glass like on a ship's wheelhouse, instead of dozens of perfectly lined-up windows.

Jesse had been adamant the home be state-of-the-art without being pretentious, saying the only people he wanted to impress were his children—catching Cadi by complete surprise, since the guy wasn't even married. That's when the idea of Winnie the Pooh had come to her—he had bought Hundred Acre Isle—and she'd realized the outside of the house had to be just as important as the inside. So she'd drawn an outdoor fire pit, a big scruffy dog, swings hanging from several tall pines, a fountain shaped like an open clamshell that would double as a wading pool, and, of course, hidden pots of honey. But it wasn't until Stanley had taken her to the island a third time that she'd added a working periscope rising up through the roof of the children's playroom, footpaths spidering through the forest, a freshwater pond fed by the spring she'd found, and a treehouse overlooking the small, sheltered beach on the south end of the island.

Oh yeah, she'd had many dreams of playing on that beach with her handsome, sexy husband and their children, not one of them wearing a wide-brimmed hat as they'd splashed around all the way up to their necks in the numbingly cold water.

Cadi turned on the shower. "I might have missed the boat—*ship*—with Jesse Sinclair," she murmured as she shed her bra and panties and stepped under the warm spray, "but after a couple of years of travel, there's no reason I can't be witty and sophisticated for when the *next* Mr. Right comes along."

Wait; why was she expecting him to come to her? Heck, there was a good chance Mr. Right was right now getting ready to head out on his own adventure, and what was to say she wouldn't find herself camped across from him in Yellowstone or Glacier National Park?

Now there was a dream with real-life potential. And how cool would it be to tell her children that she'd met their daddy in a redwood forest? Or on an airplane or a train. Or better yet, on a big scary roller coaster.

Wow. She should send Jesse Sinclair a thank-you card for making her realize it was time to get off her own comfortable couch.

Heck, maybe she'd even invite him to her wedding.

SEVEN

❧

Having found it was the only place he could get decent cell phone reception, Jesse sat leaning against a boulder atop the high ridge on his island, sipping his third beer while watching the last light of dusk fade in the western sky as he debated whether or not to install an antenna to strengthen the signal. So far he was leaning toward no, figuring a constantly ringing phone more or less defeated the purpose of having a sanctuary. But probably the biggest reason he liked not being readily available was because in his experience, whenever Sam or Ben—or in this case, *both*—left several text and voice messages asking him to please call while neglecting to mention why, Jesse knew he wasn't going to like the ensuing conversation.

Best-case scenario, he'd be heading back to New York in the morning. Worst-case, their larger corporate jet was already on its way to Maine and he'd be in Brazil this time tomorrow, trying to wrestle two of their ships away from a dock full of disgruntled longshoremen. The strike was in its third week, and despite telling their captains *last week* to get the hell out of there even without a back-load, the crews were refusing to cross the picket line to board their ships.

The email he'd sent before leaving New York had said that if they weren't at sea by midnight tonight, every last one of them was fired and could find their own way home. Looking to save their necks—as well as their generous paychecks—the captains had likely called Ben, who had in turn likely called Sam, and now both brothers were after him to fix the mess.

Jesse took another sip of beer as he pondered which one should have the pleasure of being told to go to hell right along with their captains and crews. He'd just spent three friggin' weeks dealing with the Brazilian longshore-men while paying a small fortune to house his men at a four-star beach resort in hopes of keeping them out of trouble, as well as placating a frantic logistics department fielding calls from businesses on four continents asking why their products were sitting on docks and rotting in the sun.

Jesse set down the empty beer beside the others and called Ben. "If you're going to insist on keeping a Maine address," he said the moment Ben answered, "you at least have to read the emails I send you. Specifically the ones pointing out when I'm on vacation."

"And if you insist on running off to your island, you at least have to answer your phone."

"I only just realized I can't get a decent signal here. When my phone didn't ring all day, I thought everyone was respecting the fact *I'm on vacation*."

"Who takes off in the middle of a strike?"

"Anyone who's *trying* to have a life outside the office."

"You need to go down there and fix this, Jesse."

"I didn't see your name on the vacation roster. You go down and fix it."

There was a moment's silence. "My passport's expired."

Jesse snorted. "Then I guess it's a good thing you and Mike got back from last month's fishing trip when you did, and saved Emma the trouble of having to fly her fancy Cessna under the radar to sneak you back across the Canadian border."

Another silence, then a sigh. "A word of warning, brother: a man's lying skills go to hell the moment he says 'I do.' Not that it appears you will ever have that problem."

"If I don't stay single, who's going to run all over the globe putting out fires? Because it looks to me like you and Sam are on some pretty short leashes."

"Did you really tell Simms and Poe they're fired if they didn't get out of port by midnight?" Ben asked, apparently deciding to ignore the dig. "You put it in writing?"

"I was pissed. Those longshoremen aren't about to stop empty boats from leaving. If anything, they'd consider it a victory. When Starrtech realized last week that the strike could go on indefinitely, their crews got out without any problem. So why can't our guys do the same?"

"It's called solidarity."

"No, it's called an all-expenses-paid vacation at an

overpriced resort. I say we move them to some dive up in the mountains and see how long before they decide to come home."

"Come home empty," Ben reminded him.

"Those ships aren't making any money rusting at the dock, either. If I have to go down there, I'm bringing a couple of skeleton crews willing to cross that picket line."

"Good luck finding them."

"Oh, I'm pretty sure a sizable bonus will bring them crawling out of the woodwork. It has to be cheaper than what the resort *your* secretary booked our men into is costing us."

That got Jesse a chuckle. "I think Deloris has a thing for Captain Poe. So you'll go down and fix this? Alone?"

"I can't drive two freighters all by myself."

"Offer those bonuses to our men already there."

"No," Jesse growled. "That's nothing short of extortion. If our crews realize they can hold our boats hostage, we're sunk. The only way for this to work is to leave them high and dry."

"Or you could go down and lead them across the picket line," Ben countered. "Simms and Poe are obviously betting you won't."

Jesse dropped his head with a succinct curse, knowing but not liking that Ben was right. Dammit, he didn't want to leave.

"Take Pamela with you," Ben suggested, "and finish your vacation at the resort after you get our ships on their way."

He sure as hell didn't want to do that, either. "I'm over Pamela."

There was another silence, then an equally nasty curse. "You're going to talk to someone who specializes in commitment issues if I have to drag you to the appointment myself."

"Last time I was at Pamela's, I found *wedding* magazines."

"Every mother signs their daughters up for those magazines on their eighteenth birthday. I think it's in the rule book they get when they leave the hospital with a girl baby."

"I checked the labels," Jesse snapped. "And Pamela's subscriptions started a month after she *accidentally* missed her ride home from the Henderson party. Aubrey Henderson set me up."

"Did Aubrey also make you *stay* at her niece's that night?"

Nope, not liking this conversation at all. "Nathaniel is begging for more responsibility. Why can't he go?"

"Because no one's going to take a kid who looks like he just started shaving last week seriously. You're the one who's been dealing with the longshoremen, and the only way they'll let our crews on that dock is if you're leading them." Ben hesitated. "What's going on, Jesse? Sam and I usually have to talk you out of rushing into the middle of these messes."

"This was supposed to be my first night sleeping on my island. It's gorgeous, Ben," he said quietly. "No matter where I'm standing on Hundred Acre, I can hear waves breaking on the ledges. And my contractor said he thinks there's an osprey nest at the south end, and I've seen two adult ospreys lugging fish in that direction all day." He sighed. "I've been waiting almost a year to fall asleep to the sound of waves hitting my shoreline."

"Get this mess cleaned up and you can spend the rest of the summer firing off emails to Nathaniel while listening to waves hit your shoreline."

"Fine. I'll call Regina and she can get her crew together and fly up in the morning."

"Don't bother," Ben drawled. "She somehow managed to land the Boeing in Trenton half an hour ago and should be refueled and done filing her flight plan by the time you get there."

That surprised Jesse. He'd expected to have to drive all the way to Bangor, since he'd thought only their much-smaller Lear could land in Trenton. "Just so you know, I'm giving myself that bonus. Oh, and based on the short glimpse I got of my house, I'm also going to need a hefty raise to pay for it."

"The model is done?" Ben said in surprise. "What does it look like? Send me a picture."

"I wasn't able to get a picture before it was crushed."

"Crushed?"

"Long story. I'll fill you in when I see you at Jen's bon voyage party."

"*If* there's a party," Ben said on a chuckle. "Willa called the other day and told Emma that once Sam realized how close Jennifer is to leaving, he started threatening to take an ax to the hull of her sloop. Hell, Willa said he actually tried to hide the girl's sailing prosthesis."

Jesse involuntarily shivered. "I've been tempted to

deep-six that sloop myself. But what I can't figure out is how come Willa's okay with her niece sailing solo around the world."

"Probably because she remembers being nineteen. Jennifer will be okay," Ben said, although he sounded like he was trying to convince himself more than Jesse. "That girl's as much at home on a moving deck as she is on land. And she's too smart to make stupid mistakes. Besides, I've already given her charts to our logistics department, so some of our smaller boats will be taking a few detours over the next year."

Faster, specialty cargo carriers, Jesse knew, that hadn't been part of Tidewater's fleet until three years ago, when Willa's then-sixteen-year-old niece had started planning this voyage. And near as Jesse could tell, about the only other person not worried that Jennifer—who had a prosthetic right foot—could circumvent the world solo was Emmet Sengatti, the man who had designed and personally built the *Spitfire*.

"She'll be okay," Jesse echoed, also trying to sound confident. "That boat has enough technology on board to practically sail itself." He dropped his head with a heavy sigh, resigned to the fact he'd be falling asleep tonight to the drone of a jet engine. "Give little Hank a hug from me, and tell him Unc-J is bringing him back a surprise from Brazil."

"Nothing alive," Ben warned. "We still haven't recovered from your last surprise."

Jesse couldn't help but grin. "You never found the gecko?"

"I'm pretty sure Beaker ate it. The dog started looking guilty about a day after it went missing and has been glued to Hank's side ever since. You want to spoil your nephew, just make sure he has a fleet to inherit that isn't two freighters short."

"Oh, I intend to get our boats back. I'm just not guaranteeing Simms and Poe will be at their helms. Bye, brother," Jesse added, ending the call before Ben could respond. "And thanks for nothing," he muttered to the huge orange moon peeking halfway over the ocean horizon.

Dammit, he didn't want to leave.

Although . . .

He was tempted to stop by Whistler's Landing tonight on his way to Trenton and see if Miss Glace might like her very first plane ride to be in a fast, comfortable corporate jet, with him serving as personal tour guide on her first foray into the world.

Not that she probably had a passport—expired or otherwise.

Jesse reached in his pocket and pulled out Cadi's fake engagement ring, then held it up in front of the moon as he wondered how any woman in this day and age, even one living so far off the beaten path, could be so . . . parochial. Hell, he'd bet a year's salary that instead of realizing the flowers she would have received this afternoon were to let her know he was romantically interested, Cadi would assume they were an attempt to sweet-talk her into rebuilding his models.

He probably shouldn't have kissed her this morning, but he hadn't been able to pass up the chance to see if those lips tasted as sweet in real life as they had in his dreams. He palmed the ring with a chuckle, remembering they'd tasted like bittersweet Moxie—which he'd tried today—and glazed doughnuts. He also remembered they'd gone from slackened in surprise to perfectly still, making him wonder if it had been so long since the woman had been kissed that she'd forgotten how to respond.

Or maybe she simply hadn't wanted to, worried that kissing a virtual stranger after just losing a fake fiancé was a step in the wrong direction.

Then again, maybe she didn't think *he* was Mr. Right, either.

And wouldn't that be ironic: a world-class woman-dodger being dodged by the very first woman he could see himself actually getting serious with.

EIGHT

❧

Cadi set a match to the cardboard and wood scraps she'd spent the last hour carrying out to her backyard fire pit, then stepped back and protectively hugged herself as she watched the flames creep toward the small sheet of plywood on top of the pile. But instead of the apprehension she'd been expecting, she felt surprisingly calm. Peaceful. Maybe even relieved.

No, wait. There. Were those shivers of doubt?

She momentarily stilled, then broke into a huge smile. Nope, that wild fluttering in her stomach was butterflies, she decided, batting their wings in anticipation of being set free.

And she didn't care if Beatrice did mean well, the woman had no business trying to scare her. "At least you have the good sense to get a motorhome and stay at campgrounds," her friend had said on their ride to Ellsworth three days ago, when Cadi had tried to prepare Bea for all the changes she intended to make. "Families and poor college students go camping, where there's no telling what sort of weirdos you'd run into staying at motels. But I think you should limit your travels to Maine, so you won't be too far away if you get in trouble." Bea had glanced over with an indulgent smile. "And if you truly feel daring, you could even venture into New Hampshire and Vermont. Those states are a lot like Maine."

"I'm fairly certain the whole point of traveling is to experience something *different*," Cadi had said. "And for me, that means visiting cities like Boston and New York. And I've always wanted to go to Florida and swim in ocean water that's warm."

Bea's smile had disappeared. "The sun reflecting off all that white sand will burn you to a crisp," she'd countered. "And can you imagine trying to maneuver even a small motorhome around Boston?"

"And then I'll head west," Cadi had continued brightly, determined to stay positive, "and visit Yellowstone and Yosemite and Glacier National Park. I'll camp in a redwood forest, raft through the Grand Canyon, and ride every roller coaster I come across."

"And you will," Bea had responded tightly, "with your *husband*."

"And just where am I supposed to find this great traveler," Cadi had said with mounting frustration, "when the only eligible bachelors in fifty miles are fishermen or loggers who think Massachusetts is a foreign country?"

She'd rolled her eyes. "When Bryan Fibbs mentioned his mom is planning to spend the summer with her sister, he turned as pale as a turnip when I suggested he drive Ansley to Portland instead of making her take the bus."

"Bryan gets lost driving to Bangor," Beatrice had snapped, only to take a calming breath. "People from away come here. Isn't Stanley from North Dakota?"

"From a town smaller than Whistler's Landing. All we get are retired summer people, and then usually only because they're lost." And then, for some insane reason, Cadi had added, "And it's not like I don't know anyone who lives in big cities, or are you forgetting that many of Dad's and Stanley's clients are from Boston and New York? In fact, Mr. Sinclair suggested I call him if I find myself in New York. And judging by the pictures I saw online, the personal tour he offered to give me of his beautiful home would definitely be worth battling city traffic to see. Rosebriar—that's the name of the estate his grandfather built—sits on twelve hundred acres and supposedly has eighteen bedrooms and *twenty-four* bathrooms."

Beatrice had suddenly pulled into a convenience store's parking lot, shifted the car into park, and turned as far as her seat belt would allow, making Cadi lean away from her glare. "Let me guess; I bet you told him you would love to have a *personal* tour."

Apparently still insane, Cadi had silently nodded.

"And that is exactly why you have no business traipsing all over the country alone. Not only did you willingly climb in his truck last night and let him drive you over an hour away, now you're telling me you intend to go see his home. So who else lives in this veritable palace with him? His parents? Brothers and sisters? His *wife*?"

Cadi had shaken her head. "He's not married. And it's my understanding his parents died when he was young, and Jesse has had Rosebriar to himself since his grandfather passed away three and a half years ago and his brothers got married and moved to Maine. Well, he mentioned having a cook, and I'm sure an estate that size has other staff, so it's not like he's completely alone. What's the big deal, anyway? Knowing I'm interested in beautiful architecture, I think it was nice of him to invite me to go see Rosebriar."

"Please tell me you're not that naive, Cadi," Beatrice had whispered. "Rich, handsome men like Mr. Sinclair do not invite single, blonde-haired, blue-eyed women over to show them twenty-four bathrooms."

"No, you're wrong about Jesse. He was a perfect gentleman last night, and even offered to unhook his camper and drive me all the way back home because he didn't like the idea of my staying at a motel. And trust me," Cadi had muttered, looking out the windshield, "I might not be worldly and sophisticated *yet*, but I'm definitely smart enough to know Jesse would never be interested in me that way." She'd turned just enough for her friend to see her smile, once again determined to lighten the mood. "And I also know the reason he's building on Hundred Acre Isle is because he's planning to get married and start a family. So I doubt a man focused on finding a wife is going to lure a Maine country bumpkin all the way to New York just to seduce her. So come on, already," she'd said, gesturing at the road. "This blonde-haired, blue-eyed bumpkin needs to buy herself a shiny red sports coupe. A convertible," she continued when Bea had hesitated. "One that will fit in a trailer I can tow behind the motorhome," she'd added in relief when her friend had finally started off again. "So the car will *stay* shiny."

Cadi came back to the present when the sea breeze sent several pieces of glowing cardboard swirling into the air. She added more scraps to the fire, then plopped down in one of the cedar lawn chairs. During their ride back from Ellsworth—without a sporty red convertible, since the dealership had sold the one she'd been eyeing two months ago—Cadi had managed to persuade Beatrice that she wasn't about to let every handsome man she met seduce her.

That is, right up until they'd returned home to find a huge bouquet of flowers sitting on her front porch. It hadn't helped that the card had said they were from Jesse, or that he'd offered to come pick her up in his corporate jet when she was ready to shop for a motorhome, as he knew a good RV dealership not far from Rosebriar—which, he'd added, would allow her to cross *airplane ride* off her bucket list. There'd also been a P.S. saying that despite the risk of sounding like a killjoy, he wondered if she had considered replacing her old-lady car with a sporty red SUV, as it occurred to him that a bit more road clearance might come in handy when she went looking for glaciers to walk on.

Good Lord, no wonder he was so successful; not only did the man have a memory like a steel trap, he actually *listened*. All of which had her right back to being naive, apparently, with Bea completely dismissing Cadi's argument that the flowers and plane ride were *businessman* Jesse Sinclair's attempt to get her to rebuild his models.

And now two people she loved were barely speaking to her.

For that matter, neither was Wiggles; yesterday's introduction to a harness and leash apparently an affront to the cat's ancestral wild Asian leopard genes.

"What the— Cadi, no!"

Cadi jumped to her feet with a startled gasp just as Stanley charged past.

"You said I had two weeks!" he shouted, kicking at the fire and sending burning wood scattering in a flurry of glowing embers. "Dammit, that was a model." He rounded on her when Cadi grabbed his arm. "Which one? Whose house was it?"

"Covington's," she said calmly, dragging him away from the pit. "And that wasn't a model; it was a mess of walls and windows that didn't make a lick of sense." She gave him a tug when he glanced back at the fire. "God Himself couldn't design a house for Marilyn Covington." Cadi nodded toward what was left of the plywood. "That was attempt number *four.*"

Stanley shrugged free and scrubbed his face on a groan. "I was afraid it was Stapleton's," he said behind his hands before dropping them to give her a pleading look. "Please tell me you haven't burned his model."

"There is nothing to burn except the sketchbook."

"Nothing?" he whispered, turning as pale as bleached flour. But then he brightened. "Do you at least have preliminary drawings I can use to work up something to show him?"

Cadi slipped her arm through his and started toward the house. "Not yet, unless you can make Dante's *Inferno* look like paradise."

He pulled her to a stop, having gone pale again. "Jesus, Cadi, the guy's coming here day after tomorrow."

"What? So soon? But at your meeting three weeks ago, I distinctly remember hearing you say you'd have something to show him in *September*."

"I did. But when he called last week, I . . . ah, I promised to move him to the top of the list. My plan was that once we showed Sinclair his models, I'd ask you to start on Stapleton's next. But when he called again this morning saying he was flying up to see what I've got, I was only able to stall him two days. You always flesh out your sketches after a meeting while everything's still fresh in your mind; all I need are a few drawings to prove I'm working on it."

"I came home and shoved Stapleton's sketchbook to the bottom of the pile because I thought the man was a pompous ass. Didn't I tell you not to take him on? I knew five minutes into the meeting he would be a demanding client. So how much did he offer you to cut in line?"

Stanley shook his head. "My agreeing to give him priority has nothing to do with money—at least not the way you think." He hesitated, then clasped her shoulders on a deep breath. "You know I have a brother who's been trying to open a restaurant in New York City? Well," he went on when she nodded, "Aaron ended up borrowing the startup money from Ryan Stapleton. But after eating at the restaurant last month, Stapleton said he didn't like the food and wanted his money back—immediately. All of it, including an obscene amount of interest, or Aaron would find himself feeding fish at the bottom of the Hudson River."

Cadi pulled away with a gasp. "The man's a loan shark? Your brother borrowed money from a *thug*?"

"Apparently," Stanley muttered. "But having heard Stapleton had just bought a tract of land on Long Island, Aaron mentioned he had a brother who's an architect, and Stapleton came to him a couple of days later and said he'd forgive the entire loan if I design him a house."

"Nice brother," she said, only having met Aaron once a couple of years ago, since instead of Aaron visiting Whistler's Landing, Stanley usually went to New York, claiming he liked visiting the city. "Not only was he stupid enough to borrow money from a loan shark—he didn't hesitate to get you involved."

"Aaron's all the family I got, Cads. And I imagine he thought it would be an easy fix; one house in exchange for one life."

"Did it ever occur to you to tell *me* what was going on?"

Stanley snorted. "Aaron wasn't exactly forthcoming when he called last month saying he was sending me an important client, and I thought the guy was just some rich businessman he was trying to impress. I didn't get the whole story until I called him after our first meeting with Stapleton." He snagged her hand and started leading her to the house. "Let's go through your sketchbook and maybe together we can come up with a concept I can expand on."

He scaled the rear deck stairs with her still in tow, opened the slider and led her inside, then headed directly to the large sunroom off the kitchen. "We'll work all night if we have to, and then . . ." He stopped and clasped her shoulders again. "And then I want you to pack enough clothes to last you a month and get out of here."

"What? Why?"

"Stapleton asked if he'll also be seeing you when he gets here." Stanley's usually boyish hazel-gold eyes turned troubled. "I know that sounds like an innocent question, but this morning Aaron confessed that he told Stapleton about your role in Glace and Kerr."

"Aaron knows?" Cadi said in alarm. "You told your brother what I do?"

He nodded, his face darkening. "We had a bit too much to drink the one time he came to visit, and when he saw one of your models and the plans I was working on, I apparently told him." His grip tightened when she tried to step away. "And because Stapleton also knows, I'd rather you not be here when he arrives."

"But *why*?"

Stanley released her and slipped his hands in his pockets as he turned to face the windows overlooking the ocean. "I'm worried that if he doesn't like what I have to show him, the bastard might . . ." He glanced over his shoulder at her. "I'm afraid he might come after you." He turned to face her. "You need to disappear. You said you want to start traveling, so go. Now."

"But I'm not ready *now*. I haven't even shopped for a camper yet. And the SUV I bought won't be delivered until tomorrow morning."

"That still gives us plenty of time. We'll work on a preliminary design tonight, and you can be packed and ready to go the moment it arrives."

"But go *where*?"

"Anywhere," he said, slashing a hand through the air. "Just drive." He stepped toward her. "But I don't want you telling anyone where you are, you understand? Not Beatrice and not even me. And because I don't know the full extent of Stapleton's reach, I want you to withdraw enough cash from the bank to last you a month instead of using credit cards."

Cadi took a calming breath, even as she hugged herself. "Are you sure you're not overreacting? Why do you think Stapleton is a threat to me?"

"You said it yourself, the man's a thug. According to Aaron, only idiots with a death wish get between him and what he wants. And from the look of things, the bastard has decided he wants an award-winning house designed by Glace and Kerr Architecture."

"He's not going to kill anyone over a stupid house."

"You willing to hang around and find out? Because I don't know about you, but I don't particularly care to be feeding fish at the bottom of the Hudson."

"So does that mean you're also going to leave? Because why are we bothering to work up a design if you're going to get in your car and drive away, too?"

"I can't. If I disappear, Stapleton will go after my brother."

"Then take Aaron with you," she half-growled, half-cried.

"And spend the rest of our lives looking over our shoulders?" He shook his head. "I can fix this, Cadi. If you'll just work your magic and come up with a concept that speaks to Stapleton's ego, I can draft the bastard a house even the devil would be proud to live in."

"And if he doesn't like what you show him in two days?"

"Then I buy us time by telling him that just as soon as you get back from your trip to Europe, the three of us will put our heads together and come up with something he does like. Meanwhile, you can email me alternative designs from the road."

"You're serious," she whispered, hugging herself again. "You expect me to just drive away and leave you to face Stapleton alone?"

"You expect me to let you get drawn into the mess?" Stanley whispered back, his eyes softening. "You're more than like a sister to me, Cads; for the last five years you've been my best friend. And I wouldn't be able to live with myself if anything happened to you."

"But anything *what*? I still don't understand why you're so sure I'm in danger."

"Well, for starters," he said, his softness vanishing, "Stapleton started drooling the moment you came running into the office ten minutes late the day of our meeting, and then he spent the next two hours watching you scribble in your sketchbook out of the corner of his eye. Why do you think he insisted on flying up here again when I pointed out it would be easier to just send him what I've got, if not to see you? So the *danger*," he rushed on when she tried to speak, "is that if he doesn't like the concept, I wouldn't put it past the bastard to send a couple of men here to personally escort you to New York, where he'll then force you to design his house. *While*," he added, gesturing toward her, "he also helps himself to your lovely body."

"Don't be ridiculous," she snapped. "The man's not going to kidnap me."

"Don't be naive," he snapped back. "Women disappear every day."

"God, you sound just like Bea. Does everyone think I have the brains of a chipmunk?"

Stanley took a calming breath and stepped forward, then wrapped her up in his arms and pressed her head to his shoulder. "You're not dumb, Cads," he whispered. "But you haven't exactly been living in the real world, either." He hesitated, taking an even longer, deeper breath. "And I know exactly what Ryan Stapleton is capable of, because up until nine years ago I was on my way to being just like him."

"They have thugs in North Dakota?" Cadi ended up mumbling against his shoulder when he refused to let her lean away.

"No, in Atlanta, which is where I grew up until I *wised* up and ran off to Boston. And once I got my degree, I kept running all the way to safe, boring, Whistler's Landing."

"You . . . you were a thug?"

"I was until I saw my best friend get gunned down at

his family's pizza shop when one of his drug deals went bad and I had to skip town when the men came gunning for me."

Cadi went perfectly still. "Did . . . did Daddy know any of this?"

"I told Owen about a year and a half after I started working for him."

Cadi shoved against him and broke free. "You're lying! Daddy never would have approved of our getting married if he knew your background."

"He would have if he felt that background would help me keep you safe."

"Safe from what—gang fights at potluck suppers?"

"From the world," he said gently. "Do you honestly believe your father didn't know how badly you've always wanted to travel? Hell, it was Owen's idea that I take you to Tahiti for our honeymoon." His eyes softened with his grin. "He also asked me to take you hiking up mountains and swimming in the ocean, only someplace where the water was warm. And he hoped we'd take our kids tenting, and get a sailboat so we could show them the houses he'd designed from the ocean instead of the road."

Cadi lifted her hands to cover her face, utterly speechless. All these years her dad had known about her dream to travel? He'd even known that as a kid she'd wanted to hike up Cadillac and swim in the ocean and go camping and . . . and . . .

"He died of guilt," she rasped, still hiding her face, "so I could start *living*."

"Aw, hell, Cads, don't cry," Stanley murmured, folding

her into his embrace again and slowly rubbing her back. "When we were working late a few months before he died," he went on tenderly, "Owen told me he would have followed Sandra to the grave if not for you. It was then that I realized instead of easing his stress, our getting engaged actually freed him." The chest she was tucked up against expanded slightly. "I don't think I've ever felt more accepted as when Owen told me he could die in peace knowing I'd be here for you." He ducked his head to let her see his smile. "He said I would be better than him at not smothering you, and made me promise not to smother our kids." He gave her a squeeze then stepped back with a chuckle. "He also suggested I not wait until I'm in my fifties to have them."

Using the cuff of her shirt to wipe her eyes, Cadi pounced on the chance to change the subject. "Are you going to have children?"

"I wouldn't mind having one or two, assuming I can find a woman who would love me enough to live in a safe, boring town."

Cadi felt heat creeping into her cheeks, but simply couldn't stop herself from asking. "Was there a candidate for Mrs. Kerr at your birthday party? Because I imagine any of those women would know how to keep things from being boring."

Stanley's jaw momentarily slackened, then snapped shut as he spun away—though not quickly enough to hide his own blush—and strode over to her desk. "Where's Stapleton's sketchbook? The sooner we start on that concept, the more time you'll have to pack."

"What's it like?" she asked, following him.

"What's what like?" he muttered, riffling through her organized clutter.

"Having sex with a bunch of people," she said, reaching past him and pulling a book from the bottom of one of the piles. "I couldn't decide who was having more fun—the men watching the women sprawled all over you or the women themselves."

He headed to the worktable set up in front of the bank of windows facing the ocean. "How the hell long were you standing there?"

"Long enough to realize that one of those girls probably wasn't even old enough to vote," she said, following him again.

"Lilly is *twenty*." Stanley pulled out a chair and sat down, then propped his head in his hands with a groan. "I'm sorry, Cads."

"Sorry for what?" she asked, sitting down beside him. "That I walked in on you or that I'm jealous as hell?"

He jerked his head up. "Jealous of *what*?"

"Of those women. Of their . . . freedom."

"You think they're free?" he asked, leaning back in his chair. "Cadi, one of them is a self-admitted sex addict, and one is trying to prove to her ex-boyfriend that she's sexier than the girl he dumped her for. That's not freedom; it's compulsion."

"And the third woman?"

"She goes to Machias," he snapped, "and is trying to avoid racking up huge student loans by being a part-time prostitute. Mark brought her along to make things even."

"And the men? What are their reasons for having kinky sex?"

"They're *men*. We don't need a reason, only willing women. Now focus," he muttered, reaching for the sketch-book, "so I won't be forced to dust off my thug badge and feed *Stapleton* to the fishes before you find yourself in New York experiencing kinky sex firsthand."

NINE

❧

Cadi pushed the covered litter box to the side and slid the last suitcase into the rear of her shiny red SUV, taking a deep whiff of the wonderful new vehicle smell before it vanished the first time Wiggles went to the bathroom. She mentally reminded herself to grab some tiny plastic bags so she could immediately scoop up the mess and dump it in the first public trashcan she found. Surely a cat couldn't be any harder to travel with than a baby, could it, since both ate and pooped and slept more hours than they were awake? And she could even leave Wiggles in the car alone for short periods of time, provided it wasn't hot out.

"Is there a reason you had to do this today?" Stanley asked, making her straighten to see him staring at

Beatrice speeding in Cadi's tree-lined driveway ahead of a Salvation Army truck.

"I stopped at their Ellsworth store and made the appointment Friday, when I borrowed your truck to go back to the dealership. Then the moment I got home, I started going through the house like a madwoman, deciding what I wanted to donate before I talked myself *out* of finally getting on with my life once and for all."

Stanley closed the rear hatch, then snagged her hand and led her along the side of the house. "Just as soon as they're done loading the truck, you're out of here right behind them." He stopped beside the front porch and looked back at the SUV, which had been delivered at nine that morning, parked near the rear deck. "The windows are tinted enough that Beatrice can't see you're packed. So don't tell her you're leaving, because I don't want her asking a bunch of questions you can't answer."

"Are you serious? It's *Bea.* She'll call the sheriff the moment she decides I'm missing."

He winced. "You're right." He hesitated, obviously thinking. "Tell her you're going shopping for a motorhome and expect to be gone at least a couple of weeks. Say you intend to look at dealerships in Bangor and Portland and even in Massachusetts." More thinking. "When the two weeks are up, call and say you're still searching, but always give her the name of a city far from where you really are." He went back to watching Bea approach. "Go ahead and take pictures of any motorhomes you come across, then send them to her and ask what she thinks, to back up your story. Just make sure there aren't any recognizable landmarks in the background. And whatever you do, don't actually buy a camper or give a salesman any personal information that might leave a paper trail."

Cadi cocked her head while she listened, wondering what had happened to the carefree architect she knew and loved. Did all men have a dark side? Because Stanley the thug was even more disconcerting than Jesse the high-powered executive. Where Jesse appeared to reserve that side of himself for crushing business rivals, she'd just spent all night and this morning a little scared and a whole lot in awe of Stanley. Apparently determined to live up to her father's trust in him to protect her, it was as if the guy had suddenly morphed into Batman. Lacking only a mask and cape, he'd spent the last twenty-four hours giving her a crash course on disappearing so he could stay behind and save his brother from the evil villain.

Heck, she should have drawn Stapleton as the Joker instead of the Mad Hatter.

Stay at small, no-questions-asked motels so you won't have to show your driver's license because you're paying in cash, Stanley had instructed as they'd worked into the night. Even better, buy a tent and stay at campgrounds, but move on every couple of days. Run your temporary license plate right up until it expires, then change the date on it. Purchase a prepaid cell phone and text me every so often to let me know you're okay. And if you call Beatrice or anyone, explain the different number by saying your phone got wet and you grabbed a new one at Walmart. And I also want you to buy three canisters of Mace, then find a gravel pit and use one of the canisters to practice spraying a rock without spraying yourself in the process, he'd added just before crashing on her couch around two in the morning only to wake up issuing instructions again as she'd cooked him breakfast.

No, she didn't know this Stanley at all.

"Cadi," Bea said as she got out of her car and rushed over. "These men stopped at my store asking where you lived, and I decided it was easier to have them follow me out here. They said you're donating nearly an entire house of furniture to the Salvation Army."

"I told you on our ride to Ellsworth last week that I was redecorating."

"But this soon?" Bea darted a frantic look at Stanley, then back at her. "Cadi, what if you give something away only to find yourself regretting it later? A lot of that furniture is heirloom quality and should be passed down to your children."

"I'm keeping a few sentimental pieces. But both bedroom sets and all the linens are going, along with the sofa, the chairs and lamps, and the dining room table," she explained as she started toward the truck pulling to a stop beside Bea's car.

"Stanley, do something," Cadi heard Bea hiss. "Because I hope you know this is your fault. The girl's been acting crazy ever since she walked in on you having sex with all those people. She's so embarrassed she couldn't even come to church service yesterday, and I don't remember her ever missing Sunday night Bible study."

"I can't speak to her skipping service," Stanley drawled, making Cadi halt in mid-step and cover her mouth when he added, "but I do know she missed Bible study in favor of entertaining some of *those people* when

I brought them out to meet her yesterday. That's probably why she's yawning, since they didn't leave until after midnight."

Cadi immediately dropped her hand and started off again, even as she wondered what her life would have been like if she really had married Stanley the architect/thug.

She probably wouldn't have had to worry about dying of boredom.

"Hello, gentlemen," she said to the three men standing beside the truck. "You'll find several boxes of small appliances and dishes on the dining room table, along with a couple bags of linens. I hope you don't mind that some of the furniture is on the second floor."

All three chests puffed out and their apparent leader's eyes crinkled with his grin. "You don't worry your cute little blonde curls about that, honey. These muscles have hauled a lot heavier stuff than beds and bureaus down three, sometimes four flights of stairs," he said, actually lifting his arm and flexing his biceps. He looked at his two buddies. "Virgil, you get the handtruck, and Gus, you bring the padded mats. If the furniture's half as pretty as its owner, we don't want it getting scratched." He looked over and gave her a wink. "I'll see to it personal, Miss Glace, that your stuff goes to people who'll take right good care of it."

Cadi barely caught herself from rolling her eyes at the outrageous old flirt, instead giving him a smile and a nod. "Thank you." She gestured toward the porch. "Go ahead in the front door and straight upstairs, and I'll be up shortly. The two bedroom sets and mattresses are yours to take, and anything I'm keeping is clearly marked with large Post-it notes."

"Please rethink this before it's too late," Beatrice whispered as she came up beside her. "Once it's gone, it's gone forever."

"I've been thinking this to death for fourteen months," Cadi said gently. "And I'm looking forward to refurnishing with items from my travels." She glanced back to see Stanley had gone inside. "Speaking of traveling, I intended to stop in and let you know I'm leaving this morning to go look at motorhomes. I expect to be gone a couple of weeks, but I'll text you every day so you won't worry I'm holed up in some seedy motel with a man. I'll even send pictures of ones I like so you can tell me what you think. Of *motorhomes*," she added dryly at her friend's gasp.

"This isn't a joking matter," Bea hissed. "You're moving too fast." She glanced down the side of the house, then back at Cadi through narrowed eyes. "Or maybe you're not joking. I see you didn't waste any time taking Mr. Sinclair's advice about buying an SUV, which makes me wonder if you're not meeting his corporate jet in Trenton and shopping for that motorhome in New York while getting a *personal* tour of his twenty-four bedrooms."

Cadi just barely stifled a gasp of her own. Was there a reason she'd never noticed how controlling Bea was?

Oh, that's right; she'd been too busy pleasing everyone. God, maybe she did have the brains of a chipmunk. "It's eighteen bedrooms and twenty-four *bathrooms*," she said as she headed up the walkway. "And I intend to tinkle in every one of them."

"Don't you understand the reason I'm worried is because I love you?" Bea called out as Cadi climbed the stairs. "You're like a daughter to me."

Cadi stopped on the porch and turned to face her. "Then don't you think that just like your real daughter, it's time for me to grow up, too?"

"Why?" Bea said thickly. "So you can move two thousand miles away and only bring your babies to visit *maybe* once a year?"

And therein lay Beatrice's biggest fear and greatest sorrow, and why she—as well as the entire population of Whistler's Landing—was clinging to the last town daughter with the tenacity of a bulldog. Cadi gave her a sad smile. "I'm not flying to New York, Bea; I really am driving around looking at campers. And no matter how far my travels do eventually take me, I'll always come back, because this," she said, gesturing toward the house, "will always be home."

"That's what Anne thought, too, until she went off to college and fell in love with a man from Colorado. Nobody comes back once they see all that's out there."

Cadi said nothing, since she couldn't very well argue with a time-proven truth.

Bea just as silently walked to her car and opened the door, but didn't get in. "You . . . you promise to call and text me?"

"I promise. And I'll send pictures of— Oh, sorry," Cadi said, scrambling out of the way when a man stepped onto the porch guiding the handtruck carrying her padded bureau. She turned back at the sound of an engine starting, only to sigh at the sight of her friend backing around and then speeding out the driveway.

Cadi spent the next two hours overseeing the men methodically emptying her house, gave them each a crisp hundred-dollar bill from the money Stanley had given her until she could get to a bank, then stood on the porch hugging herself as she watched a good part of her sheltered, sensible life leaving in the back of a Salvation Army truck.

"Do you think I'm going to regret it?" she asked when she sensed Stanley standing in the doorway behind her.

"It's been my experience we more often regret *not* doing something," he said, wrapping his arms around her from behind. "In fact, I sometimes regret not falling in love with you."

That made her smile. "I've never taken your lack of romantic interest personally." She shrugged inside his embrace. "Probably because I've always felt you made a better big brother than you would a husband. Or so I thought when you were nothing but a boring architect."

"And now that you know the real me?"

"Sorry," she said, patting his arm, then dropping hers. "Now you're just a *bossy* big brother who apparently likes group sex."

He dropped his own arms and stepped away with a snort. "I suppose that beats godless heathen," he mumbled, walking in the house.

Cadi followed him into the kitchen. "Who called you that?"

"Who do you think?" he said, continuing into the sunroom.

She didn't have to think long. "Beatrice. When did

she— Oh, I bet it was the night of your party. Bea actually called you a godless heathen?"

He went to the desk and picked up something, then turned with a grin. "Just before she threw my birthday cake at me. Which you would know if you hadn't run off like a scandalized virgin and left your *big brother* to deal with the mess you made."

"I wasn't the one having an orgy."

"No, you just invited the entire town to *mine*." He held up what she realized were four of her sketchbooks, his grin broadening. "And for payback, I'm taking these with me."

"I thought you were in here working on Stapleton's house, not snooping."

He shook his head. "I'll work on it tonight. But just as soon as the bastard leaves tomorrow, I have to start deciphering your drawings in order to have something to show the Covingtons when I meet them at their building site on Friday. At which time," he added, his eyes lighting with a familiar gleam, "I plan to bring along my first, and, with any luck, my *last* candidate for a partner." He went back to grinning when Cadi gasped in surprise. "I thought watching her interact with clients should be part of the interview."

"*Her?* You're thinking of taking on a woman partner? Who is she?" Cadi asked when he nodded. "How did you find her?"

"Sarah Pinsky. And I found her résumé posted on one of the online career sites I started searching the moment I got back from picking you up in Castle Cove. Sarah's been working in Denver for the last ten years, and her cover letter said she's looking to join a more intimate firm that specializes in residential design."

"And you've already spoken to her, and she's agreed to come for an interview?"

His grin turned derisive. "It's more like we're interviewing each other. I might have Owen Glace's reputation backing me up, but Sarah has more actual experience. And judging from the portfolio she sent me, the woman appears to possess an inordinate amount of boldness." He shook his head. "One of the houses she designed had a huge icosahedron-shaped cupola with windows that actually fold open like petals on a flower."

Cadi covered her mouth. "I have no idea what that is," she said behind her hands, "but if you're impressed, then so am I. Oh, Stanley," she cried, throwing herself at him and squishing her sketchbooks between them, "she sounds like your perfect complement."

"Maybe," he said. "Assuming Glace and Kerr Architecture and Whistler's Landing aren't *too* intimate for her."

"Kerr and *Pinky* Architecture," Cadi said, trying to catch the books as she stepped back.

"It's Pinsky, not Pinky," he muttered, bending to pick up the one she missed, then waving it in the air. "But I still need something to show the Covingtons on Friday."

"Oh, I almost forgot." Cadi rushed to her desk, reached into the narrow space between it and the wall, then straightened holding a long, thick roll of papers. "I thought of this last night while you were napping and planned to give it to you before I left. You don't need to decipher my Covington drawings," she explained, walking back and handing him the roll, "because I want you to build them this house."

Stanley carefully unrolled the old set of plans out on the table, then simply stared down at the front page in silence. "This is your father's house," he finally whispered, lifting uncertain eyes to hers. "The one he designed for your mother. Owen brought me in here the night of our engagement party and showed me these plans, saying he'd cajoled Sandra into marrying him by building her this house, but that it burned down on Christmas Eve ten years later."

Cadi gestured in the direction of the kitchen. "Realizing by then they probably wouldn't ever have children, they built this Cape in its place. Only Dad had to raise the roof facing the ocean when Mom suddenly got pregnant with me. Take it, Stanley," she said, nodding at the plans. "It's a beautiful home and deserves to have a family living in it. Work your own magic updating it to the twenty-first century, and I promise that Marilyn Covington will immediately recognize it as the house she didn't know she wanted."

"She asked for a coastal-cottage showpiece, not a New England farmhouse," he halfheartedly argued, looking down and reverently turning the pages.

"Marilyn was all over the place about what she wanted," Cadi countered with a laugh. "One minute she was describing a palace and the next minute a small college dormitory. She has *six* kids. Trust me, when she sees all those bedrooms and bathrooms and that huge eat-in farm kitchen, she's going to fall in love. And if you stretch the garage to three bays and add a nanny suite above it, George Covington is going to start calling you for marital advice for being able to read his wife's mind."

Stanley carefully rerolled the fifty-year-old plans and held them to his chest with a sad smile. "When he showed me these plans, Owen said he'd imagined the house filled with the children he and Sandra had hoped to have. Hell, Cads," he whispered, "I almost came clean about our deception when he said he wouldn't mind if you and I updated it for ourselves." He lifted the roll away from his chest. "Are you sure you want to give it to the Covingtons?"

"I'm sure. I'd rather see it being lived in instead of collecting dust in a corner." She headed for the kitchen. "You just make sure you write *nanny suite* in big bold letters that George Covington can't miss." She shot a smile over her shoulder. "And you might want to wear a raincoat to your meeting on Friday, because Marilyn is going to throw herself at you and burst into tears of gratitude."

"I don't remember them asking for a nanny suite," he said, following.

"Then you and George must both have selective hearing, because I distinctly remember Marilyn asking for an oversized extra bedroom with an attached bath." Cadi stopped in front of the cat carrier sitting on the counter to see Wiggles glaring out at her. "And since I doubt there's going to be a *seventh* little Covington, that little request told me Marilyn is quietly planning to hire a

nanny to help her keep track of the six she already has."
She tapped Stanley on the chest. "Which is why I'm relieved you're open to taking on a female partner, and why
I think you and Sarah should sit in on each other's meetings with clients. Men and women *hear* differently, Stanley, and I can't tell you how many times I put something
in a model that my father had overlooked even though
he'd taken pages and pages of notes."

"Sarah's going to think I'm incompetent if I ask her to
sit in on meetings." He shook his head. "I'm not sure that's
how it's done in large firms. In fact, I don't think anything
about how Owen worked with clients was normal. Hell,
I wouldn't be surprised if Sarah ends the interview the
minute she sees I still use a drafting table instead of a
computer."

"Or the woman manages to drag you into the twenty-
first century." Cadi touched his arm. "You just need to
be upfront with her, Stanley, and explain that you started
right out of school with an old-fashioned, small-town
architect, and that's why you're specifically searching for
a contemporary partner. And don't sell yourself short.
There's a good chance you can teach Sarah Pinky a thing
or two about drafting."

"It's Pin-*ski*," he corrected, tucking the house plans
under his arm to pick up Wiggles' carrier. "And now it's
time for you ladies to disappear," he said, striding onto
the back deck, "and for me to park my ass at my ancient
drafting table and flesh out that concept for Stapleton
before I find myself designing *fish* houses on the bottom
of the Gulf of Maine."

*　*　*

Swatting at something tickling her ear as she crouched in the bushes, Cadi could only hope this wasn't a harbinger of future adventures. She might be eager to spread her wings, but unceremoniously being forced to leave town had turned all those beautiful butterflies in her belly into angry bees. Cadi held her breath when she saw Stanley's boring old pickup speeding toward her and didn't start breathing again until he drove past without noticing her tire marks. She stood up and headed deeper into the woods, feeling a bit guilty for asking him to go back and check that all the cellar windows were locked, but she'd needed to buy enough time to race ahead and pull down the dirt road at the edge of her property.

Besides digging out her father's old house plans last night while Stanley had slept, she'd also filled several boxes with supplies and quietly lugged them out to the shed. It wasn't that she was being sneaky; she simply hadn't wanted to admit that if she didn't have something to keep her mind occupied, she'd probably go crazy worrying about him having to deal with Stapleton all by himself. She also hadn't wanted a drawn-out discussion on how she was going to build a model while on the run, mostly because she hadn't wanted to explain that she had absolutely no intention of moving every couple of days like a criminal. She could fabricate trees and rocks and even walls and windows, but there was no way she could pack and unpack a sheet of plywood every morning and night once she actually started assembling the model, much less fit it in the SUV with everything else.

And anyway, if chipmunks had enough brains to live in a world full of predators and not get eaten, surely she could find a safe place to set up shop.

Because honestly? She really couldn't see Wiggles sleeping in motel rooms filled with strange smells every night and being stuck in her carrier all day every day. Wigs was a Bengal—a cross between a small wild Asian leopard and a domestic short-haired cat—whose entire life revolved around coming and going at will through her cat door to spend hours patrolling the peninsula. Which meant that without a camper to call home, she gave Wiggles three or four days before the independent little bugger turned into the traveling companion from hell.

Cadi veered off the tote road when she reached her SUV, made her way through the narrow section of woods, then stopped beside a large tree and looked around. Seeing nothing but seagulls and a few immature loons bobbing on the gentle waves, she scrambled down the steep bank and ran along the beach, then scaled the bank again behind the tool shed. She calmly walked to the front and opened the double doors, pulled out the garden cart loaded with boxes, then wheeled it toward the beach path farther up the peninsula. It took longer than she expected to drag the heavy cart back along the rock-strewn beach, and the steep bank forced her to abandon it above the high tide mark and lug one box at a time up to the SUV—her huffing and puffing fourth trip making her wonder if she was having fun yet.

She slid in behind the steering wheel with a winded groan, reached a finger through the door of the crate belted into the passenger seat, and stroked Wiggles' cheek. "I'm sorry it's not the traveling conditions I promised, but try to hang in there, kiddo, and I'll see if I can't find a way to make this work." She started the engine and headed out the narrow dirt road. "Which means our first stop is going to be the L.L.Bean outlet in Ellsworth to buy camping equipment. I should probably get two tents," she went on, even as she wondered if she was going to spend the entire trip talking to a cat. "One of them large enough to set up a work table," she continued out loud, mentally reminding herself to buy a folding table. And a cooler, sleeping bag, blow-up mattress, cookstove, lantern, pots and dishes and . . . Good Lord, she needed *everything.*

She pulled onto the main road heading away from Whistler's Landing and suddenly smiled. Besides thanking Jesse Sinclair for nudging her off her comfortable couch, it would appear she also owed him for suggesting she buy a roomy SUV instead of a small, sporty coupe.

But then she sighed. She supposed she'd have to include his wife on her wedding invitation, even if it meant being outshone by Jesse's beautiful and sophisticated— and by then likely pregnant—Mrs. Right.

As for her *Mr.* Right, Cadi hoped his adventure was getting off to a more promising beginning, because she wouldn't be sending invitations to anything if the poor guy got discouraged enough to turn around before they even had a chance to meet.

TEN

Not quite ready to admit that bouncy blonde curls and sparkling blue eyes may have played a role in his decision to end his eighteen-day, four-continent flying marathon in Maine instead of New York, Jesse stopped in front of Glace & Kerr Architecture and shut off his truck, only to scowl at the closed sign on the door. Even though he hadn't been able to give an exact time, he knew Stanley was expecting him this afternoon, since the man had returned his email confirming their appointment.

And to his thinking, 1:30 p.m. was considered afternoon on any continent.

Jesse closed his eyes and rested his head on the steering wheel, surprisingly close to roaring in frustration. It had taken him longer to fly to Brazil and back than it had to wrestle his boats away from the longshoremen. But then he'd had to spend two days in New York trying to keep a frenzied logistics department from self-destructing, and two freaking *weeks* flying all over Europe and northern Africa to personally soothe disgruntled clients threatening to switch their business to Starrtech. So if spending eighteen days of his life that he'd never get back in more time zones than he could count wasn't bad enough, there was also the fact that Cadi hadn't answered any of the texts he'd sent her. And now, adding insult to injury, it appeared his architect had stood him up. So not only was the realization he might be leaving here *again* without a copy of his house plans adding to his foul mood, he'd been hoping Stanley could give him some insight as to why Cadi wasn't responding to his texts—preferably *before* he hunted her down to ask her in person.

The least the woman could have done was acknowledge receiving his flowers.

Jesse sat up at the sound of a vehicle and watched in his rearview mirror as an older-model pickup pulled up behind him, his relief at seeing Stanley behind the wheel vanishing when he realized the female passenger—whose head of wildly spiked dark hair barely showed above the dash—was *not* Cadi. He got out and walked around his truck to meet them on the sidewalk.

"Mr. Sinclair," Stanley said as he extended his hand. "I hope you haven't been waiting too long." He ended the handshake on a wince. "Our new client's building site wasn't quite as accessible as he led us to believe, and his wife insisted on showing us every page of the idea book she's spent the last two years putting together," he explained, gesturing at the thick binder the definitely petite, mid-thirtyish woman was hugging to her decidedly ample chest. "I'd like you to meet Sarah Pinsky, who as of ten minutes ago has agreed to become my new partner."

"Ms. Pinsky," Jesse said, shaking the hand she extended after shifting the binder.

"Stanley showed me photographs of your island, Mr. Sinclair," she returned, her warm smile crinkling bright green eyes framed by neon red glasses that matched her lipstick—which also matched several streaks in her spiked hair. "And although it's definitely off the beaten path, I certainly understand why you chose to build out there. The sunrises must be spectacular."

Not that he'd had the pleasure of seeing one yet. "And did Stanley also show you the plans for the equally spectacular house he designed to take advantage of those sunrises?"

"Um . . . no," she said, looking at Stanley then back at Jesse. "But if it's anything like the beautiful homes he's taken me to see this past week, I can definitely picture it sitting on that high granite ridge, where you'll have commanding views out every one of its windows."

"Actually, he tucked the house up against a lower, southeast-facing bluff," Jesse said as he also glanced at Stanley, only to wonder at the man's suddenly guarded look. He smiled at Sarah. "And it's *window*, as in one long, floor-to-ceiling wall of glass. And based on the short glimpse I got of the model a couple of weeks ago, I'm going to need a second job not only to pay for all that concrete and steel, but also to move that much tonnage across three miles of open water." The magnitude of which he'd spent a good portion of his flight-time contemplating, which would have been a lot easier if he'd had the plans and accompanying spec-sheets.

"Concrete and steel?" Ms. Pinsky repeated, looking at Stanley in surprise. "But I thought Glace and Kerr built its reputation on designing large, New England cottage–style homes."

"We have," Stanley said, grasping her elbow and turning her toward the door. "But Jesse asked for something . . . less traditional. Why don't you go on in and start officially settling into your new office while Mr. Sinclair and I take a little walk."

"*Mr. Sinclair* prefers to see his plans," Jesse said once Sarah disappeared inside.

Stanley studied him as if trying to gauge his mood, then headed across the road.

Jesse bit back a curse and followed. "Can you at least tell me how Cadi is doing? I sent her several texts over the past couple of weeks, but she never responded."

"She's traveling," Stanley said, turning onto the lane leading down to the pier. "And she didn't answer because her phone apparently got ruined a couple of weeks ago, and she's been using a prepaid phone until she decides which new model she wants to get."

"Traveling? She purchased a motorhome already?"

Stanley shot him a tight grin. "No, she took your advice and bought a sporty little SUV, loaded it with camping equipment, and left a couple of weeks ago to shop for a motorhome."

"But I thought she didn't want to travel without her cat."

"She's not." He shrugged, this time his grin derisive.

"Apparently Cadi thinks Wiggles would rather sleep in a tent than stay with me."

Jesse stepped in front of him when they reached the beginning of the pier, forcing Stanley to stop. "Then can you please give me her new cell number?"

Stanley folded his arms over his chest, his stance somewhat defensive. "I'd rather not."

Jesse felt his mood darken further at the feeling that Stanley was hiding something. But what really worried him was that he suspected it concerned Cadi. Because the easygoing architect he'd been dealing with for the last six months appeared to have vanished, replaced by an edgier, more intense, and definitely guarded . . . prevaricator.

Well, Cadi had said she intended to burn her sketchbooks to force Stanley to find a new partner. Hell, maybe she'd tossed a few house plans on the fire with them.

"Mind telling me why you'd *rather not*?"

"Because I don't want you bugging her to rebuild your models. She's on a much-needed, long-overdue adventure."

Jesse relaxed slightly. "And if I promise not to mention the models?"

Stanley's eyes narrowed again, obviously trying to decide why else he would want Cadi's number. The easygoing architect suddenly reappeared and shook his head with a grin. "Give her some time, Jesse. She's been waiting twenty-nine years for the sweet taste of freedom."

"I don't want to clip her wings. In fact, I consider her eagerness to travel one of her more appealing traits. Right up there," he drawled, "with her fondness for snooping and telling lies."

Stanley stiffened, once again turning defensive. "Why would you say—"

"Stanley! Stanley!" Sarah Pinsky shouted as she ran down the lane toward them. "You need to come. Quick!"

"Why? What's going on?" he asked, having to catch the frantic woman when she ran into him trying to stop. "Sarah, what's wrong?"

"Man in your office . . . beat up . . . says he's your brother," she stammered between huge gulps of air as Stanley held her shoulders and bent to look her level in the eye. "I went to put your mail on your desk and found him . . . tied to your chair . . . he snapped at me to go get you." Sarah Pinsky chased after him when Stanley took off up the lane. "I didn't call the police yet," she continued as Jesse also followed. "We need to call them."

"No cops," Stanley growled over his shoulder, barely dodging a car that had to slam on its brakes when he sprinted across the road without looking.

Jesse caught Ms. Pinsky in time to stop her from running into the same car and guided her over to the sidewalk, but stopped her from going inside as he looked around for . . . hell, he guessed for anything that didn't look right. "You didn't see anyone else or hear anything before going in Stanley's office? The guy didn't call out when he heard you arrive?"

The panting woman hugged herself and shook her head. "I think he was passed out and only came to when I screamed."

"Do you want to sit in my truck while I go inside?"

She shook her head again, dropping her arms and squaring her shoulders. "No, I'm over my initial shock and want to help. I'm a volunteer EMT for the town I live in near Denver."

"Okay. But if the guy really is his brother," Jesse said, leading her inside, "I think we should follow Stanley's lead until we know the reason he doesn't want to call the authorities."

"Jesus, Aaron," they heard Stanley whisper thickly, "what in hell did he do to you? And for chrissakes, *why*?"

Jesse found it interesting that Stanley obviously knew the assailant, which implied that finding his brother tied to his chair was an unmistakable message—which had Jesse wondering what sort of trouble a small-town architect could get into. An angry husband or boyfriend of one of the women at his birthday party, maybe? Jesse stopped Sarah in the lobby. "Let's give them a minute," he said softly, moving closer to the office door but staying just out of sight.

Jesse heard a pained, humorless chuckle. "Isn't it obvious? Stapleton wanted to make sure you knew what he thought of your house design."

Nope, not fallout from the orgy; this was obviously business related.

It must have been one hell of an ugly house.

A hiss sounded over the sharp creak of a chair. "Christ, go easy, will you? My hands are numb and I think some of my ribs are cracked. Do you have any idea how long a ride it is here from New York *in the trunk of a car*? I swear the sadistic driver aimed for every pothole after we left the interstate."

Stapleton, Jesse silently repeated, trying to think if he knew anyone by that name from New York, even as he moved forward just enough to see Stanley reach inside a desk drawer.

"I'm sorry," the obviously shaken man murmured, his hand emerging holding a large hunting knife. "The knots on your wrists are slick with blood. I need to cut you free."

Aaron gave another pained chuckle. "Please tell me you've got something more lethal than that tucked in the back of your belt."

Jesse looked down when he heard a muffled gasp and found Sarah had moved up beside him, her hands pressed to her mouth. He guided her away from the door just as Stanley snorted.

"I've been carrying since the morning I called you to find out what sort of trouble you'd gotten us *both* into. Quit tensing. You're making it worse."

Aaron took a shuddering breath. "He said he's going to torch the restaurant if you and Ms. Glace aren't standing in his office in one week with a brand-new design."

"I'm not letting that bastard within a hundred miles of Cadi."

Jesse felt something the size of a cargo freighter slam into his chest.

"I'm also supposed to explain that if you show up without her," Aaron added, "he's going to track down all your past and present clients and tell them what you and Owen Glace have been doing all these years. And then he said he'll . . . he'll just . . ."

"He'll what?" Stanley snapped above the sound of the chair bumping into the wall, immediately followed by more hissing. "Easy, Aaron. I'm sorry, but I figured the quicker the better. Let the blood start circulating before you try to move. Stapleton said he'll what?"

"Hell, it's circulating all over your floor." Another shuddering breath. "He said if Cadi's not with you, he'll send his men to come get her. And that he won't . . ."

"He won't *what*?"

"That once he has her, he probably won't need you anymore. Christ, I'm sorry, Stanley. I never thought anything like this would happen."

There was a long silence, then a heavy sigh. "No, you just sold your soul to a loan shark to open a restaurant."

"I was told Ryan Stapleton was a venture capitalist who helped small startups."

"And when you found out he wasn't, you sold the bastard *my* soul in return for a house."

As well as Cadi's, apparently, Jesse silently added, her sudden departure and prepaid—therefore untraceable—cell phone finally making sense. The woman wasn't out shopping for a motorhome; she was running from a loan shark. Not that he understood why Stapleton was including her in what was clearly Aaron's debt. And what sort of blackmail-worthy dirt could the bastard have on a backwater architect and his *dead* partner, anyway?

"What are we going to do?" Aaron whispered. "He's not going to stop until he gets what he wants or . . . or until we're both dead."

"He can't kill what he can't find," Stanley said. "Just

like Cadi, you and I are going to disappear until I can figure a way out of this mess."

Jesse was just about to start forward when Aaron asked, "Are you saying Cadi's not here? Christ, where is she?"

"I honestly have no idea, which is exactly what I told her I wanted. She bought camping equipment and is traveling around New England in a car with temporary plates. I made her promise to check in with me every couple of days, to only use cash and never stay in one place more than two nights, and to not come home until I give the okay."

"Hell," Aaron muttered, "you sound just like a brother I used to have. You remember that guy who was constantly pulling my stupid ass out of the wringer before he shipped me off to culinary school, then ran off to college and became a respectable architect?"

"What I remember is he died nine years ago. Now come on, let's get you upstairs and cleaned up enough to see if I need to take you to the hospital."

At the sound of the chair squeaking loudly again, accompanied by more hissing and groaning and heavy cursing, Jesse stepped into the doorway to see Stanley cradling his brother against his side as he slowly started out of the office.

Stanley spotted him and jerked to a halt. "Shit."

"Which," Jesse said tightly, "you appear to be standing in clear up to your eyeballs."

"This isn't any of your business, Sinclair."

"I made it my business the moment I heard Cadi was involved. Give me her number."

"Then you heard enough to know that's not going to happen."

"You're in over your head, Kerr."

"I wasn't always an architect. I can handle Stapleton."

"You do that. But while you are, I'll be the one making sure the bastard doesn't get within a hundred miles of Cadi. Think, Stanley," he said when the man remained silent. "I have the resources to keep her safe, which will free you up to deal with Stapleton."

"Contrary to popular belief, Cadi is a fully grown, intelligent woman who is right now proving she's capable of keeping herself safe."

"I have a two-year-old niece who's more world-wise than she is. Just give me Cadi's number and I'll make sure she *stays* safe."

Sarah stepped into the doorway when Jesse's demand was met with silence. "I'm an EMT, and even though I have no idea what's going on, I'm willing to go upstairs and help with your brother before I *also* disappear."

Jesse was back to wanting to roar, not caring if Aaron Kerr bled to death. He stifled the urge to physically take Stanley's phone from him, and instead walked over and opened the door to the stairs, then helped him carry his brother upstairs.

Sarah pushed past them the moment they settled Aaron onto a bed in a back room. "I need warm water, a couple of washcloths and towels, and a knife or large shears to cut off his shirt. Preferably," she said, glaring through her neon red glasses at Stanley when he didn't move, "before the goons who did this decide to bring their boss your *new partner* as a stand-in for Ms. Glace."

A snort came from the bed. "Stapleton's interested in a lot more than Cadi's little gift for matching the perfect house to people."

"Will you shut up," Stanley snapped, stepping toward the bed. "Your big mouth is what dragged her into this mess with us."

Upon hearing the full extent of the danger Cadi was in, Jesse was about to drag Stanley into his *fist* when the man suddenly strode out of the room. "Let me look after her," Jesse said over the sound of running water as he followed Stanley into the kitchen, "while you work on cleaning up your brother's mess. If need be, I can fly her out of the country."

"She doesn't even have a passport," Stanley said, grabbing a bowl from a cupboard.

"I'll take her to Rosebriar, then. One phone call and I can have it more secure than the Pentagon."

Stanley set the bowl under the stream of water with a snort. "That's practically in Stapleton's backyard," he said, opening drawers until he found some shears.

"Then I'll take her out to sea on one of our freighters."

Stanley grabbed towels from another drawer, shut off the water and picked up the bowl, and headed for the door—having to halt when Jesse didn't move. They eyed each other for several seconds before Stanley suddenly sighed. "All I'm willing to do is give Cadi your cell number when she calls. The choice to contact you has to be hers, not mine," he said, stepping around him and disappearing into the bedroom.

Jesse stood in the hall trying to decide if he'd built

enough of a rapport with Cadi in their short time together for her to trust him with her life.

"Jesus, Sinclair, *go away*," Stanley said as he came back out of the bedroom. "There's a good chance Stapleton's thugs are still in town, and your face regularly appears in the social and business sections of newspapers up and down the East Coast. The last thing we need is for them to recognize you as being associated with me, especially if Cadi does take you up on your offer."

"I'll leave just as soon as you explain your brother's remark about her gift of matching houses to people, and why Stapleton won't need you if he has her." Jesse stiffened when several things suddenly fell into place. "The house on my island model wasn't your design, it was hers," he said before Stanley could answer. "Cadi told me she sees things three-dimensionally and can actually walk through a structure in her mind as though it already exists. She sits in on your initial meeting with a client, then goes off by herself and builds their house one wall and window at a time, and you work up the plans from her model."

Stanley eyed him in silence again, then let out another sigh—this one sounding almost relieved. "She got so involved in designing your home she gained ten pounds living on junk food. I had to keep driving out to check that she was even alive, and I'd find her still in her pajamas despite looking like she hadn't slept in days." He shook his head. "I hired someone to go out and clean and cook her decent meals, but Cadi wouldn't even let the woman through the door."

"So that's why your brother was sent here looking like a punching bag," Jesse stated, rather than asked. "He let it slip that Cadi was the creative genius of Glace and Kerr Architecture, and Stapleton suspected she hadn't designed the house you gave him."

"Cadi decided the man was a jerk not five minutes into our meeting and warned me he'd be a demanding client if I took him on. Not knowing the whole story, she got angry when I told her I was going to anyway, and because she'd heard me tell him I wouldn't have anything to show him until the end of the summer, she went home and buried his sketchbook at the bottom of the pile. But when Stapleton called saying he was flying up to check on my progress, Cadi worked with me on some concept drawings before I sent her away."

"So if she helped with the design, why didn't Stapleton like it?"

"Because she can only create in three dimensions and often spends weeks on a house." He snorted. "And I'm fairly certain she has to *like* whoever's going to be living in it."

Jesse remembered her admitting—right after calling him Pooh Bear—that as a young teen she'd developed the habit of likening her father's clients to fictional characters. He also remembered seeing a drawing of the Mad Hatter choking a bug-eyed rabbit when he'd been thumbing through Cadi's notebook, and he was pretty sure *Stapleton* had been the name at the top of the page. "And the dirt Stapleton is threatening to take to your clients," Jesse clarified, "is that Cadi is really the one who designs the houses—her father's as well as yours?"

Stanley nodded. "Owen was a hell of an architect in his own right, but his reputation for fitting the perfect home to clients didn't take root until he started letting Cadi sit in on his initial meetings. He told me he'd taught her to fabricate his rough study models when she was only twelve, but that she kept rearranging the rooms and adding her own embellishments, insisting the flow wasn't right or that he needed to add a bathroom or move a door. Owen said by the time she was fifteen, he simply gave up and let Cadi build the models *before* he drew up the plans."

"And when you came on board, she did the same for you?"

Stanley winced and seemed to slightly relax. "She made the rough model of my very first project exactly to my plan specifications, and then she apparently built a second one to *hers*. That night Owen invited me over for a campfire, and when I got there I found two models and a bottle of brandy sitting on the picnic table. After he told me Cadi was visiting friends, we spent the evening discussing architecture in general and homes in particular, until he suddenly asked me which model I thought we should show my clients and which one we should throw on the fire. Seeing them side-by-side, all I could do was stare in awe at the one Cadi had designed. So as we sat back and watched my house go up in flames, Owen tried to explain his daughter's gift even though he admitted he didn't understand it himself. And then he asked if I wanted to languish in mediocrity or join them in what he called his and Cadi's 'little secret.'"

"So my house—the steel trusses, all that concrete, the

curving wall of glass, and cresting roofline—was entirely Cadi's vision? Was it also her idea to set it against the lower bluff?"

"Despite being absolutely certain the material and design fit you perfectly, she nearly made herself sick worrying you wouldn't like it," Stanley said with a curt nod. "And even though I argued it should go on top of the high ridge, she insisted it had to be *part* of the island rather than sitting up there dominating it."

Jesse took a deep breath, equally baffled as to how she . . . knew.

"If any of Owen's clients ever found out," Stanley continued softly, "that the houses they paid him well over six figures for were designed by . . ." He shook his head. "From the time she let her father talk her into 'their little secret,' Cadi's lived in fear not only of seeing his reputation shredded, but of his being wiped out financially if any of his clients decided to sue for damages."

"What damages, if they got the houses they wanted?"

Stanley glanced toward the bedroom when they heard a hissed curse quickly followed by an apology, then canted his head. "So you don't mind that the architect you've given nearly ninety thousand dollars to at this point, or worse, that you may have already bragged about to friends, is nothing but a glorified draftsman who probably couldn't design an award-winning doghouse?"

"What I mind," Jesse said quietly, "is that the house I'm paying for—the one I *want*—is still locked in the mind of a woman who's sleeping in a tent with her cat somewhere in New England, trying to stay one step ahead of a loan shark with the goddamned hots for her.

So give me her cell phone number or I *will* sue you for misrepresentation."

"Right now being sued is the least of my worries," Stanley countered as he headed toward the bedroom. "And *Cadi* will be the one to decide if she wants your help."

Jesse balled his hands into fists to keep from going after the bastard and silently turned and walked down the stairs. He continued through the lobby and stepped outside, then simply stood on the sidewalk in the obscenely refreshing sunshine and weighed his options.

Cadi was safe—relatively and for the moment—and there was no question she was intelligent enough to be making her own decisions, but that didn't mean he had to stand around with his hands in his pockets waiting for her to call.

It would help if he knew her better—such as where she'd gone to college before her mother had died, what trips she may have taken as a kid, and whether she felt more comfortable in touristy beach towns or the less crowded mountain and lake regions. Hell, considering the age of her parents, she'd probably never even slept in a tent before.

Was she scared? Disillusioned? Angry?

She'd been gone two weeks with only a cat for company; was she lonely?

But more importantly, would she call a man she'd spent three months getting to know intimately by simply creating his home? She hadn't hesitated to take refuge in his camper, but would she trust him when more was at stake than just embarrassment?

Dammit, he needed to talk to someone who knew her—besides her ex-fake-fiancé.

Jesse looked toward the hardware/feed store. Beatrice must be a close friend, seeing how she was the one Cadi had texted the night of Stanley's party. He crossed the road, the freighter sitting on his chest shifting at least enough for him to breathe now that he might have what should be a more cooperative source of information. He stepped out of the way to let an elderly couple exit the store, then walked inside just as Beatrice turned from the counter.

The woman's smile froze half-formed when she saw him. "Mr. Sinclair," she said flatly. "What brings you back to Whistler's Landing? Because if you're here expecting to whisk Cadi away on your fancy corporate jet, I'm afraid your over-the-top bouquet of flowers didn't do the trick." Her half-smile thawed to smugness. "Apparently Cadi wasn't all that impressed by your fast plane and fancy house, seeing how she's off shopping for a motorhome by herself."

Jesse stifled a sigh for apparently not leaving much of an impression on Cadi's *friend*, either. "Actually, since I was here checking on how my house plans are coming along," he said, making sure his smile at least appeared sincere, "I thought I'd see how Miss Glace has been faring. She was still quite upset the night I found her hiding in my camper when I reached Castle Cove, and I've often caught myself wondering about her these last three weeks. In fact, that's why I sent the flowers the next day; I thought that if a man she barely knew gave her a beautiful bouquet of flowers, she might not feel so . . . rejected."

"What do you mean you found her in your camper?"

Beatrice asked, her eyes narrowed in suspicion. "Cadi told me you came upon her walking down the road and offered her a ride."

Damn. How was he supposed to know what story Cadi had concocted? He stifled a snort—pretty sure she hadn't mentioned *spending the night* in his camper. "Considering all that had transpired," he offered, deciding to stay vague, "I can only assume Miss Glace didn't want to add to her embarrassment by admitting she'd hidden in a closet like a child."

The store owner appeared momentarily startled, then made a *tsk*ing sound and shook her head. "Oh, that silly girl; she put on such a brave front the next morning, telling me she and Stanley had both agreed they loved each other, but like siblings. She even asked me to drive her to the car dealership, and then spent the whole day assuring me she wasn't devastated."

"I've been overseas on an extended business trip, so I haven't been able to call and find out how she's doing. And since it would have been awkward to ask Stanley just now, and knowing you're Miss Glace's good friend, I was hoping you could put my worries to rest. You say she's traveling? Has she been gone very long?"

"Cadi told me she expected to be gone only a couple of weeks. But that was two weeks ago as of *yesterday*, and she's still not back."

Jesse sighed out loud. "Well, I suppose if I ever found myself in Miss Glace's shoes, I might feel that a little time and distance could help put things in perspective."

"Yes," Beatrice whispered, fingering a button on her sweater. "I guess I would, too."

"Have you heard from her?"

Beatrice nodded. "We've been talking and texting nearly every day."

"And is Miss Glace having any luck finding a motorhome?"

The store owner suddenly broke into a genuine smile as she reached in her pocket and—bingo!—pulled out a cell phone. "Cadi has checked out at least half a dozen," she said, walking toward him as she fiddled with the screen, "and even sent me pictures, asking my opinion. See?" she offered, holding the phone facing him, then peering over the top of it as she kept fumbling with the screen. "You'll have to do it," she said, handing him the phone. "Just ignore the texts and keep scrolling up to the pictures."

Jesse nearly shouted when he saw the ten numbers in the caller ID banner above the texts, and thanked God that Beatrice had kept the pictures in the conversation instead of saving them to the photo gallery.

Ten simple, beautiful, freighter-moving numbers. Not bothering with the first three, recognizing Maine's area code, Jesse memorized the last seven while slowly scrolling through the lengthy conversations to the first picture. "Wow, that's the size of a bus," he said while continuing to permanently etch those seven numbers on his brain.

"That's exactly what I told her." Beatrice moved to stand beside him, then reached over and scrolled up. "I suggested she get something smaller. There," she said, tapping the screen to enlarge the photo of a midsized motorhome. "I told her to get that one." She frowned up at him. "Until she mentioned it cost eighty-two thousand dollars even though it was used. Land sakes, if you go inland just a few miles you can buy a decent *house* for that."

Jesse nodded in agreement as he studied the photo, looking for clues as to where it had been taken, then scrolled up to the next two photos as he slowly began to suspect they'd all been taken on the same RV dealership lot. He looked through several more while checking the dates, and saw they had been sent two or three days apart—Cadi apparently wanting Beatrice to believe she'd found them in different towns.

Oh yeah, no one could accuse Miss Glace of not knowing how to tell a good lie. But then, hadn't she had everyone convinced she and Stanley were engaged for over two years? Hell, she'd pulled off an even more elaborate lie with her father for *fourteen*.

Jesse sighed out loud again. "Even if she comes back empty-handed, just shopping for a camper has to be therapeutic. And Miss Glace appears to be doing just—" He stopped scrolling on another photograph, this one a selfie of Cadi holding a copy of the *New York Times*.

She'd made it as far as New York? Sweet God, the woman had run *toward* Stapleton.

Or toward a client who had gallantly rescued her twice already?

"What's this?" Jesse asked, tilting the screen to show Beatrice the photo.

"Oh, that," the store owner said with a nervous laugh, grabbing the phone and shoving it in her pocket as she walked away. "Cadi sent me that as a joke. She's not really in New York; you can buy that newspaper in most cities in Maine."

Christ, he hoped it was only a joke. "Then why send you a photo of that particular paper?"

Keeping her back to him, Beatrice began fidgeting with something on the counter. "The day Cadi left, I . . . ah, I may have accused her of accepting your offer to look for a motorhome in New York," she softly admitted, finally turning to expose red cheeks and a sheepish smile. "The girl thinks it's a big secret, but I've always known how much she wants to travel. And since you apparently proved to be a gentleman the night you picked—the night she hid in your camper, I got it in my head she was really running off to meet you at the Trenton airport."

Jesse felt his heart rate settle down at the hope that Cadi was still in Maine. "Well," he said with a deceptively negligent shrug, "I suppose my sending flowers to a woman who had just caught her fiancé in a compromising position might make you question my motives. So maybe you shouldn't tell Miss Glace I was checking on her," he suggested, not wanting Beatrice to call Cadi the moment he left. "That way *she* won't get the wrong impression of me."

"Yes. Yes, I think that would be best."

"Well, I better get going if I want to reach Castle Cove before the marina closes so I can see about getting my boat in the water," he said, walking to the door. "But I'd like to thank you for reassuring me that Miss Glace is doing well."

"You're welcome, Mr. Sinclair."

He opened the door, but decided to add a little insurance. "My friends call me Jesse."

"And my friends call me Bea," she returned, giving

him a warm smile. "So you make sure to stop in and see me whenever you're in town."

"I'll do that," he said with a nod, losing his own smile the moment he stepped outside.

Jesse strode across the road and, with only a cursory glance at Glace & Kerr Architecture, climbed into his truck and started the engine, checked for traffic, and made a U-turn. He drove several miles out of town and pulled into a scenic turnout, then took out his phone and input Cadi's new number—only to still with his finger over the call button.

Dammit to hell; he'd been so focused on hearing her voice that he hadn't considered what to say. *Hi, there, Cadi, it's me, Jesse. Jesse Sinclair? Yes, well, I just found out you're driving around pretending to shop for a camper when you're really running from a loan shark with the hots for you. So could you please tell me where you are so I can come get you and— What's that? Yes, I know you probably don't need or particularly want a virtual stranger to come save your pretty little ass, but I really think you should . . . I thought I could . . .*

Yes, what had he thought?

Dammit to hell again; he didn't like that Stanley was right about it needing to be Cadi's decision. She definitely was a grown woman, and anyone with half a brain could see it was intelligence making those big blue eyes sparkle. There was also the fact she was highly creative, which could very well prove to be her greatest asset when it came to protecting herself.

Jesse dropped his head onto the steering wheel with a groan. If he wanted any sort of relationship with the ever-more-interesting Miss Glace, insisting he could do a better job of keeping her safe than she could probably wasn't the way to go about it.

Okay, then; he'd give her until five p.m. tomorrow to call. But that still didn't mean he had to stand around with his hands in his pockets. He sat up and dialed a pretty damn good asset of his own, then pulled back onto the road.

"I want you to find out everything you can about a New Yorker named Ryan Stapleton," he began without preamble the moment Nathaniel came on the line. "How much money he has and how he makes it, who his friends are, where he shops and eats and even what teams he roots for—everything. You can probably start somewhere in the middle of the legitimate businessman scale and work your way *down* from there."

There was a pronounced pause, then a soft, "Ohh-kay. Sounds like . . . fun."

"Also find out where he's planning to build his new house. And Nathaniel?"

"Yeah, boss?"

"You not only make sure Stapleton doesn't know he's being researched, you don't let anyone know what you're doing. And that includes my brothers."

"Yes, sir," Nathaniel snap-whispered. "This is strictly between you and me and my triple-password-protected, invisible computer."

"Just don't go skulking down any dark alleys looking for information, you got that? If you hit a dead end online, discreetly get the name of the security firm Ben used when he found out he had a teenage son three years ago and let *them* scour the alleys. Just be clear they answer only to you or me."

"Got it."

"But first off I need you to research small, unobtrusive cell phone antennas that will extend the signal and overnight one to me." Jesse glanced at the dash clock. "If I don't call you later with an address, send it to me general delivery at the Castle Cove post office. Oh, and be sure everything to make it function is in the package. I need to get that antenna up and running first thing tomorrow, and I can't exactly pop out to the nearest store for parts."

"Got it," Nathaniel drawled. "One cell antenna even an executive can put up. Anything else?"

"As a matter of fact," Jesse drawled in return, his protégé's maddeningly persistent sense of humor moving the freighter a little farther off his chest. "Check with that security firm and see if they can find out where a cell phone is located if I provide them with a number."

There was an even longer pause, and then, "Law enforcement can, but I'm fairly certain private citizens—or private security firms—can't."

"Ask anyway."

"Consider it done. Anything else?"

Jesse suddenly had a thought. "Do you know if anyone from Glace and Kerr Architecture tried to contact me while I was gone?"

Another pause. "I seem to remember seeing something in your mail," Nathaniel said distractedly as Jesse heard papers shuffling. "Yeah, here it is. Looks like a card. The return address isn't Glace and Kerr, though. It's from Cadi Glace."

Jesse felt his heart falter and then start racing. He checked his rearview mirror and pulled to the side of the road, then stared out the windshield. "What's the postmark date and town?"

"June seventh and Whistler's Landing."

"What day of the week was the seventh?"

"Ah . . . Saturday. You want me to open it and see if it's about your house?"

Jesse dropped his chin to his chest on a silent curse. That was two days after he'd sent the flowers, meaning it was a thank-you card. "No. It's personal."

"Ah . . . Cadi Glace also called," Nathaniel said—Jesse perking up at the hesitation in his voice. "Marjory recognized the name Glace and put the call through to me."

Jesse's heart shot back into overdrive. "Do you remember *when* she called?" he asked, wondering if it had been after her phone had gotten "ruined," which meant she wouldn't have had his private cell number. "What did she want?"

"I'm fairly certain the call came after the card," Nathaniel said as Jesse heard what he assumed were pages turning on a call logbook—bless the kid's borderline OCD organizational skills. "Yeah, here it is. She called on Tuesday, June tenth."

"Is there a reason I'm only hearing this *now*?"

"Two reasons, actually: first, because there really wasn't anything to tell you, and second, because she asked me not to mention she'd called."

"So Miss Glace is signing your paychecks now?" Jesse said quietly.

"No, sir," Nathaniel said, all business again. "But since she wouldn't leave a message, I thought . . ." A heavy sigh came over the line. "Do you have any idea how many people call you in a matter of two weeks? Why do you think I keep such a detailed logbook? I can usually handle most of their questions or problems, so I only tell you about those I can't. Miss Glace seemed to fall in the first category."

Jesse blew out a heavy sigh of his own. "Tell me again what day she called."

"Tuesday, June tenth, which is the day after you left for Europe."

Which was also the day after Stanley had sent her away, according to Beatrice. "Did Miss Glace happen to say what was so *unimportant* for her to call me?"

"She just asked to speak with you. I explained you were overseas but that maybe I could help, since I'm responsible for payments and scheduling and most things concerning your house. Miss Glace said her question had to do with the design and asked how long you'd be gone."

"And you said?"

"I told her I didn't expect you back for at least three weeks. But knowing how anxious you were to get hold of your plans, I offered to have you call her the first chance you got."

"And did Miss Glace give you her number?" Jesse whispered.

"No, she asked for yours instead."

"And did you give it to her?"

"Yes, but I explained it would be easier if *you* did the

calling, since there was no telling when you'd be thirty thousand feet over some ocean or in a meeting. I told her even I usually have to wait until you call."

Jesse was back to wanting to roar. "Did she give you her number then?"

"I'm sorry, boss. After all that, she decided her question wasn't really that important. But for the record, I even went so far as to say you'd probably fire me if those house plans got delayed, and she . . . she said . . ."

"She said what?" Jesse growled.

"She laughed and said to tell you that if you didn't give me a big fat raise instead—and this is a direct quote, so don't shoot the messenger—'you're going to find yourself living in a very unpretentious hollow tree.'" Nathaniel cleared his throat. "When I told her I didn't get the joke, Miss Glace suggested I read Winnie the Pooh."

Jesse felt himself grinning at the idea that Cadi wasn't any more worried about spending Tidewater's money than she was his. "And did you read it?"

"Ah, I did, actually. And I still don't get it."

"Really?" Jesse said in surprise, since Nathaniel was one of the sharpest young men he'd ever had the privilege to mentor. "Where did Winnie the Pooh live?" he prodded.

"In Hundred Acre Wood."

"And where am I building my house?"

Silence. Then a heavy groan. "On Hundred Acre Isle. But what's that got to do with a hollow—" Then came a snort. "I guess that also explains her parting shot before she hung up."

"Which was?"

"She asked if I was your assistant, and when I said yes,

she suggested having some books on beekeeping sitting on your desk when you returned might get my big fat raise *doubled*."

Jesse checked for traffic and pulled back onto the road, breaking into a full-blown chuckle. For a woman forced into running from a lecherous loan shark, Cadi didn't seem all that traumatized. In fact, it sounded as if she thought she were on an adventure.

His chuckle was answered by a relieved sigh. "So is there anything else you'd like me to do?" Nathaniel asked, apparently eager to get off the subject of Miss Glace. "Say, any actual Tidewater business, like maybe fly to Newfoundland for you and handle a small matter of marine patrol chasing down one of our ships and arresting the captain?"

It was Jesse's turn to go silent, and if he hadn't been driving, he would have dropped his head on the steering wheel. "Arrested for what?"

"It's apparently against the law in Canada for anyone to pull up a string of lobster traps they happen to be passing by, relieve them of their catch, then toss them back several miles away from where they'd been pulled."

"Who in hell is the captain? Wait, how does marine patrol even know it was our boat that snagged those traps? For that matter, what evidence do they have it was deliberate?"

"The entire crew was eating the evidence when they boarded. At least they only arrested Captain Fournier and let our ship continue on once the first mate produced paperwork showing he was licensed to command. So do you want me to hop on the corporate jet and fly up there with Tidewater's hat figuratively in hand, pay the lobsterman for his lost gear and a little something extra for goodwill, and bail out Captain Fournier?"

Poor Nathaniel; he was dying to board one of their jets as the man in charge. Hell, Jesse wouldn't be surprised if the kid brought along his girlfriend, had the steward serve champagne, and asked the pilot to take the scenic route. "Sorry, but the job I just gave you takes precedence over everything else, especially some idiot captain. Send Ben."

"I tried him first, but he said his passport is expired."

"Then send Sam."

"Willa told me, and I quote, 'Sam's a total basket case over Jen's imminent departure.'"

"Damn," Jesse muttered. "I forgot about the bon voyage party. What day is it?"

"It's a week from this Saturday at eight a.m. at the Sengatti shipyard."

"No, what day is *today*?"

"In Maine or Istanbul?" Nathaniel sighed again when all that got him was silence. "It's Tuesday, June twenty-fourth, the year two thousand—"

"You leave for Newfoundland tonight," Jesse said, cutting him off, "in the Lear. I promised the Boeing crew at least a week to recover. But you don't set one foot on that plane until after you send out my cell phone antenna. And Nathaniel?"

"Yeah, boss?" he said with unfiltered cheeriness.

"Captain Fournier takes a commercial flight back and buys his own ticket. And he pays his own bail. Got that?"

"Loud and clear. Anything else?"

"Yeah. Champagne is clichéd; you really want to impress your girlfriend, ask Charles to break out *your* private stock of Aberfeldy single cask."

The phone went so silent that Jesse thought their call had been dropped.

"Don't worry," he added. "Charles is a sharp fellow and will play along. He also knows when to close the curtain and go read a book." Jesse grinned at what sounded like a forehead thumping down on wood. "Enjoy your flight, Mr. Cunningham," he drawled, ending the call.

Jesse pressed a little harder on the accelerator and thought about why Cadi had tried to contact him. Had spending one night in a tent made her wonder if being Mrs. Sinclair came with any other privileges besides opening doors, such as maybe her and her cat hiding out at Rosebriar for a little while?

Damn, he wished she'd given Nathaniel her number, because he would have immediately sent the kid to pick her up in the Lear. Or, if she'd been shy about staying at Rosebriar without him being there, he could have talked her into driving to Sam's in Keelstone Cove or to Ben's in Medicine Gore. Both brothers would have welcomed her with open arms, no questions asked.

Jesse snorted, wondering who was he kidding; if he'd known Cadi was in trouble he would have turned his plane around and come after her himself.

Forget five p.m. tomorrow; he was giving her until *noon* to call, which gave him twenty-one hours to figure out how to persuade her to let him protect her pretty little ass.

Jesse blew out a heavy sigh, wondering if he was ever going to sleep in his camper's bed. Because as things stood now, it appeared he'd be spending the night on the high ridge where he had a cell phone signal—his only consolation being he'd finally get to see his first island sunrise.

Too bad he wasn't going to enjoy it.

ELEVEN

Jesse decided one advantage of driving Maine's back roads was that law enforcement apparently had more important things to do than patrol them for speeders. He made it to Castle Cove in plenty of time to get a post office box and give Nathaniel an actual address, and even managed to hit the marina before it closed.

The powerful cruiser he'd purchased last fall was really a lobster boat rigged for personal use, and he'd only been able to spend four days running it under the tutelage of its builder—a soft-spoken Swede named Sven—before having to put it in winter storage. But to his surprise, the marina had brought it to the harbor eighteen days ago, since he'd apparently been too busy flying all over the world to remember to call and tell them to wait until he got back.

So now he was the one waiting on a small group of what appeared to be tourists to finish ambling across the entrance to the pier. But instead of turning once they passed, Jesse froze when he spotted a woman wearing a blue hat exit a store farther up the sidewalk, and didn't start breathing again until she turned enough for him to see her face.

Talk about having Miss Glace on the brain; this was the second time since reaching town that he'd mistaken a woman for Cadi. It had to be the hats. Hell, he'd swear half the female population of Castle Cove was wearing them. But then, maybe lots of women wore hats in the summer and he'd just never noticed before meeting Cadi.

Then again, maybe they were a Down East thing.

A horn honked, and Jesse lifted his hand in apology and turned into the parking lot. He pulled into the empty slot marked with the slip number the marina had given him and shut off the truck, so damn glad to be smelling ocean air instead of jet fuel that it was all he could do not to rest his head on the steering wheel again. But the bottle of Aberfeldy in his overnight bag was enough incentive to send him in search of his boat, and with any luck he could haul his sleeping bag up to the high ridge in time to watch the sun set. He grabbed his bag out of the backseat and headed down the ramp—which was rather steep because it was low tide—to a maze of floating docks filled with recreational vessels of every size and shape imaginable. He stopped to read the sign pointing out the slip numbers, but looked up when he heard a shout and saw Oren Hatch at the other end of the long anchoring dock. The harbormaster had one arm outstretched, apparently directing a group of kayakers paddling through the congested harbor to put ashore on a narrow beach beside the boat launch ramp.

Satisfied they were following orders, Oren turned and spotted him, waved Jesse forward as he started toward him, and extended his hand when they met. "Good to see yah again, Jesse. Although hearing you was traveling overseas, I didn't expect you for another two weeks."

"I was highly motivated to cut my trip short," Jesse said as he shook his hand, having to marvel at how everyone seemed to know everyone's business in small towns. "You haven't seen my cruiser around here, have you? The marina said I'd find it in slip twenty-three."

Oren headed down the center dock. "I hope you don't mind that I put you in here," he said as Jesse followed, "what with your boat being more maneuverable than most its size." He grinned over his shoulder. "But I figured you wouldn't have no problem fitting her into a tight spot, seeing how you make your living juggling cargo ships."

"You do know they don't let me actually drive them, don't you?" Jesse said dryly, lengthening his stride when he spotted his cruiser tied to the dock three boats from the end.

Oren stopped beside it, his grin folding his weathered face into a treasure map of wrinkles. "Watching you put this beauty through her paces last fall, I admonished Sven for calling you a flatlander, since most summer folks can't row a dinghy through this harbor without fetching up on mooring lines or causing a traffic jam." His wrinkles folded into a grimace. "And don't even get me started on them fools in their sloops who come in off the reach under full sail, then send the little missus scrambling to the winches *after* they get inside the breakwater." He gave Jesse a one-eyed squint. "You ain't thinking of getting a sloop, are yah?"

"Not until I'm sure I've gotten myself a little missus with plenty of scramble in her," Jesse said with a chuckle as he climbed aboard his cruiser. He set down his bag and knelt to open the engine compartment and, despite the boat being newly constructed, stuck his head inside to check for any water seepage, as Sven had instructed. Seeing it was perfectly dry, he straightened to tell Oren the marina had said they'd left the key with him, only to find the harbormaster had disappeared. Jesse stood up and spotted him farther down the dock lifting something out of a large wooden skiff before walking back.

"Talk of your missus reminded me of this, and I figure you might as well take it with you," Oren said, handing Jesse a bicycle wheel. "Ray had one of his clerks run it over about an hour ago."

Jesse assumed it went to some piece of equipment his contractor had out on the island. "Ray?" he questioned, stowing it behind one of the seats.

"Ray Dean. He owns the hardware store down the street. Your wife brung the wheel with her this morning, and even before she docked I could see the tire was half off the rim."

Jesse froze. "Did you say my wife brought it here? This morning?"

"It's off her garden cart," Oren said with a nod. "She must'a punctured the tire and figured since she bought the cart off Ray that he could probably fix it."

Son of a bitch; Cadi wasn't driving all over New England—she was *here*.

That's why she'd called his office two weeks ago pretending to have a question about his house; the woman had been fishing for information on how long before he was coming to Maine again so she could hide out on his island as *his wife*.

Hell, he had *helped* establish her as Mrs. Sinclair before he'd left.

Jesse vaulted onto the dock and walked to the skiff Oren claimed was hers, then stared down at the leaky, paint-peeling, positively ancient . . . scow and even older motor. He schooled his features to hide his surprise. No, his shock. No, he was pretty sure that was abject horror making his heart pound. "My wife is coming and going to Hundred Acre in this boat? And you say she bought a garden cart at the hardware store . . . when?"

Oren cocked his head and squinted off at nothing. "I seen her heading out past the breakwater with the cart in her skiff . . . oh, I reckon a couple of weeks ago now." He looked at Jesse and nodded. "Yeah, it wasn't long after the marina put in your cruiser." But then he shook his head. "I remember 'cause when I noticed how she seemed comfortable around boats and more than competent, I suggested she might prefer using your cruiser instead, especially if a gale were to come up when she was crossing the reach. I told her I had the key in my office and even offered to take her out and show her how to run it."

Jesse stared down at Cadi's skiff again as he fought back his anger. Sweet God, if the woman was smart enough to hide on his island, why wasn't she smart enough to beg or borrow or even steal a goddamn *real* boat? "And my little missus said?" he whispered, looking toward his big, safe, seaworthy cruiser.

"Her eyes got all bright and twinkly and she said she wouldn't dream of driving your shiny new toy and risk putting a scratch on it. And she claimed the skiff was easier anyway, seeing how she could just run it up on the beach at the island."

"Do you know where she got it? Who sold it to her?" Jesse asked. *So I can hunt the bastard down,* he refrained from adding.

The edge in his voice must have given him away, because Oren eyed him for a short second, then shook his head. "I come back from lunch one afternoon and found it here. She must'a seen it for sale by the side of the road." He snorted. "In Fender Cove, most likely. Them outlaws are giving all us Downeasters a bad reputation with you from-away folks, seeing how there ain't a man—or woman, for that matter—in that town with enough decency to not sell a flatlander this piece of crap. So whenever you find yourself dealing with locals on anything, the first thing you ask is what town they're from. They say Fender Cove, you run like hell, yah hear?"

"I hear you," Jesse said as he turned and walked back to his cruiser, silently promising the skiff a decent burial at sea.

"Oh, I almost forgot," Oren added as he followed. "The kid that run the tire over said Ray ain't gonna put the cost of the tube or installing it on your account, seeing how your wife's more or less responsible for his selling mud boots faster than he can order them."

"My wife is buying multiple pairs of boots?" Jesse asked. *And putting them on an account I don't remember opening at a store I've never even been to?* he silently added.

"No, she ain't buying them. All the women in town are. Ever since your missus told Eva that . . . rustic clothing, I think she called it, was all the rave in New York City, mud boots and hats and anything with plaid on it's been flying off the shelves of every store in town. FedEx even had to put on a bigger truck to fit all the packages coming from L.L.Bean all of a sudden."

"Eva?"

"Eva Dean, Ken's wife. They own the grocery store up on the hill." Oren shook his head on a chuckle. "And I heard Joanne's havin' to stay open extra hours to keep up with the demand for perms and . . . highlighting, I think they call it, 'cause everyone suddenly wants blonde curls."

"Joanne?"

"Sorry. What with your wife coming and going these past couple of weeks, I forgot you ain't spent much time here yourself yet. Joanne owns the beauty shop up next to the drugstore that sits up beside the grocery store."

Okay, then; it would appear he'd not only acquired a wife while he'd been overseas, but one who was responsible for starting several new fashion trends. Not that he understood *why* she was starting them. The *how* was probably a given—as wouldn't most women living in such a remote town want to emulate a beautiful, bouncy-curled, sparkling-eyed *New Yorker*?

Jesse scrubbed his face with both hands, only to stop

in mid-scrub at the realization that Cadi's skiff being here meant *she* was here. In town. Right now.

Unless Stanley had already called her and, realizing *her husband* was about to arrive, she'd already run off.

No, Oren had said the hardware store had brought the tire back over an hour ago, and, at best, Stanley couldn't have called Cadi more than three hours ago. And Jesse was pretty sure she wouldn't leave without her cat, which meant she wouldn't have had time to go out to Hundred Acre, grab the cat and her belongings, then motor back to shore in that tired old scow and make her getaway. He dropped his hands when he felt the dock vibrate and saw the kid from the grocery store striding toward him like a young man on a mission.

"I thought that was you, Mr. Sinclair. Remember me? Paul Acton? My grandfather and dad are doing the earthwork out on your island."

"I remember you, Paul," Jesse said, extending his hand.

Apparently surprised by the gesture, Paul reached out holding a folded piece of paper. He quickly switched the paper to his other hand and shook Jesse's—a little too long and a bit too firmly, but his enthusiasm was impressive. "Since your wife's not answering her phone, I came down to check if her skiff was here so I'd know if she was in town and could give her my bill," the boy said, his chest puffing out on the word *bill*. "Even though I told her I don't mind adding my hours on the next bill Gramps was gonna give you, Mrs. Sinclair insisted on paying me personally in cash each week. And since I had to work for Mr. Dean all weekend and yesterday and today, I didn't get a chance to give her last week's bill."

"Go ahead and give it to me, Paul," Jesse said, holding out his hand, "and I'll pay you. What sort of work have you been doing for her?" he asked, unfolding the paper to find a neatly hand-written, daily accounting of hours worked and total owed. Hell, it was a good thing he'd stopped at a bank in Ellsworth and grabbed some cash— a good chunk of which was going to young Mr. Acton, apparently.

"You can see I worked four full days last week," Paul said, peering over the top of the bill. "Mrs. Sinclair already paid me for the week before, when I mostly split the firewood from the trees we cleared for your camper pad." He looked up at Jesse and grinned. "But I pointed out it wasn't near dry enough to burn yet and would pop embers at her. So my dad let me sell her half a cord of our seasoned firewood left over from last winter, and I used the cart to haul part of it to that low cliff halfway down the other side of the island. Then I—"

"Wait," Jesse said, cutting him off even as he wondered why Cadi had the kid lugging firewood to the lower bluff. "How did you get the half cord to the island? Did you haul it over in my wife's boat?"

"Not likely," the boy said on a snort, only to instantly look contrite. "I mean no, sir. I used one of my dad's boats. That's how I been coming and going to work." He squared his shoulders. "I told Mrs. Sinclair a sea kayak would be safer than that old skiff she bought, and that she could probably *paddle* to the island faster. I also explained the reach has some powerful currents when the tide's changing, and if her motor suddenly quit she could end up on the rocks before anyone could get to her."

"Don't worry, Paul," Jesse said as he pulled out his wallet. "Mrs. Sinclair won't be crossing the reach in that boat again. So what other work have you been doing for her?"

Paul looked down, his face darkening again. "I . . . it's . . . I'm sorry, but I can't say." He suddenly snapped his gaze to the bill Jesse was holding. "Oh, no. I bet the reason Mrs. Sinclair wanted to pay me personally was because we've been working on a surprise for you."

Jesse felt his heart start pounding again, only this time with excitement when he realized where better to rebuild a model than on the very island where the house would be sitting—hence the reason for hauling campfire wood to the bluff.

No, that didn't make sense. Since he doubted a finished model would fit out through the camper door, Cadi would have needed to set up a weatherproof workstation, and his camper pad was the only place open and flat enough to pitch a large tent.

"I'll settle up with you now," Jesse said, pulling eight fifty-dollar bills from his wallet and holding them out to the boy, "and we'll both let on to my wife that I thought I was paying you for the firewood. But can you at least tell me if she's been able to use the generator to run the lights and well pump?"

"Oh, yes," Paul said, stuffing the money in his pocket without bothering to count it. "I was working the afternoon she came in the store with Mr. Dean and I heard her ask him if there was someone she could hire to take her out to Hundred Acre." His chest puffed out again. "I spoke up and said my dad had to go get some equipment he'd left behind and that I could call and ask if he'd go that afternoon." He rolled his eyes. "It's a good thing he showed up at the pier with his smaller work barge, because Dad said Mrs. Sinclair had a lot of camping equipment and boxes and stuff she wanted to take, even though he explained the camper was all set up and ready to go. He told me she even brought your cat." The boy scrunched up his nose. "He said it didn't like the ride over and threw up. But even though I've only caught glimpses of Wiggles these last two weeks, she seems pretty happy now that she's got free run of the island. Anyway, Dad showed Mrs. Sinclair how to start the generator and told her to call him if it acted up or if she needed anything, including a ride back to the mainland."

"And did she call?" Jesse asked.

Paul nodded. "The next morning. But that must be the day she bought the skiff," he said, glancing down the dock, "because the only other time she called was to ask if he knew anyone who'd be willing to do some odd jobs for her." He grinned. "And Dad told her I would."

"Well, Mr. Acton," Jesse said, once again extending his hand, "I not only appreciate your helping out my wife while I was gone, but for keeping her surprise a secret. You'll be hearing from me when I need more work done."

"You call me anytime," Paul said, giving Jesse another enthusiastic handshake. "Mrs. Sinclair's got my number.

And like I told her, I'm free whenever I'm not scheduled to work for Mr. Dean," he added before turning and sprinting up the dock.

"I forgot to mention," Oren said, watching the boy run up the ramp, "that the one exception to my Fender Cove warning would be Corey Acton." His eyes crinkled with silent laughter. "But then, Corey's usually quick to point out that he lives only three telephone poles inside the town line. At least his son was smart enough to marry a Castle Cove girl. Corrine made sure Jeffrey bought a house a full ten telephone poles on the *correct* side of the town line, and even managed to talk him into selling his lobster boat and going to work for his daddy."

"Do Jeffrey and Corrine have any children besides Paul?" Jesse asked.

Oren chuckled. "A set of triplets—identical *girls*. They'd be . . . oh, twelve or thirteen now, I figure. They was the reason Corrine managed to persuade Jeffrey to give up lobstering." He sobered and shook his head. "Not that construction work is any less dangerous."

"Well, Mr. Hatch," Jesse said with a nod. "I appreciate your also keeping an eye on my wife, and for letting her tie up at the dock whenever she comes to town."

Oren frowned in confusion, then suddenly grinned. "Your missus insisted her skiff deserved a slip of its own. But when she tried to pay me and I told her what it cost," he continued with a chuckle as he started up the dock, "she said to just go ahead and add it to your bill."

Jesse boarded his cruiser and set his overnight bag inside the cabin, then hopped back out. But then he hesitated, and instead of following Oren, he walked down to

Cadi's boat. He knelt and unhooked the fuel line from both the motor and the small gas tank, then tossed it onto the deck of his cruiser on his way by as he finally followed Oren to his office. He got his key and then headed into the heart of town on foot, figuring all he had to do was stop any woman wearing a hat and ask if she had seen Mrs. Sinclair today, and if so, could she kindly tell him where.

Jesse suddenly realized he was smiling, the freighter that had been sitting on his chest all afternoon having completely vanished. And this time it was anticipation making his heart race as he pictured the welcome home he was about to receive from the *little missus*.

Which had him wondering . . .

Since Cadi seemed quite fond of helping herself to his name—along with his camper and island and apparently also his wallet—maybe he should just go ahead and marry her for real.

TWELVE

❧

"You're not at all like I was expecting," the bubbly, twentysomething hairdresser said as she pumped up the chair Cadi was sitting in.

Cadi looked down at herself—specifically at the hat she was holding on her lap, since the rest of her was hidden under a salon cape. "What were you expecting?"

"Well, for starters, you dress like a Mainer."

Amazed at how quickly this particular little fib had taken on a life of its own, Cadi used the mirror to smile at Joanne standing behind her. "That's because *rustic chic* is all the rage in the Big Apple right now. So I guess you're dressed like a New Yorker."

"Living forty miles past the end of nowhere doesn't mean we can't keep up with the latest fashions," Joanne said with a laugh. But then she sighed. "Although getting any woman over forty in this town to try a new hairstyle is like pulling teeth. Even the younger women are reluctant to get a few highlights." She shot Cadi a smug smile. "Until recently. Now all of a sudden everyone wants perms and color. You're really here for a cut?" she asked, running her fingers through Cadi's hair. "I would think you'd only let—" Her eyes widened. "You're a natural blonde. And these curls didn't come from a bottle, either."

Cadi shrugged. "What can I say? My mother contributed the curls, but the blonde hair and delicate skin are compliments of my Scandinavian father."

"Delicate skin?" Joanne repeated, frowning at her in the mirror.

Cadi lifted her hand. "I think I was born wearing a hat."

"That's why you're always wearing one? Instead of for style, you're afraid to sunburn?"

Cadi also frowned. "It's either buy sunscreen by the case and walk around feeling like a greased pig or carry my own shade."

"You can't be wearing that hat all the time, because you're already well on your way to a beautiful tan. My God, with a little effort you could be a bronzed goddess. No, seriously," Joanne added, moving around the chair when Cadi turned to gape at her. "I have several clients with delicate skin, but I also have several natural blondes who are a deep, rich brown by the end of the summer. So long as they don't overdo it until they build up a good base tan," she clarified. "Tell me, do you have to use unscented laundry detergent?"

"No, I usually just buy— I leave that sort of thing up to our housekeeper," Cadi said, catching herself in the nick of time. She tucked her hair behind one ear and studied her face to see she *was* tanned—only to realize she hadn't really looked in a mirror for almost two weeks! And now that she thought about it, she rarely wore her hat out on Hundred Acre, usually just plopping it on her head once she got to town.

"And do you have to use hypoallergenic makeup?"

"Um, no. But I don't wear makeup very often. Mostly just when I attend social and business functions with Jesse," she quickly amended.

Joanne nodded. "Then in my professional opinion, your skin isn't at all delicate."

"But even in winter my father couldn't stay outside twenty minutes without turning as red as a beet"—which her parents had reminded her on a daily basis right up through her teens.

"Then curly hair isn't the only thing you inherited from your mother," Joanne said as she reached for a spray bottle. "Looks to me like you also got her skin."

Undecided if she was dismayed to have spent her whole life hiding from the sun or excited by the idea that she no longer had to, Cadi caught Joanne's wrist just as the woman started spraying her hair with water. "You really think I could get a nice tan?"

"You are tanned." Joanne set the bottle on the counter, then grasped Cadi's hand and slid down the cuff of her long-sleeved blouse. "See? You've got a faint line already. And I bet if you look under—oh, you're not wearing a wedding ring."

Fully prepared for this little fib, since Joanne wasn't the first person to notice that Mrs. Sinclair was missing some important jewelry, Cadi gently pulled her hand free with a laugh. "I took it off because I've been digging in the dirt out on the island. My diamond used to belong to Jesse's mother, and I'd never forgive myself if anything happened to it."

Joanne picked up the bottle and started spraying again. "Malinda told me she only got a short glimpse of your husband, and then only from a distance, but what she did see nearly had her drooling." The hairdresser rolled her eyes at the mirror. "But Mal just turned sixteen, and any male old enough to shave usually makes her drool."

Oh God, was Jesse in town? Because not only was he supposed to be gone at least another week, but Cadi was counting on a backlog of work waiting for him in New York to buy her another one or two. "Malinda from the grocery store? Isn't she Oren Hatch's granddaughter? When did she see Jesse?"

"Mal's also my second cousin," Joanne said with a nod. "Or maybe my first cousin once removed—I can never remember. Anyway, Mal told me she saw him the night the two of you camped in the parking lot a few weeks back. She said he has really broad shoulders, a strong sculpted jaw, and the most beautiful blue eyes she's ever seen."

"All that from a short glimpse from a distance?" Cadi said dryly to hide her relief.

Joanne set down the spray bottle and picked up a comb and scissors. "No, the girl ran straight home that night and Googled *Jesse Sinclair*. And based on the pictures she found, Mal said he's even dreamier in a tuxedo."

Cadi went back to being alarmed at the realization that

she'd never thought about anyone doing an Internet search. So just how was she supposed to explain the lack of information on *Mrs.* Jesse Sinclair? Good Lord, this little charade could very well explode in her face and she really could find herself in jail for trespassing. And probably also larceny, since she'd been opening accounts in Jesse's name all over town. Well, unless an understanding judge bought her defense that she intended to pay them off just as soon as she could use her checkbook again.

Heck, if she'd known how much disappearing would cost, she would have taken a lot more money out of the bank. Forget day-to-day living expenses; what with all the camping equipment she'd bought and that poor excuse of a boat, she'd spent almost three thousand dollars already! And that wasn't counting the two hundred she'd already paid Paul or the four hundred she owed him for last week.

"I know what Malinda means," Cadi said, making sure she sounded dreamy. "Jesse was wearing a tuxedo the first time I saw him."

Joanne's smile turned sheepish. "I, ah, did a little Googling myself. My God, you're married to a handsome man. And you live in a *palace*." But then she frowned. "Only I didn't see any pictures of you." Her face suddenly darkened as she began combing Cadi's hair. "In fact, there were a lot of pictures of your husband with . . . other women," she added softly.

Cadi laughed, making Joanne look at the mirror in surprise. "The competition was fierce," she drawled, "and I thought I was going to have to beat some of them off with a stick, but I'm the one Jesse comes home to every night." She sighed dramatically. "Except when he's gone on one of his extended business trips. Most of those pictures are several years old, Joanne. Heck, you know stuff stays on the Internet forever."

"But I didn't even see pictures of your wedding. I bet it was elegant," Joanne went on, sounding a bit dreamy herself. "What was your dress like? How many bridesmaids did you have? Were you married at . . . What's the name of your estate? Roses-something?"

"It's called Rosebriar, named after Jesse's grandmother Rose. As for my wedding, I wore two pair of long johns under a heavy sweater and down-filled parka, and my bridesmaids and groomsmen were penguins." Cadi smiled at Joanne's look of surprise. "We'd been dating only a few months when Jesse surprised me with a trip to Antarctica this past January, since that's when it's summer down there. And while we were standing at the South Pole, the big sap got down on one knee and proposed, and two days later we got married standing on a glacier," Cadi told her, actually *feeling* dreamy. But hey, this was her lie to embellish, wasn't it? "That's why you didn't find any photos; it was just the two of us, a minister Jesse had secretly brought along on the tour ship, and a colony of penguins. Which, come to think of it, were the only ones dressed in formal wear."

"That is so romantic," Joanne whispered once she'd stopped gaping.

"Yes." Cadi sighed past the sudden lump in her throat. Lord, she hoped a for-real Mr. Right was out there somewhere, waiting for her to come find him.

"Well," Joanne said, "if your husband isn't wearing

his ring when he comes in town, I'm afraid you might have to dig out that stick again." She began snipping the ends off Cadi's curls. "You should have been here last summer when word spread that a handsome, *young*, and obviously rich man was out looking at Hundred Acre Isle. By the time the real estate broker brought him back to shore, I swear every unmarried female in Castle Cove between the ages of sixteen and fifty was out on the pier, holding fishing poles." She stopped cutting, arching a brow with a cheeky smile. "And trust me, it wasn't mackerel they were trying to catch."

Wow, maybe she really was doing Jesse a favor by posing as his wife.

Joanne sighed and went back to combing and snipping. "But then you showed up here with him this spring, and all the push-up bras and short-shorts everyone had bought over the winter got put back in their closets."

"Including yours?" Cadi asked, also arching a brow.

That got her a laugh. "Nope. I'm happily married to my own dream guy, thank you very much; two years as of next month."

"So where's your ring?"

Joanne used the comb to point at a cupboard, then went back to snipping. "It gets safely tucked in my purse every morning and doesn't come back out until I go home at night. I don't imagine it's anywhere near as fancy as yours, but I cherish my diamond too much to expose it to the chemicals I use." She stopped in mid-snip. "Please don't repeat that or I'll never sell another perm. What I use is perfectly safe for my clients, but they're not exposed to it all day long. Anyway," she went on as she resumed snipping, "the diamond kept ripping the latex gloves I wear when I'm doing color."

Well, since she was into this fib for a dime already, Cadi figured she might as well jump in for a dollar. "Actually, my ring is a simple gold band." She smiled at Joanne's disbelief. "Even though we'd only known each other a few months, Jesse had quickly figured out I'm not a very showy person."

"But you said he gave you his mother's diamond."

She had?

Oh God, she really needed to stop coming to town. Every time she met someone new she kept right on expanding her fibs to the point she couldn't remember them two minutes later! "Ah . . . the band is inset with tiny diamonds. I don't think his parents were all that financially well off when they were first married, and—"

Cadi was saved from having to dig herself out of this particular hole when the bell over the door jingled and Sally Barnes, who owned the drugstore next door, came rushing inside.

"Mom," Joanne said in surprise. "What are you doing here?"

Her face flushed with excitement, Sally went to one of the two hairdryers beside Joanne's workstation and sat down. "Don't let me interrupt," she said, setting her tote on her lap. "Mary Ouellette mentioned she saw Cadi going into your salon and I thought I'd come say hi."

"Hi, Sally," Cadi said, waving her hat as she looked at the smiling woman from the corner of her eye, since Joanne was snipping her hair again. "Is that a new tote?"

"As a matter of fact, it is." Sally proudly ran her hand

over the plaid outside pocket of the leather bag. "And we won't tell your father I ordered it from L.L.Bean, will we?" she drawled to Joanne, rolling laughing eyes as she looked at Cadi again. "I don't want Roger having a heart attack when he inevitably checks the catalog to see how much I paid for it." She turned slightly serious. "If a thirty-year veteran of marriage can be so bold as to give a new bride a little advice, Cadi? Always have at least one credit card of your very own, and never, ever, use your husband's card to buy anything *he* would consider frivolous."

Joanne stopped cutting, her own laughing eyes going to Cadi's in the mirror. "Mom gave me my own credit card for a wedding present."

"Damn right—pardon my French," Sally said. "You work your heart out making this salon a success and deserve to buy yourself a few frivolous things." She went back to smiling at Cadi. "And if that handsome husband of yours ever asks how much a new purse or pair of shoes costs, you tell him not nearly as much as that fancy boat of his floating down in the harbor."

"Mother," Joanne admonished. "Mr. Sinclair isn't going to worry about how much his wife spends on shoes."

"No, don't stop her." Cadi looked at Sally from the corner of her eye again. "My mother died when I was twenty, so I never really got any marriage advice from her. Can I ask what a wife's supposed to do if she doesn't have a job? I mean, even if she comes into the marriage with money of her own, how do husbands and wives divide up the household expenses?" She stifled a snort, only able to imagine what it must cost to run Rosebriar. "Does a woman keep dipping into her savings to contribute her fair share? Because if that's the case, I'm probably going to run out of money before our *fifth* anniversary."

Come to think of it, what were her chances of finding her for-real Mr. Right if he was stuck in some office fifty weeks of the year?

Sally blinked at her, clearly nonplussed. "Ah, well . . . I guess . . ." She shrugged. "I'm afraid you're going to have to ask someone else about that, Cadi, since I've never *not* worked. Even when my children were little I kept a playpen in the back office of the drugstore. Maybe your mother-in-law can help. Does she work?"

"Jesse's mom died when he was young."

"Oh, I'm sorry," Sally murmured.

Cadi waved her hat with a laugh, wanting to lighten the mood again. "I'm sure Jesse and I will figure it out. I really love that tote, Sally. You said you ordered it from L.L.Bean; do you know if it comes in a smaller size?"

The bell over the door jingled again and Eva Dean came rushing in clutching a cell phone to her chest. "Oh, good, I haven't missed it," she said in a winded rush as she sat down at the dryer next to Sally.

"Hi, Aunt Eva," Joanne said—Eva being Ken Dean's wife and therefore Sally's sister-in-law. "What haven't you missed?"

"Oh. Ah . . . Cadi!" Eva blurted to her niece before giving Cadi a smile. "I was gone to the post office when you stopped by the grocery store earlier, so when Lindsey Beckman mentioned you were heading to Dee's for a haircut, I decided to run over and say hi before you went back to the island." Music started coming from Eva's chest, and she held her phone at arm's length and squinted at it. Sally leaned into her to also see as Eva slid her finger across the screen with a murmured, "Excuse me, I just need to read this text."

Cadi watched from the corner of her eye as Eva returned the text, whatever she typed causing Sally to giggle just as the bell over the door jingled wildly again. Joanne froze in mid-snip and Cadi looked in the mirror to see two women she recognized but couldn't immediately place rush inside.

"Oh, good, we didn't miss it, Mary," one of them said as she pulled her companion over to Eva and Sally. She practically pushed Mary into the shampoo chair, then walked to the line of chairs Joanne had for waiting customers and dragged one over between the dryer and shampoo station. She sat down and shot Cadi a smile. "You may not remember me, Mrs. Sinclair," she said, pulling off her blue canvas bucket hat, then fluffing her heavily highlighted hair. "I'm Janie Dean. Ray's wife? I was in the hardware store the day you purchased the garden cart and all those rolls of surveyor tape." She gestured at the woman in the shampoo chair when all Cadi could do was mutely nod. "And this is my sister, Mary. She works at the Between the Covers bookstore."

"I showed you our selection of field guides," Mary piped in, "and searched online for that book on beekeeping you then ordered." She frowned. "I tried calling you yesterday and again this morning to let you know it came in, but you didn't answer."

"Cell phone reception is spotty on the island."

"I left you several voice messages."

Cadi felt her cheeks fill with heat, remembering how she'd gone up to the high ridge last night to text Bea and also watch the sunset, only to discover her phone battery was dead. "My phone's out on the island plugged into my solar charger. I remember you both," she rushed on, moving her eyes to include Janie to find the woman had *her* eyes trained on the front windows. Good Lord, what was going on here? "But thank you, Mary, for coming to tell me in person that the book is in."

"Oh, it's nothing," Mary said, her own cheeks flushing. "I needed to get something at the drugstore anyway."

"Will it be okay if I pick up the book the next time I'm in town? I need to leave for Hundred Acre just as soon as I'm done here, so I don't miss the tide."

"That's fine," Mary said. "If I'm not there when you come in, just tell whoever's working that it's right under the counter."

The door opened again and three women—one carrying a toddler—came rushing inside to the cheery jingle of the bell. They stopped and looked around and blew out what sounded like a collective sigh of relief, then two of them sat in the two remaining chairs and the young woman with the toddler walked behind Joanne and plopped down at the second workstation.

"Can someone please tell me what's going on?" Joanne asked her suddenly full salon.

"We all just wanted to come say hi to Mrs. Sinclair," Janie Dean said, standing up and walking to the window. She glanced up and down the parking lot, then suddenly turned and all but ran back to her chair, her lips pursed as if she were fighting not to blurt out something and her eyes bright with excitement as she looked at each of the women.

Cadi once again decided she really needed to stop coming to town. Everyone in Castle Cove had been super friendly to her these last two weeks—some, like Oren Hatch, Jeff Acton, and Ray at the hardware store being exceptionally helpful—but this was bordering on bizarre, especially considering she didn't recognize any of the last three women. "Please, all of you, call me Cadi. And it's really sweet of you ladies to want . . . For you to rush up here just to . . ." Every one of them was looking at her so intently that she simply couldn't go on. So she shrugged and shot them all a big, warm smile. "Hi."

"Hi," the last three arrivals all said in unison.

"So, Cadi, how's your aunt?" Eva asked.

Cadi wracked her brain trying to remember when— and for crying out loud, *why*—she ever would have mentioned having an aunt. "My aunt?" she repeated.

Eva nodded. "Ken told me you had to rush home the morning you stayed in our parking lot because you got a call that your aunt wasn't feeling well."

Good Lord, she had to remember *Jesse's* lies, too?

Eva suddenly smiled. "She must have recovered quickly, since you were back less than a week later." But then her smile turned sad. "Only Ken found you in your car in our parking lot, crying because your husband had left before you got back." She glanced at the door again as several of the women did the same, then looked at Cadi with bright eyes. "You poor newlyweds are like two ships passing in the night. How long did you say you expect him to be away?"

"Jesse has one more week overseas, and I'm assuming it's going to take him at least another week to plow through all the work that's been piling up on his desk in New York."

"Jeepers, Jo, get those scissors going," Sally piped up. "We can't have the poor girl sitting there with half a haircut."

"Yeah," Janie added. "And turn her chair toward the back wall so we can watch."

No longer bizarre, Cadi decided; this was getting creepy.

Joanne made eye contact with her in the mirror and gave an apologetic shrug, then turned the chair toward the second workstation and started combing and cutting again.

Cadi found herself facing an adorable toddler sitting on her mother's lap, staring at her from huge, bright blue eyes as she quietly gnawed on a pink rubber pretzel. "Is she teething?" Cadi asked over the sound of scissors snipping and excited whispers and shushes behind her.

The mother—who barely looked twenty—mutely nodded, her entire complexion turning as pink as her daughter's pretzel.

"I'm sorry to have to ask," Cadi said, "but have we met?" She laughed softly. "I've met so many new people in the last two weeks, I realize now I should have been taking notes."

The young woman shook her head. "We haven't met,

Mrs. Sinclair. But you probably know my grandfather, Oren Hatch. The harbormaster?"

"You're Malinda's sister?"

"No, Mal's my cousin. My dad and her mom are brother and sister."

"Please, call me Cadi. And it's nice to meet you . . . ?"

"Oh, I'm so rude! It's Mandy. Mandy Hatch." She smiled down at her daughter. "And this little gremlin is Abby."

"Oh, my middle name is Abby. She's adorable. And so quiet."

That got Cadi a snort, which immediately kicked Mandy's blush up again. "I'm sorry, Mrs.—Cadi, but Abby's usually about as quiet as a flock of seagulls circling a picnic. And my mom says that once she starts—"

The bell suddenly jingled again and Mandy's eyes widened as her gaze shot to the door. Joanne stopped snipping, and Cadi closed her own eyes as the jingling slowly faded to utter and complete silence, even as she wondered how many more women the salon could hold.

Oh yeah, she definitely needed to start buying her groceries in Fender Cove.

"Excuse me, ladies. I was told my wife might be here?"

THIRTEEN

❧

Cadi snapped open her eyes at the undeniably familiar voice, then immediately shut them again. Oh please, God; if wishes really could be horses, could one come galloping to her rescue, like *right now*?

"There you are, sweetheart," that deep, masculine voice said, moving closer.

Cadi clutched the arms of her chair when she felt it swing around, then opened her eyes to see Jesse standing in the middle of the salon, his arms held away from his sides as he smiled at her . . . expectantly.

Well, she certainly didn't need to feign shock, because—

Wait, he'd said *my wife*.

He *knew* she was running around town pretending to be Mrs. Sinclair?

His deep, masculine chuckle broke the utter and

complete—and pregnant—silence. "I can't believe I've finally managed to shock you speechless." He stepped closer and spread his arms wider. "I realize we have an audience, but I'm sure we're all friends here. Come on now, honey, don't be shy. Show everyone how much you've missed me."

Dressed in jeans and a slightly wrinkled flannel shirt, his jaw shadowed with a couple days' growth of beard, and his own hair in need of a cut, Cadi could almost believe this was the man she'd designed a house for—if not for the competition-crushing gleam in his eyes that said he'd stand there all day if he had to, waiting for her to run to him.

"Cadi," Joanne whispered in her ear, giving her a soft nudge. "Don't ruin his surprise."

"For gosh sakes, Jo," Sally said, "take that ratty old cape off her."

"The poor thing's not shocked," someone added. "She's embarrassed."

No, Cadi was fairly certain she was shocked.

"Yeah," someone else said. "No woman wants her husband to catch her not wearing makeup and having wet, half-cut hair."

So what, Cadi wondered, was the minimum sentence for impersonating a . . . person?

"I'm afraid I have to disagree," Jesse drawled, that gleam intensifying as he continued to stare at her, still holding out his arms, "as I can't imagine my wife ever looking more beautiful."

Joanne ducked down close again. "Go on," she whispered just as there was a soft ripping sound and the cape disappeared and the chair sank with a loud whoosh. "Put the poor man out of his misery."

Near as Cadi could tell, *she* was the only miserable person present. And since that horse didn't seem to be materializing—although she doubted even a figment of the imagination would dare push its way past Jesse-the-businessman—Cadi finally stood up. She started toward him on legs threatening to buckle, but suddenly stopped. Because really, even if he had discovered she'd been racking up bills in his name all over town, what was the worst he could do to her?

Not much, she decided, if he ever wanted to see his house plans.

She canted her head. "I'm sorry, have you been away? I guess I hadn't really noticed," she added over the collective gasp of their audience, "what with being so busy traipsing all over Hundred Acre looking inside hollow logs for pots of—"

Cadi barely had time to register the brief flare of his eyes before he closed the distance and lifted her clean off her feet, his deep, masculine laughter vibrating every cell in her body as he gave her the mother of all bear hugs. "I can explain," she whispered, taking advantage of the fact that her mouth was right next to his ear as she gave him a very wifely hug in return.

He lifted his head; not to respond, but to kiss her to the collective *sigh* of their audience.

Cadi was only peripherally aware of someone's excited clapping being cut short, what with her being so busy kissing Jesse back, because . . . well, because she was *not* a virgin. And because she did need the practice for when she finally met her for-real Mr. Right.

Except she probably shouldn't be practicing on a man she'd spent three months dreaming about, because she really didn't want to start thinking he could be Mr. Right *Now*.

"Eww, Mama! No-no! Ew—mmm."

At the sound of the toddler's protest ending in a muffled growl, Jesse broke the kiss and slowly lowered Cadi down the length of his body until her feet touched the floor. "That's what I rushed home for," he said to more sighs from their audience, while graciously letting Cadi hide her face in his shirt until she stopped blushing from boldly kissing him back.

Well, and from finally realizing what all the women were doing here. Good Lord, text messages must have started zinging through the airwaves the moment someone realized Jesse Sinclair was back in town two weeks before his wife was telling everyone he would be, and they'd all rushed up here to see him surprise her.

Cadi stepped away when the bell over the door jingled madly again and four women rushed inside, only to bump into each other as the first one stumbled to a halt. "Dang, we missed it!" their leader cried, turning to the women behind her—every last one of them well on the north side of eighty years old. "Jehoshaphats, Maude, didn't I tell you nobody waits for a light to turn green if there ain't no cars coming? You made us miss it."

Maude, who had to be ninety if she was a day, lifted her chin defiantly. "And I told you that if I mess up one more time, they're going to take my license away. Or need I remind you that you'd still be back at the diner if I hadn't swung by and picked you up?"

"At least I wouldn't be deaf from Fran's caterwauling when you run up on that curb."

"Ladies," Jesse said, the gleam back in his eyes, "would an instant replay help?"

Jehoshaphats, another kiss like that and she'd be permanently sunburned! "Now behave yourself," Cadi said with a laugh, gesturing at Abby, who was quietly gnawing on her pretzel again. "Not *everyone* wants to see that again," she added into the disappointed sighs of the newcomers. Cadi walked over and sat down in her chair, then gave Jesse a very wifely wave of dismissal. "I'll be a few more minutes, so why don't you go visit Ken and I'll come find you when I'm done."

Everyone *else* likely bought that wounded look. "Knowing how much I love kids," he said as he walked past, "you honestly believe I'd leave this poor little cherub scandalized?"

What she believed is that he expected her to run the moment he left.

"Uppy!" Abby cried when he stopped in front of her, the poor little cherub so scandalized by the kissing man that she dropped her pretzel and lifted her arms. "Uppy!"

"May I?" Jesse asked Mandy, holding out his hands.

"I . . . I think her pants are wet," Mandy whispered in obvious embarrassment.

"Uppy! Uppy!" Abby growled as she squirmed against her mother, her little cherub fingers opening and closing with each demand.

"Having a niece and nephew under three years old, it won't be my first wet shirt," Jesse assured her, chuckling when Abby hurled herself at him the moment Mandy loosened her grip.

And just what, Cadi wondered, was the sentence for assaulting a man for making his fake wife's heart melt at the sight of him holding an adorable little girl in his large, masculine hands?

More sighs filled the salon as every last feminine heart present also melted.

Eva, Sally, Janie, and Mary suddenly stood up; Cadi's relief that half their audience was leaving was short-lived, however, when they merely gave the four older women their seats.

"So, Cadi," Jesse said as he started walking and bouncing Abby as the little girl ran her fingers over his bristly jaw, "how have you been occupying yourself while I've been gone? I'm especially curious what you and Paul Acton have been doing out on the island that requires a garden cart."

A soft snort came from the side wall. "I'm more curious as to what she's doing with all those rolls of—"

"It's a surprise!" Cadi blurted out. She shot Janie Dean an apologetic smile for cutting her off, then gave Jesse a very wifely scowl. "Which you ruined by arriving *two weeks early*."

"Now, now," Eva Dean chided just as Joanne wrapped the cape around Cadi again. "You can't be mad at a man for wanting to hurry back to his new bride. You two have been married, what . . . only a few months?"

"Almost five," Cadi rushed out when Jesse stopped bouncing Abby.

"You got married in February?" Sally Barnes said in surprise, her gaze darting between them before stopping on Jesse. "I hope you took her someplace warm for your honeymoon."

"He took me to Antarctica," Cadi answered before he could.

"Only she didn't know it was their honeymoon," Joanne interjected as she grabbed the bottle of water again, "because they'd only been dating a couple of months when he surprised her with the trip. But when they were at the South Pole he suddenly got down on one knee and proposed, and they were married while standing on a glacier two days later by the minister he'd secretly brought on the cruise ship." She started dampening Cadi's hair again. "And they had a whole colony of penguins for bridesmaids and groomsmen."

Cadi watched through the gentle spray of water as Jesse resumed walking around the crowded salon while bouncing Abby again, but instead of being able to read his mood, all she could see was her impending jail time expanding exponentially.

"Oh, you romantic rascal, you," one of the women said—Cadi presumed to Jesse, since she'd closed her eyes as her little charade continued slowly exploding around her. "It takes a very confident man to spring that kind of surprise on a woman."

"Really?" Jesse said curiously. "And here I thought I was merely desperate."

"Desperate?" someone repeated.

Cadi heard Jesse stop walking. "You obviously don't know my wife well enough yet to realize she's the one who's full of surprises. That's why I decided I better whisk her off to the end of the Earth before some *other* Mr. Right came along."

And just when had she mentioned—

Okay, she was never drinking around Jesse ever again; not if he was going to remember *everything* she said. Yeah, well, he better remember he'd not only gone along with her being Mrs. Sinclair three weeks ago, he'd actually added several embellishments of his own. Come to think of it, it was his fault she'd come up with the idea of hiding out in Castle Cove.

"All done," Joanne announced as the cape disappeared and Cadi opened her eyes to find herself facing the mirror. "Well, what do you think?"

"I wouldn't have thought it possible," Jesse said as he walked behind them and handed Abby to her mother. "But you've somehow managed to improve on perfection." He reached in his rear pocket and pulled out his wallet. "How much . . . Joanne, isn't it?"

"Ah, fifteen," Joanne said, flushing at his compliment. "And I didn't really do . . . I only trimmed a little off the ends."

Jesse handed her a twenty. "Don't bother making change," he said when she rushed to the counter and opened a drawer. "And you can look for me to stop by later this week for my own haircut."

"It's perfect, Joanne. Thank you," Cadi said as she walked up to the mirror. She turned her head back and forth while fluffing her curls and tried to decide if the fact that she wasn't being carted off to jail meant Jesse was going to give her a chance to explain, or if he was waiting until they didn't have an audience before calling the sheriff to lead her away in handcuffs. Figuring there was no avoiding the inevitable, Cadi picked up her backpack and canvas tote full of groceries, then straightened facing the women. "It was wonderful seeing all of you again."

Jesse took the backpack from her and slung it over his shoulder, then took the tote in one hand and *her* hand in the other.

"Before you go, Cadi." Eva Dean glanced at Jesse, then moved closer and lowered her voice. "My oldest daughter, Samantha, has been trying to get pregnant for over a year now, and I was wondering if you can tell me the name of those mushrooms that increase a man's . . . well, you know—the ones that helped you get pregnant."

"Excuse me?" Cadi said on a gasp, spinning toward Jesse to see him arch a brow. "I'm not pregnant!" She turned back to Eva to find the woman blushing to high heaven. "I'm not pregnant," she said calmly.

"Yet," Jesse added as he possessively tucked Cadi up against his side. "But considering I can't eat a salad without my bride smothering it with mushrooms, I'm pretty sure the first room we'll need to finish in our new house will be the nursery."

Eva looked at Cadi. "So what's their name?"

How was she supposed to know? This was Jesse's lie; *he* could answer. Wrapping her arm around his waist as she melted into him, Cadi pinched his side—*not* noticing it was like pinching granite or that he didn't even flinch.

"Most any mushroom is good," he told Eva, "but Cadi's friend said medicinal cordyceps did the trick for her. Although you might want to warn your son-in-law they taste pretty much like they look," he added with a shudder, shuddering Cadi with him. "I'll have our cook send you some along with the address of the market where she gets them."

"Oh, thank you," Eva said, her embarrassment replaced by a beaming smile.

Cadi stepped away from Jesse and gave a general wave good-bye as she headed for the door. "I'm sorry to have to run, but we really don't want to miss the tide."

Not that she was looking forward to spending even one night on an isolated island with Jesse. Well, except she supposed it was better than spending it in jail. And right now a hundred acres was preferable to a salon full of women expecting to see two long-separated newlyweds acting all touchy-feely—a role *her husband* appeared to be enjoying far too much.

Which he proved by capturing her hand again as he caught up with her at the door.

"Cadi, wait," Joanne called out. "You forgot your hat."

Cadi slipped free and ran back and took the hat from Joanne, then walked over and plopped it down on Abby's head, only to laugh when it covered the cherub's eyes. "She'll grow into it," she told Mandy. She then turned to Joanne and shrugged. "I figure what's the fun of having a perfect haircut if I'm going to keep it covered up. Thank you for giving me back the sun," she added softly, squeezing Joanne's arm on her way past.

Cadi then grabbed Jesse's hand before he could grab

hers. "Come on, you desperate rascal, you, let's go home and I'll make you a nice huge salad for supper," she drawled, leading him outside to a final round of sighs, several gasps, and at least one excited applause.

The little missus may have recovered from her shock quickly enough, and even managed to bring him up to speed with some of the stories she'd been telling, but Jesse could feel the tension in her grip as she all but dragged him down the parking lot.

"I can explain," she repeated.

He gave her hand a squeeze. "You don't have to. I just came from Whistler's Landing." He turned to her when she stopped walking. "Stanley hasn't called you yet?" he asked, only to realize that was a dumb question, considering she was still *here*.

She dropped her gaze to his chest. "My phone died yesterday afternoon and it's back on the island, charging."

He started them walking again. "Your ex-fiancé must be going crazy with worry that you're not answering," he said, making sure not to sound as pleased by that notion as he felt.

She pulled him to a stop again. "Why?"

Jesse looked back to see the women spilling out of the salon and started them off again. "Because Stanley found his brother tied to his office chair this afternoon," he said, deciding not to mention Aaron's condition at the time as he used his grip to keep her walking when she tried to stop again. "Apparently Ryan Stapleton didn't care for his house design and sent Aaron with the message that if

Stanley *and you* aren't standing in his office in New York in one week with a house he does like, he's burning Aaron's restaurant and sending his men to . . . fetch you."

Jesse looked over when she didn't respond and bit back a curse when he saw how pale she was. He led her to the side of the parking lot entrance and set down the tote bag, then pulled her into his arms. "It's going to be okay, Cadi," he murmured, pressing her head to his shoulder. "Stanley and Aaron are going to disappear, and I'm going to stay right here with you until Stapleton is no longer a threat." He leaned away to smile down at her. "You have no idea how relieved I was to discover you've been hiding out on Hundred Acre these last two weeks instead of driving all over New England with your cat."

"Why?"

"Why what?"

She lowered her gaze to his throat, a bit of color returning to her cheeks. "Why do . . . What's it to you that I'm not driving . . . Why should you care?"

He tucked her against him again with a chuckle. "Because even slow-witted bears dream of being heroes." He snorted. "Even in absentia, apparently."

It took him a moment to realize she wasn't responding again, a bit longer to notice she'd gone rigid, and definitely too long to decide she was scared. Of Stapleton? Or of him?

Hell, was she afraid he was going to kick her off his island?

Or was she worried about staying on it *with him*?

"Hey," he said, ducking to look her in the eyes, "you know me well enough by now to realize I'm not the kind of guy who would take advantage of a woman or expect anything in return." He immediately let her step away when she apparently needed physical proof of his claim, leaving him to wonder what she was thinking as she picked up the tote and strode off down the road.

"Did you come back early because you heard some woman was going around Castle Cove pretending to be Mrs. Sinclair?" she asked when he fell in step beside her.

"No, I cut my trip short because I missed my island." *And you,* he silently added.

"So you just found out what I've been doing?"

"About an hour ago," he said, nodding when she looked over at him. "When I went to the docks, Oren gave me a repaired wheel from a garden cart, saying I might as well take it with me. I thought it went to a piece of Corey Acton's equipment, but Oren said my wife had brought it with her from the island this morning."

She looked at the road ahead. "And you didn't set him straight?"

"I told you, I was relieved." He guided her up onto the sidewalk when he spotted a truck heading toward them, then took hold of her hand again and kept walking. "I'd texted you several times while I was overseas but didn't find out why you never answered until this afternoon, when Stanley told me you'd changed phones a couple of weeks ago. But it wasn't until his partner came running down to the pier to tell us she'd found Aaron tied to a chair in the office that I learned why Stanley was refusing to give me your new number."

"He told you what was going on with Ryan Stapleton?"

"I got most of the story from listening to the conversation

between him and Aaron, and Stanley filled in the blanks when I confronted him and suggested he let me worry about keeping you safe while he dealt with Stapleton."

She gave him a quick glance before staring ahead again, but it was long enough for him to see what she thought of that idea. "So you also believe I have the brains of a chipmunk."

He stopped walking. "Excuse me?"

She shrugged her hand free and continued down the sidewalk.

"Hey, you can't take my being worried as an insult," he said, rushing to catch up. "I thought you were hiding from a loan shark who has the hots for you by aimlessly driving around with your cat and staying in a tent. How was I to know you were sleeping in a big cozy camper with electricity and running water?" He angled closer and gently bumped her arm, hoping to lighten the mood. "And running all over Castle Cove starting fashion trends."

She picked up her pace. "For your information, I haven't so much as set foot in your camper. And I only run the generator long enough to fill my water jug."

"What? Why aren't you using the camper?"

"Because I *like* sleeping in a tent with my cat." He heard her take a calming breath. "Wiggles and I will be packed up and gone on the morning tide."

He pulled her to a stop just as they reached the pier parking lot, then clasped her shoulders to hold her facing him. "I don't think you have the brains of a chipmunk, Cadi. In fact, it was the intelligence sparkling in your eyes that first caught my attention back in February.

I made that offer to Stanley because I was worried you'd spent the last two weeks disillusioned and lonely and . . . scared." He flashed her an arrogant grin. "And because I'd read somewhere that the quickest way to get a girl's attention is to ride to her rescue."

It wasn't exactly intelligence sparkling in those big baby blues at the moment, but rather confusion. "Why?"

Honest to God, his niece and nephew said *why* less often. "Why what?"

"Why would you want to get my attention?" He felt her stiffen. "You said you're not the kind of guy who expects something in return."

Now he was confused. But only until he realized she was comparing him to Stapleton. "I'm not," he said quietly.

"Then give me one good reason you're willing to let me continue hiding out here as your wife if you're not expecting me to return the favor by rebuilding your models."

Jesse dropped his hands and stepped away before he could act on his urge to give her a shake, pretty sure being mercenary was on par with being a lech. "For the same reason I sent you the flowers: to let you know that unlike the man you were engaged to for two years, I *am* interested in you romantically."

Her jaw momentarily slackened, just before it snapped shut and she strode off. "So instead of brainless, I'm a *naive* chipmunk," Jesse heard her mutter as he followed.

"Naw," he drawled, his anger giving way in light of hers. Well, and because Miss Glace in a snit was a glorious thing to see. "I'm thinking you're more of . . . an otter." That didn't score him any points, if the scowl she shot him over her shoulder was any indication. "Hey, river otters are beautiful and playful and *smart*." *And they have great senses of humor,* he silently added.

He'd actually intended to go with *ferret*, since besides being infamous snoops with the attention span of . . . well, ferrets, the fearless little creatures were cute and cuddly and really quite clever. And just like Cadi had figured out how to hide in plain sight, the ferret he'd given Ben's long-lost son, Mike, for his sixteenth birthday was a master escape artist.

Unlike Hank's gecko, apparently.

Hell, Sam had called Willa a little brown partridge— though not to her face—when he'd first laid eyes on her battling Tidewater's bag-eating elevator.

But figuring Cadi might take being likened to what was basically a glorified rat as less than flattering, he'd gone with otter. Because, hey—he'd rather she believed he was a jerk instead of a mercenary, since he was pretty sure women considered jerks redeemable. And anyway, he preferred her angry over her being scared.

Especially since they were about to have their first real fight of their fake marriage.

FOURTEEN

❧

Still trying to wrap his mind around the fact that he'd lost, Jesse watched from his cruiser as Cadi maneuvered her skiff into the small cove on the southwestern end of Hundred Acre in time to ride a cresting wave clean up onto the beach. Lost, hell; he'd folded like a house of cards when instead of snapping fire at him, those big baby blues had turned vulnerable. "Would an otter," she'd quietly asked, "agree to trap itself on an isolated island with a man it barely knew?"

And just how was he supposed to counter that? Which meant either Cadi truly was unsure of him or else she knew him far better than he knew himself, because not in a million years would he have thought there was anything she could have said to make him back down.

But this *definitely* was the last time she crossed the

reach in that boat. Now that he'd actually witnessed her making the treacherous commute—which she'd done only God knew how many times in the last two weeks— he was standing firm even if she started crying, since he doubted *he* would survive another crossing.

Running an unsteady hand over his face and taking his first decent breath in half an hour when he saw Cadi finally step onto solid ground, Jesse figured that instead of falling asleep dreaming of sparkling blue eyes, he was in for at least a month of nightmares. He grabbed the wheel and braced himself, then pushed on the throttle and turned the cruiser into an oncoming swell, hoping a fast ride would calm him down and clear his head enough to think of a solution they both could live with.

Having found himself following Cadi through the congested harbor, his first thought had been to let someone else be the bad guy by simply making her boat disappear and suggesting it must have been stolen—until he'd realized that for a lie to work it at least had to be *believable*. Next he'd thought about messing with the motor—until he'd pictured Cadi *rowing* to the mainland. His plan to burn the damn boat had died half-formed, however, when she'd passed the breakwater into the choppy reach and he'd gotten real busy alternating between remembering to breathe and shouting curses at Stapleton, at Stanley and Aaron Kerr, and more than a few at God.

But mostly he'd cursed himself, wondering what could have possessed him to buy an island. Because if a grown woman had him sweating bullets, how did he hope to survive a passel of sneaky teenagers constantly wanting to motor over to the mainland?

Jesse sent a silent apology to his brother for not understanding why Ben had turned into a veritable bear after receiving a letter three and a half years ago saying he should come to Maine to meet the fifteen-year-old son he hadn't known existed. Eighteen now and already in his second year at MIT, Mike was older and wiser and frighteningly smarter than all three Sinclair brothers combined, and definitely as wily as his great-grandfather.

Rounding the southern tip of Hundred Acre to be greeted by five-foot swells pushing straight in off the Gulf, Jesse shuddered at the thought of the havoc Bram and Mike would have caused had they ever gotten together. He shot up the windward shoreline while eyeing the lower bluff, only to realize the house Cadi had designed would barely be visible from the water for blending into the landscape. He pulled the throttle halfway back when he caught sight of something red at the base of the short cliff, not ten seconds later spotting Little Miss Independent approaching what must be her campsite.

Hell, she really was sleeping in a tent.

With her cat.

Seeing her stop and look in his direction, Jesse pushed the cruiser back to three-quarter throttle and turned his attention to the windswept ridge crowning the north end of the island, still undecided if he might be getting unpretentious at the expense of a truly commanding view.

How fortuitous, then, that he happened to be married to the lead designer of his house, who just happened to be camped on the exact spot where she wanted it built. Was it mere coincidence she'd chosen to hide out here? Karma? Fate? Guilt?

Had Cadi even once considered the long-term ramifications of pretending to be his wife? Because even a chipmunk would realize the position she'd put him in; in particular how he was supposed to explain what had become of Mrs. Sinclair when she went back to being Miss Glace. Hell, he could already see the cadaver dogs searching Hundred Acre for his missing wife.

Jesse shook his head as he rounded the north end of the island, willing to bet a year's salary that guilt had made Cadi immediately jump to the conclusion he was expecting something in return for letting her continue the lie. She should feel guilty, dammit, and happily rebuild his model for intending to walk away from the mess she'd made of his life.

Not that he intended to let her.

He pulled back on the throttle as he approached the mooring Ken Dean's son had placed just off the beach below his campsite, bracing himself when the wake caught up with the cruiser as he fought the urge to roar. Instead of calming down, he was twice as angry. He still wasn't over watching Cadi cross the reach, and the long-term ramifications of having a fake wife were only just now dawning on *him*.

Jesse shoved down on the throttle with a curse and headed around the island again.

"Here's a news flash for you," Cadi said as she spooned cat food into the colorful ceramic dish. "We no longer have the island to ourselves. Yes," she muttered, setting the dish on the ground, "the lord of the manor missed his island so much he came back two weeks early." She snagged a bag of Cheetos and a bottle of warm Moxie out of the tote bag, then collapsed into her canvas chair with a sigh. "I don't know what to do, Wigs. Jesse said we could stay and is even playing along with our being married, but I don't know if I can keep it up now that he's actually here. I didn't have any problem being a fake fiancée because it was Stanley, but I'm afraid Jesse is going to take his role in our little charade much too seriously."

Not that she understood why he was willing to play the part of her husband. After looking positively thunderous when she'd accused him of expecting her to rebuild his model, did he truly think she would believe he was interested in her romantically?

"He called me an otter," she told her pet as she wrestled the bag of Cheetos open. "To my face. Well, to my back, since I was walking away from him at the time. Am I supposed to take that as a compliment? Or was it his way of making sure I didn't start scheming to keep the title of Mrs. Sinclair permanently?" She drove her hand into the bag. "Everyone knows otters are about as sophisticated as two-year-olds." Popping several Cheetos in her mouth, Cadi furiously chewed as she tried to decide what sort of animal best described Jesse. She'd designed a house for a carefree, *likeable* bear, but businessman Jesse was a . . .

Shark was too clichéd. Tigers were too beautiful. Hawks too majestic. Lions . . .

Heck, likening Jesse to any predator was too complimentary.

Weasel then. Or ferret. Yeah, ferrets were sneaky little rats that always seemed to have an agenda, were always sticking their wet little noses into everything, and always popping up where they shouldn't.

Okay, then; if he called her an otter again, she was coming back with ferret.

Cadi polished off half the bag of Cheetos and most of the warm soda, then walked to the top of the bluff. She spent several minutes taking in the view, then scanned her campsite below. "What do you suppose my chances are of getting Jesse to stay away from this section of the island?" she asked when Wiggles silently leapt onto the boulder beside her. "Probably not good," she said with a sigh, "since ferrets *listen* about as well as two-year-olds."

Cadi picked up her cell phone and solar charger off the boulder and headed back down the bluff, wanting to grab a warm fleece for her hike to the high ridge so she could call Stanley and find out exactly what was going on with Stapleton.

Jesse beached the small motorized raft he kept on the cruiser and stepped ashore, still unable to believe it had taken him three trips around Hundred Acre to come up with an argument Cadi couldn't possibly counter. But if by some miracle she did, he was marrying her for real first thing tomorrow and giving her his seat on Tidewater's board of directors.

He dragged the raft up across the beach above the high tide mark, then tied it to a tree, grabbed his overnight bag, and headed up the road to his camper. A bit disappointed at not finding a tent pitched on the gravel pad that meant Cadi had been building models during her stay, he opened the door and stepped into his camper, even more bummed to see she really hadn't been using it. But from the looks of the small oak branches and fallen green leaves on the ground indicating there'd been a couple of good storms since he'd been gone, she at least could have ridden them out in the camper instead of a tent. It just didn't make sense that she would borrow his name but not use any of the creature comforts that came with it.

Jesse tossed his bag onto the couch, remembering she hadn't been shy about opening accounts in his name to purchase . . . well, okay, tools. She'd bought a cart and mud boots and probably gloves, and the hat she'd given the cherub. He walked to the utilities panel by the door and started the heater to take away the coastal chill, making him wonder what Cadi was using for heat when it got chilly at night or a fog bank rolled in.

Was she really that stubborn?

I like sleeping in a tent with my cat, she'd said. So maybe she did, and was simply trying to turn a bad situation into an adventure. Yeah. Maybe she was practicing for her real adventure by pretending Hundred Acre was one of the national parks she was so anxious to see. And he had to give her credit for finding a place where . . . What was the cat's name? Wiggles. Yeah, she'd found a place to hide where Wiggles would be able to roam free.

Jesse went to his bedroom and grabbed a jacket from the closet, then slipped it on as he headed outside, figuring he had enough daylight left to check his email and make a few calls. He started up the path to the ridge as he decided he could get away with holding hands and kissing Cadi in town, but wondered how he should go about starting a real—and preferably private—relationship with her.

Well, he supposed he should make sure she *stayed* on the island long enough for them to get to know each other better, which meant he should probably take a little walk tonight after dark and steal the fuel line off her boat again. She might get pissed, but at least she'd be pissed *here*. And all he really needed was a day or two to persuade her that he . . . what? Offering to give her all the space she wanted might be a good start, so long as she promised not to cross the reach without telling him first. Then he'd give her back the fuel to prove he trusted her, and she would see that she could trust him in return. And if he didn't mention his models again, she might even start to relax around him.

And maybe he could get her interested in wanting to hang around even longer by sharing some of his plans for Hundred Acre. He could talk to her about the deep-water dock he intended to have built, ask what she thought he should do with the high ridge and that spectacular view if the house wasn't going up there, and even ask her questions about the house itself—without using the word *model*—such as what the inside would look like.

Okay then. If he considered today their second date—they had kissed, after all—then he was actually making progress. And he'd noticed some wild rosebushes growing along the cove where Cadi had beached the skiff; maybe tonight when he stole the fuel line he'd pick a whole pocketful of rose petals and scatter them outside her tent for her to find in the morning.

No, that might creep her out, and he'd wake up to see

Cadi *rowing* across the reach in that old scow loaded to the gunwales with camping gear—and her cat.

Despite it still being daylight, Jesse emerged from the trees to be greeted by a thin crescent moon hanging high over the top of the barren ridge, but stumbled to a halt when he saw Cadi sitting almost directly beneath it, leaning against a boulder and talking on her cell phone. He realized she'd spotted him when he saw her say something and end the call, then lower the phone to her lap.

She watched him the whole time he walked up the steep ledge, but it wasn't until he was almost to her that Jesse noticed her features were drawn with worry and her unusually large eyes were welling with unshed tears. Guessing it was too soon in their one-sided relationship to pull her into his arms and comfort her, he settled for sitting beside her to also use the boulder for a backrest, then stared out at the ocean in silence.

"I guess I really am naive," she said nearly two full minutes later, her voice sounding as though she were still fighting tears. "Whenever I've watched those forensic or police shows on television, I've always assumed they kept exaggerating the . . . evilness, trying to one-up each other for ratings." She looked over at him, her eyes troubled and still thick with moisture, and smiled sadly. "And I always felt that even if half of what they showed was real, I didn't have to worry, because it was too far away to ever affect me." She looked down at her lap and pulled in a shuddering breath. "But it *is* real, and the evilness has found its way to Whistler's Landing—and me."

"It can't affect what it can't find," Jesse said quietly, finally giving in to his urge to slide an arm around her shoulders, only to take a deep breath of his own when she immediately leaned into him.

"That's pretty much what Stanley's been saying since he first sent me away." She lifted her hand holding her phone, and let it flop back on her lap. "And what he said again tonight."

"Did you tell him you're here with me?"

"No. He still thinks I'm driving around. He just gave me your cell number and told me basically what you did, that you'd offered to keep me safe while he dealt with Stapleton."

"And the offer's still open. You can stay here and continue keeping yourself safe just like you've been doing for the last two weeks. I only ask that you let me stay here with you."

"Don't you have a job to go to?"

Jesse rubbed a hand along her arm when he felt her take another shuddering breath, and softly chuckled. "You honestly expect me to get any work done knowing you're back here sleeping in a tent? Hell, I'd probably create more messes than I would clean up." He stopped rubbing and gave her a gentle squeeze. "Will you agree to stay, Cadi?"

She sat up and looked at him. "Will you agree to stay away from the southern half of the island and let me come and go as I please?"

Damn. "I can respect your privacy, but I've got a problem with the coming and going part." He fought a grin when those big baby blues went from *troubled* to *he was in trouble*, and Jesse held up his hand to stop her from responding. "It's not that I mind you going to the mainland alone; it's what you're going *in* that bothers me."

She lost the scowl, looking sincerely baffled. "I really don't understand what the big deal is. I know my skiff might be a bit past its prime, but it hasn't failed me yet. And I always check the weather before I leave, and if ten-knot winds are forecast, I stay put. And after the first couple of trips, I figured out that instead of constantly fighting the tide, I could actually use it to my advantage. I come to the island only during a rising tide and go to the mainland when the tide is falling."

Jesse grinned. "So I saw earlier. You timed it perfectly and rode that incoming wave far enough up onto the beach that all you had to do was step out and tie the skiff to a tree. It's not your skill as a seaman I'm questioning, Cadi, it's that boat."

She turned back to stare out at the ocean, and he heard her sigh. "I underestimated how much it costs to live day-to-day without being able to use my checkbook or credit cards." She gave him a quick glance—Jesse assumed to see if he knew about the accounts she'd been opening in his name—then sighed again. "That old skiff was all I could afford, and then I paid twice what I should have for it."

More like ten times, Jesse figured. "My offer to keep you safe—to *help* keep you safe—encompasses more than just stopping Stapleton from finding you." Okay, time for an argument she couldn't counter. "After watching you cross the reach this afternoon, and hearing Oren Hatch's reaction to seeing you coming and going these last two weeks, I believe I've come up with a solution we can both live with."

He grinned again when her eyes narrowed in suspicion. "The locals might understand you not being comfortable driving my cruiser, but have you considered," he asked, shaking his head, "what they'll be thinking, especially now that I'm here, every time they see my wife chugging out of the harbor in that skiff when I can obviously afford to buy her something safer?"

Jesse almost laughed out loud when Cadi suddenly scowled—not at him, but at herself—even as she started shaking her own head. "I can't let you buy me a boat. That's taking your wanting to help me too far. And besides, I only expect to be here another week."

He gestured at her phone. "That was your timeline *before* today. What if a week ends up being a month?" he asked quietly.

"A boat's too much," she repeated, shaking her head again.

Jesse leaned back against the boulder and folded his arms over his chest. Oh yeah, he was definitely winning this one. "It's been my intention to buy a sporty little runabout anyway, so I won't have to bother taking my cruiser off the mooring just to zip over to town. I plan to build a deep-water dock, but I'm also going to have a set of floating docks anchored directly off the beach in order to have quick access to a smaller boat. So I'd really be purchasing the runabout for myself, but it'll be yours to use for as long as you're here."

She went back to scowling as she dropped her gaze to her lap and slowly rolled her cell phone in her hands. And when she finally looked up again, Jesse had all he could do not to high-five himself when he saw the sparkle in her eyes—even though she tried to appear nonchalant by shrugging. "Works for me." She suddenly stood up, then looked down at him with a lopsided grin. "You might have a bit of explaining to do, though, when someone in town tells your future wife that she's coming and going in a hand-me-down boat."

Jesse stood up with a chuckle. "Unless I save myself the trouble and go ahead and marry you for real. Do you want me to walk you back to your campsite?"

"Thank you, but no," she said, either not hearing what he'd said or pretending not to. She shoved her phone in her jacket pocket and pulled out a small headlamp, which she held up for him to see, a bit more sparkle escaping. "I came prepared. And I won't be alone, anyway."

Seeing hints of the Miss Glace he'd gallantly rescued from her burning crappy car, Jesse merely arched a brow as he bent at the waist as if trying to look in her pocket. "You got another slow-witted bear hidden in there I don't know about?"

That got him the laugh he was looking for, the disillusioned, frightened woman from a moment ago almost completely gone. She gestured toward the bottom of the ledge. "Wiggles followed me here."

Jesse scanned the perimeter of the trees fifty yards below. "Where is she?" He looked at Cadi and arched a brow again. "I've heard an awful lot about this cat, but I've yet to see her."

"And you probably never will. She doesn't like strangers. She was sprawled on the boulder behind my head earlier but suddenly took off. I thought she'd spotted something interesting, but now realize she must have heard you coming."

"I assume Wiggles was a good part of your reason for choosing to find an isolated place to roost instead of staying in public campgrounds," Jesse said. "So that she wouldn't have to spend most of her time in a crate. But if the cat doesn't like strangers, how is she going to like traveling all over America, even in a motorhome?"

"I'm hoping traveling will help Wigs break out of her safe little world, too," Cadi said as she shoved the headlamp back in her pocket. She started down the ledge, but hadn't taken two steps before she stopped and turned, the impish smile she shot him hitting Jesse square in his chest—making him fold his arms again. "Speaking of which," she added, "since I don't know if you've been back to your office and saw the card I sent you, I'll just thank you in person." That smile widened, lighting up her entire face. "Thank you for the lovely bouquet of flowers. And for the good advice, which you'll be happy to know I took. Well, the part about buying an SUV instead of a sporty coupe. The one thing I didn't say in the card, though, was thank you for kicking me off my comfortable couch."

"Excuse me?"

She nodded, even as she scrunched up her nose. "I'm not sure I can explain it properly, but when I left you that morning in Castle Cove, I could barely wait to get home and give my entire life a makeover. For three days I went through every inch of my house and donated half of everything I owned to the Salvation Army. And if Stanley hadn't come to me saying I had to disappear, I was going out the next day to find a motorhome and head off across America the moment I got it packed." The sparkle in her eyes intensified, even as she shrugged. "I'd really planned to thank you by inviting you to the wedding. And your wife, of course."

What in hell was she talking about? "Forgive me if I appear confused; whose wedding are you inviting me—and my wife—to?"

"Mine."

"Sorry," Jesse said with a slight shake of his head. "Still confused here. Can I ask when this wedding is taking place? No, wait; I'm more interested in *who* you're marrying. And also," he rushed on when she opened her mouth to respond, "who *I'm* married to."

Jesse bit back a laugh when Cadi looked more confused than he was. "You'll be married to the woman you're going to have a passel of kids with," she said. "Your Mrs. Right."

"Have I met her yet?"

"How would I know that? Are you dating anyone?"

"Not at the moment. Although not from lack of *trying*," he said dryly. "Would you happen to have someone in particular in mind?"

Confusion turned to impatience—with maybe a touch of anger. "Why don't you just Google yourself," she said, slashing a hand toward the sky, "and choose one from the hundreds of women in all those pictures of you at political dinners and fund-raising parties."

Jesse gave a heavy sigh. "Let's get back to who you're marrying. Is he anyone I know?"

"*I* don't know him yet. He's still out there somewhere," she said, this time gesturing toward the mainland, "waiting for me to pull my motorhome into a campsite across from him in Yosemite or Yellowstone or Glacier National Park."

"Ah, I see," Jesse murmured. He cocked his head. "You know, I just realized you and I have a lot in common."

She snorted, apparently not over her impatience *or* anger. "We have nothing in common. You're a majority stockholder of an international shipping mega-company, there probably isn't a country you haven't been to, you're on every important guest list for events all over the world, and you seem to have money growing on several trees in your twelve-hundred-acre backyard."

Not sure how they'd gone from teasing to arguing, and despite knowing it wouldn't further his cause, Jesse couldn't help get a little angry himself. "You're not exactly a pauper."

"Not by most measures," she agreed with a curt nod. "In fact, I could probably purchase my own island if I didn't mind eating what's on sale and living in a tent for the rest of my life."

She was so indignant, Jesse burst out laughing. "Welcome back, Miss Glace."

That appeared to take the wind out of her sails. "Huh?"

He closed the distance between them and hugged her before she could realize his intent. But he made it a quick hug, then stepped back. "If I'm going to be sharing an island with you, I'd much rather it be with the Miss Glace

I met three weeks ago—even when she's in a snit—than with a frightened or sad fake wife. And you're welcome," he added when she continued staring at him in confusion, hoping to confuse her more.

Because hell, he was pretty sure making her mad wasn't winning him any points.

"Ah . . . welcome for what?"

"I believe you turned back to thank me for the flowers and kicking you off a couch. So, you're welcome. It was my pleasure. You ever feel like you need another kick, you know where to find me," he drawled, turning and walking down the path leading to his camper. "Sweet dreams, Mrs. Sinclair," he added, giving a negligent wave over his shoulder.

FIFTEEN

❧

Jesse exited his camper, then immediately turned around and went back inside. He grabbed his jacket off the kitchen chair where he'd tossed it last night, then checked the outside temperature on the panel by the door before exiting the camper again. He slipped on his jacket as he headed in the direction of Cadi's camp, mentally reminding himself to start looking out the window before going outside. If he'd noticed the fog, he would have been expecting it to be twenty degrees colder than it should be for the end of June on a Maine island.

He didn't have any trouble following the crude trail he assumed led to the lower bluff halfway down the eastern side of the island, figuring Paul must have made at least a dozen trips with the garden cart full of firewood from the looks of it. Hell, considering the rough terrain, he should probably give the kid an extra fifty the next time he saw him. And while he was at it, he should talk to Corey about having some gravel paths built that were wide enough for a golf cart, since he was going to have to lug groceries and suitcases and who knew what else to the house. That's why he'd placed the landing and camper pad on the northwestern end, because at the time he'd *thought* his house was going up on the high ridge.

And he still wasn't convinced it shouldn't.

Fifteen minutes and one unsettling tumble later with no sign of the bluff, Jesse decided he needed to have a talk with Paul about the difference between working hard and working *smart*—right before handing him *two* extra fifty-dollar bills. Sweet God, the kid had dragged that heavy cart up and down small knolls and around countless boulders and fallen trees, across a couple of shallow brooks and one small ravine, over a spongy peat bog, and down the steep, moss-covered ledge responsible for the wet stain on his bruised ass.

Jesse took off his jacket when he realized he was starting to sweat, and remembered lying in bed this morning thinking about *not* putting up the cell phone antenna, because one, he still didn't want his phone ringing every ten minutes, and two, he liked the idea of bumping into Cadi when they both had to climb the ridge to call or send emails. But now he was rethinking his thinking, because he really couldn't see making this treacherous hike every time he wanted to ask her something. And what if she twisted an ankle or took sick or had a tree fall on her or something and couldn't call for help because she didn't have cell phone reception?

It was decided, then: he'd pick up the antenna at the post office this morning and put it up this afternoon. He also better go to the hardware store and buy a really long extension cord on the chance he couldn't set the antenna close to his camper, as well as see if Ray could order him a solar system to power it so he wouldn't have to constantly run the generator.

All of which meant he'd have to find some other way to bump into Cadi.

Jesse's relief at finally spotting the bluff soon turned to bewilderment, however, when he stopped at the bottom of the western end of the small cliff. Not quite sure what he was seeing, all he could do was frown at the maze of various colored tape crisscrossing the clearing that had been cut below the entire length of the shallow bluff, in the middle of which Cadi was standing, scowling down at an open sketchbook and muttering to herself. He then caught sight of movement just off to her left at the same time she did, which caused her to look up and scan the sky directly overhead.

"I promise, Wigs," she said with a laugh, looking back at the base of a boulder the size of a small car. "Ospreys eat *fish*, not cats. But they'll keep harassing you if you don't quit prowling those pines where they're nesting, because they don't know you don't eat baby ospreys."

Jesse heard a low, rather chilling feline growl just as he saw a large gray cat with black spots eyeing him as it edged around the boulder in slow motion and then turned and disappeared into the bushes one second before he heard a loud human gasp.

"No!" Cadi shouted as she raced through the maze of tape toward him with her arms outstretched. "You agreed to not come here. Go away. Go away!" she cried, now waving the hand holding the sketchbook while still futilely trying to block his view with her other hand.

Feeling about as bright as a chipmunk, Cadi was almost to him when it finally dawned on Jesse exactly what he was seeing. "Son of a bitch," he shouted, striding toward her and plucking her off her feet when she slammed into him with a whoosh of expelled air, then swinging her in a circle. "It's my house! You're not rebuilding my model—you're laying it out at full scale!"

"Put me down," she growled while repeatedly swatting his back. "And *go away.*"

He stopped turning. "Sweet God, you're a genius," he said thickly as he started walking toward the center of the maze.

She quit fighting and dropped her head to his shoulder with a heavy sigh, and he wasn't sure, but he thought he heard her mutter something about ferrets always ruining everything.

He stepped around clusters of bush stumps and grade stakes before finally having to stop when he came to a dead end. He lowered Cadi to her feet but quickly tucked her against his side and gave her a squeeze. "It's my house," he whispered reverently as he looked around. "Which room are we standing in? Is this the living room? It's . . . small."

"It's one of the guest bedrooms. That's the living room," she said, *not* reverently, as she pointed to their left. She wiggled free and headed back to where he'd picked her up. "And if it's not big enough, complain to Stanley."

"Hey, I'm sorry, okay," he said to her back. "I know you asked me to give you privacy, but this morning I realized we didn't have any way to communicate. So I thought it would be okay if I came over *this one time* to tell you I'm putting up an antenna to give the entire island cell phone reception. And also to ask if you want to go to town with me this morning when I go pick it up." He spread his arms and gestured at the tape stretching out in every direction as she straightened from picking up her sketchbook. "I never dreamed you didn't want me down here because you were building a full-scale model of my house. I'm sorry," he repeated when she said nothing. "And thank you. I don't think anyone's ever given me a nicer surprise."

He was pretty sure he caught the hint of a blush as she silently picked up his jacket and walked to a large pine tree, where she hung it on the remains of a tiny branch that had broken off.

"So this is what Paul Acton's been working on with you?" he asked, scanning what appeared to be an attempt to clear and level the ground in front of the cliff using only a shovel and a handsaw. "Wouldn't it have been easier to get Corey or Jeff to come in with a chainsaw and cut down these trees," he said, gesturing at the pine and two smaller oaks in the middle of his living room, "and bring in their bulldozer to push the boulders out of the way and level the site?"

"I didn't want to disturb the ground any more than we have," she said as she walked back to him, "because I didn't know if you agreed the house would even be going here, since you never got to study the model."

Jesse made his way to the living room and quietly stood staring toward the ocean, soon realizing that with a bit of selective cutting and pruning down the gentle slope and along the craggy shore, the view looking out would be pretty damn spectacular while still keeping the house nearly invisible to anyone looking in. "Why here?" he asked quietly, continuing to stare at the ocean as he felt her walk up beside him. "Stanley told me you're the one who wants the house to be set here instead of up on the ridge."

"Because no matter how unpretentious a home Stanley designed you," she said just as softly, "if it's up on that ridge it would constantly shout *Businessman Jesse* every time you approached Hundred Acre, where down here the forest will whisper to you, *Welcome home. Now go in and change your clothes; it's time to play* the whole time you drive one of those silent electric golf carts here from your dock."

Still looking at the ocean, Jesse couldn't decide if he wanted to kiss her or back away making the sign of the cross. How in hell did she *know*?

He did decide, however, not to tell her Stanley had admitted she had designed the house.

"Okay, then," he said, rubbing his hands together as he turned to her. "Give me a quick tour, then I'll help you—What are those poles for?" he asked when he noticed at least a dozen twenty-foot-long saplings that had been stripped bare of their branches leaning against the cliff.

She walked over and pulled one of the poles away from the cliff and thumped the end of it into the ground as she frowned in the direction of her tent—which appeared to be pitched in the middle of another room. "I'm trying to figure out how to show the second floor layout and also give a sense of the overall height of the house."

"There's a second floor?" Jesse said in surprise. "I realize I only saw the small version, but I assumed the raised roof on the east end was a cathedral ceiling." He lifted his gaze to the area above her tent. "What's going to be up there? My office?"

"No, your passel of kids."

Jesse frowned at her. "Where's the master bedroom?"

A sparkle lit up her eyes as she gestured at her tent. "I'm camping in it."

He made sure not to show how pleased he was by that notion—or how turned on. "Well, why not, *Mrs*. Sinclair," he drawled, grinning when she suddenly turned away and leaned the pole back against the ledge. He shook his head when she turned back to him. "But I'm pretty sure I told Stanley I didn't want a two-story house. What if there's a fire, especially if I'm not sleeping upstairs with the kids?"

"There's a nook in the master suite for a crib, and the second floor will be level with the top of the cliff," she explained, moving her arm in an arc from her tent to the bluff. "It will have four bedrooms surrounding a large center playroom. In my—in the model I built from Stanley's design, the children will be able to exit the playroom by way of a short catwalk straight onto the top of the cliff."

Jesse couldn't help but notice she'd nearly slipped up, and shot her a grin. "And when they're teenagers? Instead of a fire exit, they're going to use that catwalk to sneak out of the house so they can steal my boat and motor to the mainland to meet their friends."

She shrugged, her eyes sparkling again. "Then I guess you better put a secret alarm on the door that sends a signal to your cell phone."

Jesse chuckled and slowly turned in a circle, then stopped when he was facing the water again, unable to believe he was actually standing in his living room. "Yes, here," he said thickly. "I want it built here." Hearing a sigh of relief behind him, he turned and rubbed his hands together again. "So what say we spend a few hours figuring out how to set those poles, and then head to town and see what the marina has for runabouts? I'll even buy you lunch."

Honest to God, she looked like he'd just offered to buy her a bottle of rat poison. "Or," she said with far less enthusiasm, "*you* could go to town *now* and see what the marina's got for runabouts, and I'll figure out the poles by myself."

"But I want to help."

"But I don't need help."

"You obviously do, or you wouldn't have hired Paul."

"Yesterday in the salon you said something about Paul working with me; how did you know, anyway? Did Oren Hatch tell you?"

"No, Paul did. He came down to the docks looking to

see if your skiff was there so he could give you last week's bill. Which I paid," he added, walking around a wall of tape when she suddenly strode toward the tent. "So why is it okay for Paul to help you but not me?"

She grabbed her backpack off the folding camp table. "Because Paul isn't going to be living in the house, so he doesn't question every wall or window we're laying out."

"And you think I will?"

She pulled a wallet out of the backpack, then turned and simply arched a brow.

He held his hands up, palms forward, fighting a grin. "I promise not to ask a hundred— Wait," he said, looking around the maze of tape, then back at her. "If the second floor is dedicated to the children, then where's my office?"

"It's wherever you want it to be—so long as it's not in the house." She used the wallet to point north. "You've got a hundred acres to choose from, so pick a spot and make a few drawings for Stanley of what you want your office to look like."

"I can't draw."

"Then get a computer program that can."

"Why can't *we* pick a spot and *you* make some drawings for Stanley?"

"Because I'm rather busy making a full-scale model of your house right now. And just as soon as Stapleton is no longer a problem, I'm climbing in a motorhome *with my cat*," she said rather smugly, "and leaving to go look for Mr. Right."

Jesse wasn't rising to the bait, mostly because he wasn't exactly sure why she was baiting him. "It's a moot point, anyway. Because I'm sure if Stanley checks his notes from our meeting in February, he'll see that I mentioned one of the rooms *in the house* had to be sound-proofed for me to use as an office."

She tossed the wallet on the table and faced him fully, planting her hands on her hips. "I was at that meeting, and what I remember is hearing you mention that this home is supposed to be your *sanctuary*. And when I checked the dictionary to make sure I wasn't confused, I couldn't find *office* anywhere in the definition." Jesse knew he was sunk when her eyes suddenly lit up again and she pointed toward the footpath while moving her fingers to mimic walking. "Just think about smelling ocean air and pine pitch and rich humid dirt, and hearing waves crashing and birds singing and gravel crunching under your feet as you commute to work." Her smile suddenly outshone her eyes. "In your pajamas."

"I don't wear pajamas."

The smile faltered briefly, but she quickly recovered. "With your closest neighbor being three miles away, you can walk to work buck-naked if you want. At least until you start embarrassing your children."

"And when it's raining?"

"Then I guess you won't have to bother showering before you leave home."

Yup, inexplicably, unequivocally sunk. "So where is this office I'm going to enjoy commuting to supposed to be?" he asked as he looked around. He looked back at her and sighed. "And please tell me it won't cost as much as a cargo ship to build."

She pulled a roll of tape from her jacket pocket, then started tying the end of the tape to one of the grade stakes. "I'm afraid both of those concerns are your problem. Since Stanley obviously didn't know what big-time executives need for an office, I guess he left it up to you to decide what it looks like and where you want it built." She headed to another ground stake near the base of the cliff, unrolling the tape as she walked. "I only know that if I spent a good chunk of my day staring out my office window talking on the phone, I'd want a lovely view." She stopped walking. "So long as it's not on top of the high ridge."

"Why not up there?" Jesse asked, despite knowing he wasn't going to like the answer. "If I can't have that view from my house, I should at least get to enjoy it at work."

"Sure," she said as she started walking and unrolling again. "If you don't mind ruining a perfectly beautiful island. Or," she went on as she wrapped the tape around the stake and headed to another one, "if having that view for *work* is more important to you than having campfires and sleeping out under the stars up there on hot summer nights with your family."

Damn, she was good. "Wait. You sketched a clubhouse rising up out of the ground; why can't we hide my office the same way, and I'll only raise it when I'm working?"

She stopped in mid-step and turned to him. "How deep *are* your pockets? Or can you operate out of an office the size of a bathroom? Speaking of which, it's nearly impossible to set plumbing in solid granite." She arched a brow. "Or are you planning to whiz in the woods?"

Not really sure how he'd lost two arguments to her in

two days, Jesse folded his arms over his chest and looked around again. "So where should it go?"

"Wherever you want it to go," she said as she went back to walking and unrolling. "So long as it's not anywhere near the sheltered cove where I beached my skiff."

"Why not there?"

"Because you and Paul are going to spend this summer building a treehouse *there*."

"Excuse me?"

She used her teeth to break off the tape, shoved the roll back in her pocket, then tied the end of the tape to the final stake—the fact that she wasn't looking at him making Jesse suspicious. "Since I can't imagine you sitting at your campsite counting seagulls all summer, I thought you might enjoy designing your future children a treehouse—you know, like the one on Treasure Island?— and hiring Paul to help you build it." She darted a glance in his direction when he said nothing, then shrugged again. "Or you could start laying out some island paths."

"Am I supposed to build this treehouse," he said dryly, finally realizing what she was up to, "before or after I pick a site for the office that I'm *also* supposed to design?"

She wanted to get rid of him. The only part he wasn't sure about was if he was bugging her sexually or messing up her creativity.

She turned and planted her hands on her hips again. "I'm certain the first thing they teach competition-crushing executives is how to prioritize. But I suggest you start with the treehouse before you attempt to design an office."

Figuring there was only one way to find out, Jesse

walked straight up to her and touched a finger to her cheek. "Any suggestions on where I should start," he said quietly, "since I could write what I know about treehouses on the face of a dime?"

He found himself touching empty air when she shot over to a pile of grade stakes. "You . . . ah, start with the tree," she said—sounding like she'd swallowed a frog—as she scooped up several stakes and then hugged them against her chest like a shield.

Oh yeah, definitely sexually flustered. Which might be a problem, he realized, if it interfered with her creativity. Hell, if he didn't leave her alone with her tape and stakes and three-dimensional imagination, he could find himself living in an unpretentious *hovel*.

"Are you saying you and your brothers never built a treehouse?" she asked from behind the safety of her stakes. "What did you do as kids if you didn't run all over Rosebriar's twelve hundred acres playing war and building clubhouses to hide in to read your *Playboy* magazines?"

"We . . . After our parents died in our early teens, we mostly studied and followed Bram to the office to learn the business."

"And before you were teens?" she whispered.

He shook his head with a grin. "We used Rosebriar as one big giant clubhouse and tried out our pranks on the poor staff before springing them on Bram."

"You played *inside*?"

"Not always. Sometimes we went sailing, and for five summers after our parents died, Bram and Grammy Rose took us to a falling-down cabin on a lake up in the Adirondacks." Where, come to think of it, they had tried to build a treehouse—until a branch had broken and Bram had gotten a concussion, scaring them so badly they'd never gone near that tree again.

"Was it always just you and your brothers?" she asked. "Didn't you ever have friends over? Or join clubs at school or participate in sports?"

"Not after we went to live at Rosebriar. Hey," he said at her stricken look, "we had wonderful childhoods."

"You played with staff. And you studied and worked all through your teens. My God, you were more smothered than I was."

"We were as happy as three kids who'd lost their parents could be. No, dammit, we were *happier*."

"And are you still happier now?" she asked softly.

"What in hell kind of question is that?"

She smiled sadly, a picture of calm to his growing anger. "Do you ever travel other than for business, Jesse? Or have any hobbies? Do you hunt? Fish? Skydive?" She shifted the stakes to free one hand and gestured at the woods behind him. "Or do you go around buying islands on which to build safe, insulated cocoons for your future children?"

"No," he snapped, "I buy them so women—and their cats—can hide out from loan sharks who have the hots for them." He turned and walked away before he said or did something he'd regret, swiping his jacket off the tree on his way by, even as he found himself wondering how he'd lost *another* argument to her.

He was just scaling the ass-bruising ledge again when it finally dawned on him what was going on, and Jesse stopped and scrubbed his face with a groan. Every time he tried to talk Cadi into seeing something his way, she somehow managed to turn the discussion back on *him*.

Further proving she really did know him better than he knew himself.

It was as if she saw him as two distinctly different men: Jesse the family man and Jesse the big-time, competition-crushing executive. And whenever she found herself butting heads with the *executive*, she simply started asking the man she'd designed the house for a bunch of questions he either couldn't or didn't care to answer. Would *he* willingly place himself on an island with a virtual stranger without any means of escape? Would *he* put an office in a home he was building for the sole purpose of instilling wonderful memories in his children? And would *he* like someone butting into a project he was working on, or, if he couldn't come right out and tell the jerk to get lost, would he simply find something else for him to do?

Hell, forget giving Cadi his seat on the board of directors; if he let her anywhere near Tidewater, Sam and Ben would give her *his job*.

Cadi watched Jesse disappear up the path leading to his campsite, not sure what had just happened. All she'd wanted was to prevent him from redesigning her—okay, his—house, but she was afraid doing so may have just cost her a friendship she'd been coming to cherish.

Good Lord, she might not have ventured far from home growing up, but at least she'd had friends. So how was it possible that a highly educated, financially privileged, well-traveled man didn't realize there was more to life than work? Was he truly expecting to bring his family here every summer, only to stand in the window of his soundproof office talking on the phone while catching glimpses of his equally friendless passel of kids running wild on the safe little cocoon he'd built them? When Jesse had asked Stanley to design a house that would instill wonderful childhood memories in his children, at the time Cadi had thought he'd been looking to relive his own childhood, whereas now she wondered if he wasn't trying to rewrite it instead.

Only the guy didn't seem to know how to go about it; not if he didn't understand he actually had to *participate*.

SIXTEEN

❧

Cadi didn't hear from Jesse for a full forty-eight hours after he'd stormed off in a huff, and then it had been a text—he'd gotten the antenna up as promised, apparently—asking if she'd please come to his campsite at her earliest convenience for a quick lesson on driving her fast, safe, sexy new runabout. So right around this time yesterday morning she'd abandoned the second story layout she'd been wrestling with and bolted for the north end of the island, not even glancing back when she'd heard poles falling like dominoes behind her. Because really, that old skiff she'd bought scared the bejeezus out of her far more than it did Jesse. In fact, she'd nearly kissed him that evening on the high ridge when he'd pointed out that buying her a better boat would allow him to save face with the townspeople, his added argument that he'd been planning to buy one anyway allowing her to accept without actually conceding.

Cadi remembered reaching his campsite yesterday and standing on the rise above the beach trying to catch her breath and pressing a hand to the stitch in her side, utterly amazed at what one very determined man with very deep pockets could accomplish in forty-eight hours. She also remembered snorting, wondering what had made her think she'd needed to come up with a project to keep Jesse busy enough to stay out of *her* business.

Good God, there had been a huge barge anchored just off the point of land at one end of the beach driving pylons for what she'd realized would be a permanent deep-water dock, a crew of four men anchoring a series of floating docks—stretching no less than fifty feet into the water to accommodate the rise and fall of the tide—next to the gravel landing ramp at the other end of the beach, and two men installing solar panels next to an antenna just above where *another* crew was building the abutment for the deep-water dock. And if that hadn't been enough to make her head spin, she'd noticed a transport barge chugging toward Hundred Acre from the mainland, which she'd later learned was carrying a shiny new ATV, enough lumber to build a treehouse big enough to hide a dozen *Playboy* bunnies, and Eva Dean and her daughter, Samantha.

All of which was why it had taken Cadi a good ten minutes to spot Jesse standing in *her* shiny new runabout, along with a man holding what appeared to be a half-rolled-up set of plans they were looking at while drifting near the pylon-driving barge. It wasn't until the man had

gotten on the barge and Jesse had idled up to his new
floating dock that he'd spotted her sitting on a rock on top
of the rise, her chin resting in her hands, still watching
in amazement.

He'd waved her down, placed her at the wheel of the
center console the moment she'd boarded, then stood behind her with his hands on her shoulders—which she was
too excited to notice felt wonderfully warm and strong
and steady. After explaining all the fancy electronics he
apparently thought were needed to cross three miles of
water, Jesse had walked to the back of the boat and sat
down—Cadi still too excited to notice how bummed she
felt now that his hands were gone—and told her to give
it a test run over to the mainland and back.

Good Lord, it hadn't taken one tenth the time it did in
her skiff, and they were back on the island tying up to
the floating dock just as Jeff Acton was nosing his barge
onto the gravel landing beside them. Having spotted Eva
Dean and her daughter standing at the rail smiling at
them, Jesse had given Cadi a very long, very husbandly
kiss—that she certainly hadn't been too excited to savor.
He'd then jumped out of the runabout and walked up the
dock and over to the landing to graciously help the women
down the barge's metal ramp. After saying hello and apparently meeting Samantha for the first time while Jeff
drove the ATV down the ramp and parked it on the beach,
Jesse had then gotten on the barge and Jeff had backed
away without off-loading the lumber, then turned and
headed toward the southwestern end of the island.

Left to deal with their guests, Cadi had sat the women
in lawn chairs she'd dragged over to the rise overlooking

the beach. She'd then run inside the camper she was supposed to be living in and, after a bit of frantic searching, had come back out carrying three plastic tumblers of Tang and a package of Double Stuf Oreo cookies. With her guests politely munching and sipping the odd offering, the three of them had chatted about fashion and families and first years of marriage while watching all the various crews working.

It wasn't until the empty barge reappeared nearly two hours later and they headed down to meet it that the women had gotten around to apologizing for popping in unannounced, blaming their rudeness on wanting to say thank you in person for the mushrooms Eva had received that morning. Jesse had helped them climb the ladder onto the barge from the floating dock, and as they'd started back across the reach Eva had shouted that since they had cell phone reception now, she'd make sure to call before she came out again. And Cadi wasn't certain, but she thought the woman also shouted something about stopping by the bakery first.

Taking advantage of the fact that one of the workers needed to talk to Jesse, Cadi had escaped to her campsite to take a nap, exhausted from two hours of smiling and nodding and trying to remember all of her and Jesse's lies.

It was now ten o'clock the next morning, and twenty minutes ago she'd received a text from Jesse asking if she would like to join him for a campfire up on the high ridge this evening. A second text had followed shortly, offering to bring her home on the ATV so she wouldn't have to make that treacherous hike back in the dark. So here she was sitting on top of the lower bluff facing nearly a dozen cockeyed poles pretending to be second-story walls, trying to decide if she should go. The problem was that her heart and brain couldn't agree with each other.

Yes, go, her heart had been whispering for the last nineteen minutes, apparently having needed all of one minute to decide.

No, no, absolutely no, her brain had started shouting even before the second text.

Give me one good reason why not, Heart had just now asked Brain.

Because even a country bumpkin would know what that invitation is really about, and if we have sex with him, you're going to start wondering if he can't be our Mr. Right, Brain said. *And then where will we be if you're broken when we meet our for-real Mr. Right? Heck, we might as well stay in Whistler's Landing and get a dozen more cats.*

I agree with Heart, a voice Cadi had never heard before piped in. *I say we go.*

"Hey, who are you?" Cadi asked out loud, only to glance around and then close her eyes on a groan. Really, she'd been talking to Wiggles way too much.

I'm your lady parts, the newcomer drawled. *And I hope you know I have a stake in this decision, too. I mean, really, it's been six freaking years. Or don't any of you care that I'm turning into a dried-up old prune down here?*

I care, Heart whispered. *That's why I'm saying yes. We all need the practice for when we meet our real Mr. Right.*

And I can't think of anyone I'd rather practice on, Lady Parts purred.

Yeah, Heart sighed in agreement. *And if we go into this knowing it's not going to lead anywhere, we'll all walk away happy.*

Brain snorted. *You fell half in love with the man while I was designing his home, and living on his island these last three weeks sure as hell hasn't helped. So what do you think will happen if we actually have sex with him? And you, Lady Parts; what happens if you can't even remember how, and you make a complete fool of us? You get to go dormant again and Heart gets to go hide in a corner, which leaves me to deal with the embarrassment.*

I don't care, Lady Parts growled. *I say we vote. I vote we go!*

I vote we go, too! Heart shouted as it started racing.

Brain said nothing.

Cadi looked down at her phone and reread the text message that had awakened her at six this morning: Problem solved. You can go home now, Cads. I'll return next week.

Except she had an even bigger problem now, because she didn't want to go home.

Cadi reopened Jesse's text message. She took a deep breath and typed, I'll meet you on the high ridge at seven o'clock, and quickly hit send.

Now you've done it, Brain muttered. *Just don't any of you come crying to me when Mr. Wrong stops by to say hello next summer with his beautiful, sophisticated, pregnant wife and finds us still in our pajamas hunched over one of Pinky and Kerr's bold, modern models.*

* * *

Jesse thought about tossing another stick on the fire, but
decided he'd better ration the firewood he'd lugged up on
the ATV right after Cadi had texted him back this morning, as he'd hate to have to call it an early night just because he ran out of wood. He smoothed his hand over the
other half of the triple-folded blanket he was sitting on,
making sure a sneaky pebble hadn't crawled under it since
the last time he'd checked. Satisfied Cadi wouldn't get a
bruised behind, he opened the cooler to make sure the
fire wasn't melting the ice under the *one* bottle of bubbly
red Moscato, which he hoped was supposed to be served
chilled, and decided the ice would probably last longer
than the wine did once he popped the cork. He closed the
cover and ran his fingers through his newly cut hair, then
checked his watch and saw that Cadi was running a little
late for their third date.

Not that *she* was counting, Jesse thought with a grin
as he scanned the cozy scene he'd created, since she didn't
really know about their first two. But he was pretty sure
he'd read somewhere that if a guy managed to make it to
date three, it was perfectly acceptable to see if the woman
might be interested in more than just kissing.

He snorted, remembering all the women who hadn't
waited until the end of date *one* to let him know they were
interested. Hell, his town car hadn't made it past Aubrey
Henderson's gate before Pamela had crawled onto his lap
and stuck her tongue down his throat. Oh yeah, he'd bet
a year's salary she'd subscribed to all those wedding
magazines the very next morning.

Jesse suddenly stilled when he spotted Cadi standing at the edge of the woods below, and then scrambled to his feet, wondering how long she'd been watching him. Obviously realizing he'd spotted her, he saw her take a deep breath and start walking up the barren ledge with all the enthusiasm of someone going to a hanging. He sighed and started down to meet her, also wondering if he shouldn't have brought *two* bottles of wine.

Then again, maybe he could interest her in a glass of Aberfeldy.

"Did you take a tumble on that mossy ledge?" he asked when he saw the mud on her knee. He held out his hand to help her up the steep slope, only to find himself holding an ungodly heavy backpack that also had mud on it.

"I tried taking a shortcut," she said, continuing up the ledge unaided. "Turns out that little ravine the trail crosses becomes a big ravine toward the center of the island." She stopped and held her hands over the fire for a few seconds, then sat down on the triple-folded blanket and began brushing the mud off her knee. She stopped brushing and shot him a smile when he sat down beside her. "I'm sorry I'm late." She gestured at the backpack he'd set on the ground beside him. "But maybe you'll forgive my rudeness when you see what I brought you."

"Is there a scraped or bruised knee under that mud that I should take a look at?" he asked as he lifted the heavy pack onto his lap—remembering too late the bottom of it was also covered in dry mud. "Did you hurt yourself when you fell, Cadi?"

"I didn't fall. The mud splashed on me when I dropped the backpack just as I started climbing out of the ravine."

This time her smile was derisive as she nodded at the pack again. "One of the plastic flutes cracked, but the wine survived."

Jesse slid open the zipper, barely stifling a snort when he reached inside and pulled out a bottle of wine and laid it on the blanket between them, then reached inside again and pulled out a *second* bottle. Hell, he was going to have to see about buying this stuff by the case.

"Keep going," she said after he pulled out the two plastic wineglasses. He set them beside the bottles and reached inside the pack again. "I still have one more to give you," she added when his hand emerged holding five books. "I had to order it, but it's in now and I'll pick it up the next time I go to town."

He tossed the empty pack on the ground beside him, then held the stack of books so he could read their spines and saw they were all New England field guides: one on birds, one on seashore creatures, another on the night sky, one on wildflowers, and a general guide on forests and wetlands.

"I . . . ah, thought they might come in handy when you explore Hundred Acre with your kids," she said rather huskily when he said nothing. He sensed more than saw her shrug. "Or for your guests to learn about the island's environment."

"Thank you," he said, his own voice sounding a bit thick to him.

She shrugged again when he looked over at her. "They're just books."

"If you had to order one and it's in," he said, setting them on his lap and picking up the bird guide and leafing through it, "then you must have purchased these before I showed up."

"Um, yeah. My plan was to leave them in the camper for you to find when you got back *a week from now.*"

He stopped leafing and looked at her.

She picked up one of the bottles of wine and started peeling the foil off the neck. "If you don't mind, I'd like to use the runabout to go into town tomorrow morning."

"You're going to have to," he said with a chuckle, "since your old skiff is halfway to becoming a pirate ship that's laying siege to a treehouse." He set the books on the ledge, then took the bottle away from her when she kept twisting the cork wire in the wrong direction. "And you don't have to ask my permission. The boat's yours to use whenever you want. Tell me," he added as he took off the wire and started wiggling the cork, "if my assistant told you I'd be gone three weeks when you called *three weeks ago* trying to find out when I would be returning to Maine, how come you weren't expecting me to show up for another week?"

"I assumed you'd have a huge pile of work on your desk that you'd have to deal with first," she said, lifting the cracked wineglass to examine it. "I was going to call again right around now and see how close you were to coming back."

"And had you given any thought as to how I was supposed to explain my wife's sudden disappearance to the good folks of Castle Cove?"

She lowered the glass to her lap, her cheeks turning as red as the wine bottle. "I thought I'd leave that part up to you." She shot him a sheepish smile. "Since I remembered how quickly you came up with a fake aunt I had to go tend, and how you hadn't wanted me running off with the pool boy, I figured whatever lie you came up with would probably be better than mine."

"There are a couple of glasses in the cooler beside you," he said just as the cork popped free and shot toward the trees. "So while I was supposed to be telling everyone my wife . . . Oh, let's go with her getting hit by a bus while crossing Fifth Avenue as she rushed to a rustic boot sale," he said before she could answer. "So while I would be here fending off condolences, you would be climbing in your motorhome and driving away?" he asked—even as he wondered if this conversation wasn't counterintuitive to starting a *real* relationship with her. But dammit, he wanted to know what had been going through that creative mind of hers when she'd made the decision to hide here by pretending to be his wife. Was it because she truly did feel she knew him well enough to borrow his name, or did she see him as just another rich client who was more than capable of dealing with the consequences?

She froze in the act of opening the cooler and slowly turned to him, then dropped her hands to her lap and stared down at them. "I'm sorry," she whispered. "My only defense is that when I found myself sitting in an Ellsworth parking lot with my car full of camping equipment and Wiggles staring up at me from her cage, I panicked." She looked at him with eyes that appeared slightly panicked right now. "I didn't know where to go or what to do. And right then I realized that for the very first time in my life, I was completely alone. Until . . . until I . . ."

Jesse carefully set the wine down on the other side of the books, then reached over and gently pulled her onto his lap and pressed her head to his chest. "Until you what?"

"Until I remembered the night I hid in your camper and how you made me feel like everything was going to be okay." She tilted her head back to look up at him, and Jesse was relieved to see the hint of a smile. "I imagine you weren't very happy to find yourself dealing with a drunken woman who'd just been jilted, but I think you should know you probably saved my life that night." Her smile blossomed when he arched a brow. "I'm not exaggerating. You gave me the courage to stop *dreaming* about leaving and *just leave*, which saved me from dying of sheer boredom before my fortieth birthday. And you know how?"

"How?"

"That night and the next morning when you treated me like a grown, intelligent woman, I finally started feeling like one." She dropped her gaze and actually snuggled into him. "And then I remembered how safe and peaceful I'd felt the three times I'd visited Hundred Acre, and I thought . . . Well, I started my car and headed back down the coast, confident that if I could just get to your island I wouldn't be alone anymore. But when I reached Castle Cove and found out you weren't here, I panicked again."

She glanced up, not a hint of a smile in sight. "Ken Dean found me sitting in his parking lot, slumped over the steering wheel of my car, bawling like a baby. It wasn't until he called me Mrs. Sinclair that I realized even though you weren't here, the island was still a perfect hiding place for me and Wiggles." She dropped her gaze again. "I'm sorry," she repeated.

"I'm not," Jesse said as he tightened his embrace on a heavy sigh. "In fact, I'm glad your first instinct was to come to me."

She looked up, her eyes skeptical. "I've wondered since you walked in that salon why you're not freaked out about the mess I've made of your life."

"Oh, Mrs. Sinclair," he drawled, leaning forward while draping her over his arm and lowering his mouth to within inches of hers. "Are you not aware your husband makes his living cleaning up messes?" he finished in a whisper, his lips not quite brushing hers.

And that's where he stayed—hell, he even stopped breathing—as her eyes searched his while she appeared to have a conversation with herself, which apparently ended when she muttered something about being outvoted and her hand slipped around his neck and she lifted her head.

It took Jesse two full heartbeats to realize *she* was kissing *him*, another heartbeat to confirm he wasn't dreaming, and one more to decide he was skipping dates three through five and moving directly to six.

Date six was when they got to spend their first night together, wasn't it?

Only this time in bed *together*.

Damn. He was so busy planning his next move he hadn't realized she'd broken the kiss. And he definitely hadn't heard what she'd said. "Excuse me?" he asked when she hid her face in his neck, her cheeks feeling unusually hot against his skin. "I'm afraid I missed that"—although he was pretty sure he'd heard the words *make* and *love* in there somewhere.

Sweet God, was attention deficit disorder contagious? Because he'd never had a problem staying focused before, and sure as hell not when he had a beautiful woman in his arms.

"I . . . I said I want to make love to you," she whispered into his shoulder.

Here? On top of a cold granite ledge? Or can you wait until we get down to the camper and my comfortable, warm bed?

Jesse realized he'd said part—if not all—of that out loud when Cadi suddenly stiffened one second before he nearly rolled into the fire when she just as suddenly shoved him away.

Would someone *please* tell him when he'd forgotten how to seduce a woman?

Oh, right. In college, when Bram had made sure any coed majoring in husband-hunting knew his handsome, wealthy grandson was available, and Jesse had started focusing on running from women instead of chasing them.

"What the—hey!" He scrambled to his feet when he realized the one woman he *did* want was walking away. "Look, I'm sorry," he said, chasing after her and catching hold of her sleeve. "I didn't mean that the way it came out."

She stood facing the woods. "No, I'm sorry," she rasped, sounding like she'd swallowed an entire pond of frogs. "I knew coming here tonight was a mistake."

"Then why did you?" he asked, letting go of her sleeve.

"Because I thought . . . because . . ." He saw her pull in a deep breath, and Jesse actually took a step back when she turned to face him, even as he fought a grin. "Because my *tiny otter brain* finally came up with a reason my heart and la—that my heart couldn't dispute."

"Which was?" he said carefully, still unsure whether she wanted to smack him or kiss him again. And what was she talking about, that her brain had come up with a reason? No, her *tiny otter brain*. He couldn't believe he'd called her an otter out loud—which probably made him about as bright as a gecko.

"It reminded my—me, that for as much as I might need the practice, I'd already learned my lesson about recreational sex back in college."

"Recreational sex?" Jesse repeated, getting a little angry himself. "As opposed to what—procreational sex?"

"No, as opposed to the intimacy two people share when their relationship is heading somewhere."

"Like to the altar?"

"Yes," she snapped. He saw her take another deep breath. "And since you obviously don't need the practice," she said calmly, "I think I'm better off focusing on getting my *mind* ready for when Mr. Right comes along and leave the sex part for when I finally meet him."

"And how do you know *I'm* not Mr. Right if you won't even give us a try?"

Her chin lifted. "Contrary to popular consensus, I'm not so naive as to believe you'd marry someone like me, so what would be the point for our sleeping together?"

Pretty sure they'd had this conversation already—and not particularly liking it this time, either—Jesse folded his arms over his chest to keep from grabbing her. "What makes you think," he quietly asked, "I would never marry someone like you? Like you *how*?"

"Old-fashioned," she snapped, spinning around and marching down the ledge again as she continued listing her shortcomings. "Unsophisticated. Untraveled. Unworldly." She stopped and spun back to face him, her cheeks now blistering red. "You'll find the *future* Mrs. Sinclair's runabout tied in your harbor slip one hour after sunrise tomorrow morning."

"You forgot unethical," he said as she started to turn away, making her face him again.

"What are you talking about? I'm a highly principled person."

"So if you see your fake engagement to Stanley and pretend marriage to me as harmless, is it safe to assume you don't see anything wrong with clients paying over six figures for homes they thought were being designed by a licensed architect?" He walked toward her. "You started designing houses for your father when you were *fifteen*, and for the last five years you've also been designing them for Stanley. Including *mine*."

"Wh-who told you that?"

She'd turned so suddenly pale, Jesse was a bit worried she might actually faint. But he stopped three paces away, because . . . hell, because he still wanted to grab her. And because even if he had to take an ax to that brand-new runabout, he wasn't letting her leave this island until she got over the notion she wasn't good enough for him.

This was one argument he refused to lose, dammit, because he refused to lose *her*.

"A man has a lot of time to think while flying to four continents in eighteen days, and I believe I was somewhere over the Mediterranean when it finally dawned on me that Stanley hadn't designed the house I saw in that model."

"You can't know that," she whispered. "You're guessing."

"I make my living following my hunches. Like when I realized a thirty-year-old bachelor who's into orgies wouldn't stay five days, much less five years, in Whistler's Landing unless he was hiding from something or someone. And then there's the fact that a man who *is* hiding would never design a house made almost entirely of glass." Jesse dropped his arms to his sides and closed the distance between them, careful not to show his relief when she stood her ground. "And only a woman," he said softly, gently clasping her chin to lift her gaze to his, "would worry about creating a child-friendly outdoor patio nearly as big as the house itself, or bother with little details like a huge fire pit and a sunken wading pool shaped like an open clamshell disguised as a fountain, or think to put a real working periscope rising out of the roof."

"You . . . you saw all that on the small model in only a short time? Even the periscope?"

"The first thing we competition-crushing executives learn," he said with a slight nod, "is to pay more attention to the small details than the large ones."

She pulled her chin free but didn't step back—or drop her gaze from his. "How do you know I didn't just add those details when I built the model from Stanley's plan?"

He shook his head. "The entire house was designed

around the children—beginning with its location." He grinned when her eyes flared briefly in surprise. "You didn't want a passel of kids sitting up on that high ridge exposed to everyone and everything; you wanted them to feel the island wrapping around them like a security blanket, giving them a safe place to land after spending the day exploring their hundred-acre playground." He chuckled. "Hell, I just realized that catwalk is both a physical and metaphorical means of escape." He lifted his arms away from his sides. "You didn't make a mistake coming here tonight, just like following your instinct to come here three weeks ago wasn't a mistake. Come to me again, Cadi. Let me be your security and your bridge to the world."

One heartbeat. Two. Three.

Well, hell; it would have been nice if his brothers had dropped him a clue about how hard it was to actually *catch* the woman of your dreams.

Four. Five. Damn, his chest was starting to hurt.

Six. Jesse caught Cadi with a groan of relief that came out as a whoosh when she threw herself against him, then swept her off her feet before her brain could start talking again and carried her back up the ridge to the fire. He sat down on the blanket without letting her go, then cupped her face and tilted her head to look at him. "Starting now, let's agree to ignore anything weird the other one says. Deal?"

"Deal," she said hoarsely, lifting her hand to his jaw. "And we'll also agree to ignore anything . . . awkward either of us does, okay?" she whispered, looking a bit worried.

Figuring that *awkward* fell in the *weird* category, since he didn't have a clue what she was talking about, Jesse nodded. "Definitely a deal."

Worry faded, but skepticism walked in. "So if some . . . ah, some of our parts seem a bit rusty, we'll just pretend not to notice?"

Did the woman have *any* idea in how many directions he could run with that question—not one of them suitable even for his ears? He touched his forehead to hers with a heavy sigh. "Oh, thank God. I was a little worried you'd start laughing when I started creaking from an old high school football injury," he said, only to remember too late he'd already admitted to never playing football.

Yup, he knew he was sunk when he saw that I-know-a-secret smile; the one responsible for lighting those big baby blues with a nearly blinding sparkle.

The same one that had haunted his dreams since February.

"Oh, poor Pooh. Show me where it is and I'll kiss it."

Fully focused now and intending to stay that way, Jesse shifted so that they were lying side by side, then slowly started unzipping her jacket. "Well, I'll show you my rusty parts if you show me yours," he whispered. "And I'll see what I can do about getting them lubed," he couldn't stop himself from adding—which caused Cadi's hand to still in the act of unzipping his jacket. "Ignoring weird, remember?" he said, rolling forward and kissing her slackened mouth before she could respond.

Although Jesse couldn't seem to ignore Cadi's admission that her brain had already convinced her heart once this evening that this wasn't a good idea, or that she'd murmured something about . . . something being outvoted. That meant there had to be a third player with an opinion and a tie-breaking vote. Trailing his lips down over her jaw to her neck—earning him a nice little mewling sound—Jesse decided to keep *every* part of her too busy to talk to one another.

So while exploring each tender spot on her neck and cheek and the little indent beneath her ear—getting short, shallow pants mixed in with the mewling—he went back to parting Cadi from her clothes. And damn if she didn't start helping him shed his own in the process. Which meant he either wasn't keeping her well enough occupied or he kept getting so distracted by each beautiful, baby-soft piece of skin he exposed that he then had to stop and explore.

It wasn't until he felt the distinctly damp chill of deep water fog on his bare ass that he realized they were both completely naked—on an exposed ridge on an island three miles out in the ocean—and that the sun had set and his campfire was down to embers. He stopped exploring the tender, tasty trail that had been leading down to Cadi's breasts, and rolled to his side and propped his head on his hand while keeping his other hand rubbing her baby-soft hip.

Except he had to stop rubbing in order to capture her hand headed for his midsection, then—while still holding it prisoner—reach over and nudge her chin to lift her *gaze* from his midsection to his face. "I realize I may be a little late in asking, but would you like to go to the camper? To a nice warm bed?"

"Are you kidding?" she said, her eyes filled with . . . yup, that was definitely fully-engaged, no-turning-back lust making them sparkle like stars as she wiggled her hand free and waved it in an arc over them. "This is the very reason you have to keep this ridge just the way it is. Why do you think the glacier scraped it smooth eons ago, if not for lovers to enjoy?"

Five minutes; he'd give a year's salary for just five minutes of seeing the world through those gorgeous, creative eyes. "Okay," he said with a chuckle, reaching for the packet he'd had the wherewithal to slip out of his pocket when he'd shed his pants. "But I'm stashing an air mattress and sleeping bag up here somewhere for next—"

"Stop talking, Pooh," she growled at the same time she pounced. "I've got six years' worth of rust that needs lubing."

And as his deep-belly laugh ended on a whoosh when she landed, Jesse was *completely* sure Maine had just ponied up another Sinclair bride.

SEVENTEEN

Cadi woke up to the realization she was scratching her thigh, and moved her left big toe to scratch the itchy inside of her right anklebone as she opened her eyes to find herself in Jesse's camper, in his big, warm, comfortable bed, covered by no fewer than three puffy blankets. Also realizing she was in bed alone, Cadi broke into a huge, proud-of-herself smile. She'd done it! She'd actually lived her salacious dream of making love to Jesse on top of the high ridge.

Why, she even had the mosquito bites to *prove* she'd done it! Twice!

Well, okay; the second time had been here in the camper, after Jesse had slid into his boxers and gathered up all their clothes—swatting mosquitoes and cursing like a sailor the entire time—then shoved the clothes at her—while she'd been swatting and laughing—and wrapped her up in the blanket, tossed her onto the ATV, and zoomed down the path while swatting his bare arms and chest and occasionally his face and definitely still cursing.

In fact, Cadi had learned some new words.

But then she felt her huge, proud-of-herself smile falter. So now what? Were they dating?

Did *Jesse* think they were dating?

Or worse, would Jesse think *she* would think they were dating?

Cadi felt her smile disappear completely. The guy had said he was interested in her romantically. So did that mean as in happily ever after, or was that just the modern, sophisticated term for wanting to have sex with someone?

Well, of course it is.

Oh, you're awake, Lady Parts! Heart gave a little giggle. *I would have thought you'd be sleeping in this morning? How are you feeling? You sound . . . different.*

Sounds pretty darn bossy to me, Brain grumbled.

Well, one of us had to take charge last night, Lady Parts said dryly. *Or we'd be waking up alone in that cold tent again.*

Oh, yes, this is much better, Heart said on a sigh. *This bed is so cozy and warm and doesn't keep deflating on us. I hope we can stay here again tonight.*

Brain snorted. *Like that's going to happen. Or are you forgetting all those pictures of all those women on the Internet? Now that Romeo got the goods, he'll be heading back to New York to look for his next conquest,* Brain went on with great authority. *Don't any of you know it's the chase men relish? And this guy's, what . . . thirty-four? It's obvious he doesn't have a clue what to do with a woman once he's caught her, or he'd have two passels of kids by now.*

Stop trying to scare Heart, Lady Parts growled. *You're no longer the queen bee here. We're through being shoved aside so YOU can go around pleasing everyone. Well, Miss High and Mighty, here's a newsflash for you—the real Cadi Glace has finally emerged from her cocoon!*

Heart started thumping loudly. *I'm with you, Lady Parts! We have wings! We're never pleasing anyone but ourselves ever again!*

Hey. Hey. Calm down, Heart, Lady Parts soothed. *Let's not go overboard here. There's a fine line between being self-assured and being selfish.*

And you crossed that line last night, Brain countered, *when you selfishly threw both Heart and me under the bus just for one night of sex.*

Great sex, Lady Parts purred, apparently undaunted. *Wasn't it, Heart?*

Heart giggled again. *I certainly got a workout. I mean, geesh, I haven't pounded that hard and that long in for-ever. You remember that one time, when he was doing that . . . thing to you? I thought I was going to have an attack.*

Come on, Brain, admit it, Lady Parts cajoled. *You had fun, too. If I remember correctly, I heard you screaming right along with the rest of us when we had the best damn orgasm EVER.*

Twice, Heart added. *We screamed twice. So, are we going to get to do it again tonight?*

Why wait until dark? Lady Parts asked. *I know I wouldn't mind getting a look at that buff male body in the daylight.*

"Enough!" Cadi said with a laugh, throwing back the three blankets. "This island is going to be crawling with workmen all day." She grabbed the top blanket, wrapped it around herself, and tiptoed down the hall. She stopped at the top of the steps and looked down the length of the camper to see it was empty, then continued to the living area and looked out the large window. Too late. The men were already here. She could see the runabout tied up to the pylon-driving barge and Jesse standing beside the man she now knew was Eva Dean's son, Jason, as they watched a pylon being hoisted upright in preparation of being driven into the seabed.

Workmen carrying coolers suddenly emerged from the road leading up from the beach, and Cadi stepped back from the window when she realized they had to pass right behind the camper to reach the point of land where they were building the anchoring abutment. She turned and looked around for her clothes, finally spotting them sitting semi-folded on the island counter with her muddy mud boots sitting on the floor beneath them. So just how was she supposed to sneak out of the camper without being seen?

And why would Mrs. Sinclair need to sneak out of her own camper? Lady Parts asked.

"Oh, that's right," Cadi said, scoffing up the clothes

and heading back up the stairs. "Thank you for reminding me, LP."

There was a deep sigh. *You sure you wouldn't prefer to go with SB, for Smarter Brain? I not only made last night happen, but I got us through it without embarrassing ourselves.*

You jumped the man's bones, Brain scoffed. *The first time almost before he got the condom on.*

Yes I did, LP-SB said smugly. *Just like those sexy, confident heroines in the steamy romances you're always scolding our Cadi for reading.*

Heck, if it hadn't been for the three she read before Jesse got here, Heart piped in, *SB might have forgotten what to do.*

But it was my idea she drive farther up the coast looking for a town with a bookstore, Brain apparently felt compelled to point out. *Can you imagine what the Castle Cove gossip mill would have had to say about Mrs. Sinclair buying romance novels?*

"Okay, okay, quiet down, gals," Cadi said with a laugh, dropping her clothes on the bed, then tossing off the blanket. She started sorting through the clothes looking for her panties. "Those books were entertaining, inspirational, and educational. Where are my panties?" she grumbled, lifting her jacket and shaking it.

Probably halfway to Nova Scotia by now, LP purred.

Or already lining some seagull's nest, Brain added in a snicker, *because Mr. Macho Man left them on the ridge.*

It was dark and the mosquitoes were descending in

droves, Heart said, defending him. *And he sacrificed his very own blood by wrapping us up in the blanket.*

Our hero, LP said on a sigh. *I say we reward him by having sex again tonight.*

Cadi finished pulling on her jeans—minus panties—but didn't bother fastening them, then stared down at the warm, comfortable bed. "I agree," she whispered almost in unison with Heart. "Okay, time to get this show on the road," she added, slipping her fleece on over her head. She picked up her bra and shoved it in her jacket pocket, and, not seeing any sign of her socks, headed to the bathroom.

Honest to God, she actually moaned when her bottom touched the warm, perfectly shaped toilet seat. Pulling her jeans up again and this time fastening them, Cadi actually felt tears welling in her eyes as she longingly stared at the shower stall. She muttered one of the new curse words she'd learned, grabbed her jacket off the vanity, and headed for the kitchen.

She eventually found a pen and a pad of paper with a grocery list already started in one of the drawers, added Double Stuf Oreo cookies to it, then tore off a bottom page and wrote Jesse a note. She wasn't sneaking off before he got back, she told him, but was going to feed Wiggles; adding she'd see him later this morning when she returned to borrow the runabout. She drew a smiley face at the bottom instead of signing it, reread the note as she walked to the bedroom, then set it on the pillow.

"There, that sounded like a confident, contemporary woman. So confident, in fact, I'm not making the bed," Cadi told anyone who was listening as she headed into the hall—only to stop and look inside the fully appointed, surprisingly roomy bathroom again.

She heard a snort. *You're not making that bed because you figure all those women on the Internet wouldn't,* Brain said.

Uh . . . maybe you should go back and make it, Heart said softly. *You know, just so he won't think we're a slob or anything. I bet it would really please him.*

"Enough! Not one more word from any of you again today," Cadi said, turning away from the beautiful bathroom. Good Lord, why had she bought a handbook on backcountry camping—which showed how to dig several different outdoor latrines—instead of a little chemical toilet? And that stupid black plastic bag with the hose coming out of the bottom; it would have been nice if the box had mentioned it was only a solar shower on days the sun wasn't hiding behind a freaking fog bank thick enough to cut with a knife.

Oh yeah, she was buying the most luxurious motorhome she could afford.

Jesse lowered the binoculars once Cadi was safely inside the lee of the island, then bolted down the short trail leading from the antenna to the camper to change his shirt *again*—having already soaked one through watching her head to the mainland four hours ago. He might as well permanently mount a scope on the deep-water dock, he decided, since buying a safer boat apparently wasn't enough to stop him sweating bullets every time

Little Miss Independent felt like going to town. Hell, if he got chills just thinking about the times she'd crossed the reach before he'd arrived, he'd probably start breaking out in hives now that he'd made love to her.

Or rather, had *tried* to make love to her. Cadi, however, had seemed more focused on making up for the time she'd lost during her fake engagement.

Jesse chuckled as he scaled the camper steps, willing to bet it had been a hell of a lot longer than two years since she'd gotten naked with a man. And he did seem to recall hearing what had sounded like *six freaking years* just before she'd pulled him on top of her while he'd been trying to get the damn condom on *despite* her awkward attempts to help. And the last coherent thought he remembered having—until a big fat mosquito had taken a big fat bite out of his bare-naked ass—was that sometimes doing things Cadi's way was better.

Jesse tucked his shirt in his jeans while exiting the camper and headed down the road to the beach, turning his attention to Cadi's passenger and wondering what in hell Nathaniel was doing here. He jogged the length of the dock and caught the gunwale of the runabout when Cadi cut the motor, completely failing to stifle a grin when he saw the lingering terror on Nathaniel's face as the kid sat in front of the console clutching his precious briefcase to his chest. He should have grabbed an extra shirt, Jesse realized when he noticed his protégé's cherished power suit was wet with sea-spray. "Am I going to have to take the keys to the Lear away from you, Mr. Cunningham?" he drawled as he tied the bow rope to the dock cleat.

"For wh-what I do for you," Nathaniel shot back through chattering teeth, "you should give me the keys to the *Boeing*."

"Welcome to Hundred Acre, Nathaniel."

Nathaniel slapped his wet briefcase in Jesse's outstretched hand, then scrambled over the gunwale like a sailor headed for shore leave after six months at sea. "Along with that raise *your wife* offered me several weeks ago," the kid muttered as he staggered up the bouncy dock with all the grace of a sailor coming *off* shore leave three days later.

Figuring the last thing Nathaniel needed right now was a boss firing questions at him, Jesse turned his attention to a much more pleasant subject, only to find Cadi sitting with her head resting on the steering wheel.

"Another rough day in town starting new fashion trends?" he asked. "Or another gossip-mill ambush?"

"No, him," she said, waving toward shore without lifting her head. "I don't think I've ever been more embarrassed in my life."

Jesse set the briefcase down with a sigh, stepped one foot in the boat and lifted Cadi up and stood her on the dock, then stepped out and clasped her shoulders before she'd finished gasping. And then he ducked his head to look her in the eyes, since she was looking at her feet. "What did Nathaniel do?"

"No, I embarrassed myself. Mr. Cunningham was perfectly gracious." Even though her face appeared in danger of bursting into flames, she managed to lift her head enough to give him a good scowl. "And he's right, he does deserve a raise. He not only didn't say anything to give us away when Oren said he was in luck and could just hitch a ride to Hundred Acre with *your missus*, he didn't even bat an eyelash when . . . when I . . ."

Jesse stopped her from glancing toward shore by using his grip on her shoulders to turn her toward him. "When you what?"

Her gaze dropped to his chest again. "Don't you think you should go check on him? I'm fairly certain this was the first time he's ever been on a boat in salt water, and he—"

"He'll be fine in a few minutes. And trust me, the last thing Nathaniel would want is for my wife or anyone else to see me coddling him."

"But he's just a boy."

"I know he looks nineteen, but he's only six years younger than me," Jesse said, slashing her a grin when her eyes shot to his. "So come on, tell me what you did to embarrass yourself."

Apparently sorry she'd said anything in the first place, she went back to scowling. "I blurted out that he couldn't be your assistant because he was African-American. And I kept right on making a fool of myself by saying the gentleman I spoke with three weeks ago hadn't sounded the least bit . . . he hadn't . . . Oh!" she huffed as she covered her face with her hands.

Jesse didn't know if it was embarrassment or anger not letting her finish a sentence, but he did know she'd never looked sexier. Well, except for this morning, when he'd opened his eyes to see her tousled blond curls and beautiful, sun-kissed face on the pillow beside him.

"Now do you understand why this will never work

between us?" she muttered. "The first fancy party you took me to, I'd say or do—" She dropped her hands when he couldn't stifle a chuckle and smacked him on the shoulder. "Don't you dare laugh at me! It's not one bit funny that I was so shocked just to be *speaking* to an African . . . to a person of . . . to a . . ."

"The term you're dancing around is *black*, Cadi," Jesse said, pulling her into his arms and grinning again when she buried her blistering face in his clean, dry shirt. "So tell me, how did Nathaniel react when you blurted out he was African-American?" he asked, already knowing the answer but wanting to hear hers. "Did he appear insulted?"

"No, he appeared surprised and looked down at himself and said he'd always thought he was *Iowan*-American, since he was born in . . . Cedar Rapids," she trailed off in a whisper.

Jesse fought not to laugh again as he glanced over to see Nathaniel sitting on a rock at the base of the road, his elbows resting on his knees and his head cradled in his hands. Jesse kissed the top of Cadi's head, then let his mouth linger in her soft curls. "Is Nathaniel the first black man you've ever spoken to? Surely you were exposed to a diverse range of people in college."

He felt her nod and lifted his mouth away when she tilted her head to look up at him, pleased to note her blush had settled down to just two flags of pink. "There were lots of foreign students and people from big cities in my classes, but I was too shy to actually talk to them," she admitted. "They all seemed so confident and sophisticated and worldly, and I was afraid I'd say something

stupid like . . . like I did today." She looked at him again.
"Now do you understand what I've been trying to explain? I need to travel so I can become confident and worldly, too."

"But you don't need to do it alone."

She smiled sadly and shook her head. "So if I insult or embarrass a visiting Tidewater client, you're not going to mind when they switch their business to Starrtech? Or when there's a picture of us in the newspaper after a fundraiser, you're just going to ignore the caption below it that wonders if Jesse Sinclair isn't buying his dates out of the L.L.Bean catalog now?"

"Ah, Cadi, Cadi, Cadi," he said on a chuckle, clasping her to him again and squeezing until he heard her squeak. "Just like everyone in Castle Cove, the men are going to fall in love with you, and the women are going to show up at the next fund-raiser wearing mud boots." He sobered, letting her go to clasp her shoulders again. "But the only way you're ever going to believe me is if you *try*. That's all I'm asking for—that you give us a chance by letting me take you to some of those parties and fundraisers. I promise, by the third one you'll realize that half the people there are as fake as your engagement was, and the other half are just going through the motions—just like I am—out of obligation."

She silently stared up at him, her beautiful baby blues unreadable. "Will you at least try?" he whispered. "For me—no, for *us*? When this thing with Stapleton is over, will you let me take you to Rosebriar?"

More silence, more staring, and still unreadable. "I . . . I'll think about it," she finally whispered. She then stepped

out of his grasp, picked up the tote and backpack off the
backseat of the runabout, and headed to shore.

She was halfway down the dock when she suddenly
stopped and turned to face him, and Jesse perked when
he caught the hint of a sparkle in her eyes. "How about
if we make a deal? I'm not promising I'll go to one of
those parties, but I will go with you to Rosebriar if you
agree to rent an office on the mainland instead of building one here on Hundred Acre."

Jesse felt his jaw slacken when he realized she was
serious. "Why in God's name would I want to cross three
miles of water just to go to work?"

"For me—no, for *us*?" She canted her head. "And for
yourself."

"What in hell does that mean?"

She eyed him for several seconds, then shrugged. "It
was just an idea," she said, turning and walking away
again.

Jesse actually felt his heart pounding as he watched
Cadi stop in front of Nathaniel, who immediately stood
up. They conversed for several minutes before she gave
a laugh as she reached out and patted his arm and then
headed up the road—whatever she'd said to Nathaniel
leaving the kid grinning like a simpleton as he watched
her disappear around a curve. She was just emerging from
the woods at the top of the rise when Jesse called her
name, making her stop.

"Deal!" he shouted.

She stared down at him for several heartbeats, then
silently nodded and turned away.

Jesse closed his eyes on a curse when he saw she was

walking in the direction of her campsite, then dropped his head on another curse at the realization she'd done it to him again. Son of a bitch; just when he thought he was making headway she'd turned it back on him *again*.

"Should I assume the mail boat sank with my invitation, or is a boss not inviting his assistant to the wedding the latest version of the pink slip? Because personally," Nathaniel continued when Jesse snapped his head up, "I prefer good old-fashioned email—preferably before I nearly drown trying to be the best damn assistant you've ever had or ever *will* have."

"What I have is an assistant who better have a damn good reason for being here," Jesse said by way of answer as he snatched up the briefcase and strode down the dock, "or the jet fuel you just burned and the crew's salaries are coming out of yours."

"Hey, it's not my fault your *little missus* has your tighty-whities in a twist," Nathaniel said, falling in beside him when Jesse strode past.

"Is that an *Iowan* expression?"

"Naw, I think missus is universal."

Jesse started to glare at him but changed his mind when he saw Nathaniel wasn't looking like the damn best anything at the moment. "You remember when Miss Glace called the office several weeks ago? The reason she wouldn't give you her number," he went on when Nathaniel nodded, "was because she was only trying to find out when I'd be returning to Maine."

Nathaniel stopped walking. "She used me?"

Jesse gave him a nudge and started walking again. "Cadi's got this little habit of helping herself to other people's stuff—including their names. And since she needed someplace safe to hide—from Ryan Stapleton, actually—she's been living on Hundred Acre as my wife for the last three weeks." This time Jesse stopped. "Speaking of which, and assuming I'm correct in guessing the little project I gave you is why you're here, is there a reason you simply couldn't email me what you found? Hell, you've been dying for a legitimate excuse to use that encryption program you put on my laptop."

"Two reasons, actually," Nathaniel said, all business again as he squared his linebacker shoulders inside his soggy suit. "One, because I wouldn't put half the stuff I uncovered in an email encrypted by the Pentagon. And two, because I didn't feel it was an appropriate way to ask if you wanted me to continue researching a dead man."

Jesse turned off the burner under the pot of Tang he'd been heating, figuring Nathaniel needed something sweet as much as he needed something hot, then lifted the pot and poured the Tang into two large mugs—because hell, he was chilled to the bone himself. He grabbed the bottle of Aberfeldy out of a cupboard and gave each mug a couple of shots, then carried the odd toddies to the table just as Nathaniel came down the stairs rolling up the sleeves of his stretched-tight borrowed sweatshirt. Jesse slid out a chair and sat down to hide his grin when he saw the cuffs of the jeans he'd lent him were also rolled up.

Nathaniel was about the same inches under average for a male that Jesse was over average, and even though Jesse had most of his shirts tailored to fit his slightly wider than average shoulders, he didn't come close to his protégé's linebacker build. In fact, that build had gotten Nathaniel an Ivy League education he'd somehow managed to stretch into a master's degree. But what really impressed Jesse was that the kid had jumped on his offer of employment after graduation instead of the NFL's.

"What is this stuff?" Nathaniel asked in a winded rasp as he set the mug back on the table, having taken a sip before he even sat down.

"Just drink it. It's hot, it's sweet, and it will put hair on your chest."

Nathaniel pulled out the chair opposite Jesse. "Women don't like hairy chests," he said, sitting down and nearly bursting the sweatshirt's seams when he puffed out the chest under discussion. "Which makes up for all the ribbing I got in the locker room for not having *any*," he added, just before taking another drink of the steaming Tang, which led to more coughing.

"Now can you please explain that statement down on the beach?" Jesse asked.

Nathaniel set his mug to the side and reached for the briefcase Jesse had placed on the table. He undid the buckles and pulled out a thick file, but suddenly looked around. "Is Miss Glace still here? Or do I call her Mrs. Sinclair?"

"No, she's at the other end of the island. And you don't have to worry about calling her anything, because as soon as you tell me what you came to tell me, you're out of here, got it?"

"Oh, I'm fairly sure I got it," Nathaniel said with a grin, not the least bit intimidated. "Unless you're in the habit of wearing pink socks when you're away from the office."

Jesse turned in his chair to look at where Nathaniel was looking and saw one of Cadi's socks on the floor between the couch and wall of the slide-out.

"But you're taking me back to the mainland in that boat I saw parked on the mooring out front," Nathaniel added when Jesse turned back to him. "Which I assume is the big, fast cruiser you couldn't stop talking about all last winter."

Jesse arched a brow over the rim of his mug as he took a large gulp of Tang, then took his time setting the mug down as he fought the urge to shudder all over. Damn, that was nasty. Hot and sweet and definitely bone-thawing, but really nasty. "Show me what you've got," he said once he was sure he could talk without sounding like he'd swallowed a frog.

Nathaniel turned all business and opened the file. "Ryan Stapleton wasn't anyone even the mob would do business with," he began as he shuffled through several papers before pulling one from the pile. "Probably because he was in the habit of changing the rules in the middle of any scheme he was running. Mostly real estate deals, but he'd been known to traffic people, drugs, and"—Nathaniel snorted—"of all things, exotic fish."

"Get to the part about him being dead."

"I will," Nathaniel said calmly. "Right after I tell you about Stanley Kerr."

"I already know Stapleton was blackmailing Kerr into designing him a house. What I don't know is when and *how* Stapleton died."

Nathaniel spun the page he was looking at and slid it in front of Jesse. "Mr. Kerr didn't exist until he suddenly showed up in Boston nine years ago with his supposedly three-years-younger brother, Aaron. But in reality," he went on, still calmly, when Jesse started to protest, "they were Steven and Aiden Shasta, fraternal twins born thirty-five years ago in Miami, which is where they lived until their father and mother and younger sister were gunned down at the family restaurant *nine and a half years ago.*" He tapped the newspaper article Jesse was staring at, which had a picture of an upscale restaurant with crime-scene tape cordoning it off, along with three inset photos of a middle-aged man and woman and a girl in her late teens or early twenties. "The two brothers were attending a friend's bachelor party at the time of the shooting, but were never seen again after they dropped the groom off on his doorstep. Speculation was they were dead, which was later substantiated when their wallets showed up at the local news station with photographs of their beaten, bloody bodies—which were never found."

Nathaniel slipped several more pages, fanned out like playing cards, in front of Jesse, then leaned back in his chair. "It was decided the restaurant shooting was an execution," he continued softly, "intended as an example to anyone needing to know that there was a new crime boss in town who didn't appreciate Mr. Shasta not giving him the respect he felt he deserved."

"You were supposed to be researching Stapleton," Jesse said quietly, lifting his gaze from the photo of the two mutilated male bodies. "I don't think I once mentioned Stanley or Aaron Kerr in our discussion."

"You didn't. All of this," Nathaniel said, gesturing at the papers in front of Jesse and the pile in front of him, "came off Ryan Stapleton's personal computer."

"Then how did *you* get it?"

Nathaniel lowered his gaze and began looking through the pages in front of him. "When I read on the newsfeed that an unidentified body was found on a piece of land in East Hampton, and realized it was the land Stapleton was planning to build on, I . . ."

Nathaniel hesitated. He took a drink of his Tang. Then he finally looked directly at Jesse.

"There's a twenty-four-, sometimes forty-eight-hour window of opportunity to hack into someone's computer after they die, before a family member or business partner thinks to erase the search history or wipe the hard drive clean or simply take it off-line. So I slipped in through that window and took a little look around Stapleton's computer and found this," he said, gesturing at the papers scattered between them again.

Jesse scrubbed his face in an attempt to scrub away those images, then folded his arms over his chest and looked directly at his protégé—whom he obviously didn't know a damn thing about. "Would you mind telling me," he said quietly, "how you would even *know* about that window of opportunity, much less how to hack into someone's private computer?"

"I was set for college because I was a kick-ass football player, but my little sister wasn't very good at sneaking through the line to sack the quarterback. So when we couldn't find any schools that gave full scholarships to kick-ass cellists wanting to major in education, I finally just invented one for Tessa and worked nights at a hacker's den to fund it."

Jesse had met Tessa several times, since she taught in Manhattan at a private elementary school and would often stop by the office. "And she never found out?"

Nathaniel snorted, even as he grinned and shook his head. "I think she's having too much fun pretending she doesn't know, but I'm fairly certain she figured it out by her sophomore year. I suspect that's why she's promised me lifetime babysitting once I have kids, but she said she's limiting it to two at a time if they're boys." Jesse saw Nathaniel pull in a breath, and when he blew it out he was all business again as he started sorting through his pile of papers. "The main reason I felt I needed to tell you this stuff in person is—"

"Wait," Jesse said, holding up a hand on a sudden thought. "When did you read the newsfeed that said Stapleton is dead?"

"The article about the body being found came out yesterday, but the identity only came out in this morning's feed."

"Did it make it into this morning's *print* newspapers, too?"

"And it's on the national news," Nathaniel said with a nod, "because of where he was found, which is smack in the middle of several estates of the famous and wealthy. And because of the weird way he'd been— Hey, where are you going?" Nathaniel asked, having to shout the last part because Jesse was already halfway out the camper door.

Jesse sprinted around the camper and up the narrow

trail to the antenna. "I need to shut this off," he said when Nathaniel caught up with him. He opened the door for the solar power system and scanned all the dials and switches. "Did Cadi receive any calls or texts when you were with her?"

Nathaniel reached past him and turned a dial, then flipped two switches. "No," he said as a humming stopped at the same time several lights on the panel started flashing. "Why?"

Jesse closed the door and headed back down the trail. "If it made national news, then Stanley Kerr also knows Stapleton is dead. But I need to buy myself some time to think before he calls Cadi and tells her it's safe to go home."

"Yeah. That's probably a good idea," Nathaniel said as he followed, "as Mr. Kerr is the main reason I felt it was important to come here in person."

They entered the camper and Nathaniel immediately went to the table and sat down and started leafing through his papers again. He stopped and pulled out one page and shoved it in front of Jesse when he sat down.

"I was able to learn through a source better left unnamed that Ryan Stapleton was found . . . planted on his property," Nathaniel said quietly. "Vertical, head pointed down, naked, and with only his feet and legs from the knee down—or rather up—visible."

Jesse wasn't sure what he was looking at, until halfway down on the page of run-on words he saw *Miami, Florida,* and then a date from nine years ago.

"The scenario struck a chord, and I remembered seeing something similar in Stapleton's research on Stanley

Kerr," Nathaniel continued softly. "So I started doing a little research of my own on Steven Shasta." Nathaniel shifted uncomfortably, then rested his arms on the table and clasped his hands together. "You remember the Miami crime boss? Well, it appears that about a month after the restaurant execution, he was found planted upside down on his estate about two hundred yards from his house, naked, with just his feet visible. The difference between that body and Stapleton's is that both feet of the Florida man had been beaten to bloody pulps. It's too early to know about Stapleton, but the autopsy from Florida indicated that guy had still been alive when he was buried."

Jesse moved his gaze from the page in front of him—that he wasn't even seeing—to the pile of papers under his assistant's arms, then over to the laptop peeking out of the soft-sided leather briefcase, then finally to Nathaniel. "Is there any way anyone can find out that you were inside Stapleton's computer?"

"No. Mine really is invisible. I can get in and out without anyone knowing I was even there."

"And is any of this," Jesse asked, tapping the pile of papers when Nathaniel leaned back, "actually *on* your computer?"

"No. I printed everything directly off the Internet. And even though it was a computer in Jamaica that looked inside Stapleton's, I wiped my entire hard drive clean anyway. And before I backed out of that window, I also wiped Stapleton's hard drive clean." He used his eyes to gesture at the papers. "That's all there is. Somebody would have to start a brand-new search from the very beginning, and then they'd have to know what to go looking for in the first place."

Jesse very slowly started gathering the papers into a pile. "So what is it going to cost me to wipe *your* memory clean?" he asked conversationally.

He heard a soft snort. "Yeah, about that; while sitting on your beach trying to convince myself that I would also survive the boat ride back to the mainland, I decided I really did deserve the keys to the Boeing. But I changed my mind after Miss Glace stopped to talk to me."

Jesse quit gathering papers. "Talk about what?"

Nathaniel shook his head, one side of his mouth lifting as he slipped his hand inside his briefcase and pulled out a book. "She asked if I'd ever built a treehouse. And when I told her I'd built one with my dad when I was six, she offered to design me my very own home in exchange for taking one of my vacation weeks this summer to come back here and work on the treehouse you're building."

"Why?" Jesse cleared his throat to get rid of the frog and started gathering papers again. "Did she say why?"

"I asked her why. I told her I know what it costs to have a house designed because I've been writing the checks for yours. And even taking into account that the price lessens in proportion to the size of the house, I tried to point out that her offer still didn't make sense. And she laughed and said, 'You probably won't think so by the end of your week's vacation,'" he repeated, trying to pitch his voice to sound like her. "'But sometimes, Mr. Cunningham, competition-crushing executives *and* their assistants need to be six years old again.'" Jesse saw the kid's face darken. "I hate to admit it's the second time she's tripped me up, but putting it together with her offer about your office, I finally got it."

Nathaniel snatched up the pile of papers in front of him just as Jesse was reaching for them. "So here's *my* offer to you," he continued calmly. "Instead of the keys to the Boeing, I'm willing to give myself a virtual lobotomy in exchange for you agreeing to keep this one. She's the real deal, boss," he said gruffly. "I think she's . . . good for you. *And*," he added, holding out the papers but not letting go when Jesse tried to take them, "since I can't have you thinking I'm a complete idiot, I also want a Disney cruise to Castaway Cay for six adults and one child, and the Lear to go pick up my mom and dad in Iowa and then fly us all to the departure port and back."

"Who's the child?"

"Tessa and Lionel just took in a five-year-old foster kid." He grinned, still not releasing the papers when Jesse gave a little tug. "Ajax's only been with them for a few months, and he's already declared that he's staying."

"So you'll forget everything you found in your research in exchange for taking your family on a Disney cruise?"

"No, that's for my nearly drowning getting here. Forgetting everything is in exchange for you keeping Miss Glace."

"Deal," Jesse said at the same time he gave a sharp tug on the papers. He stood up, gathered all the pages into one pile, then strode to the kitchen. He stopped and opened a drawer and grabbed a lighter, then headed outside. "Is there anything in these I should read that I haven't?" he asked as Nathaniel followed.

"You know all the important stuff." Nathaniel stopped beside Jesse in front of the small metal fire pit. "I'm just the messenger; what you do with the message is up to you."

"This is what I'm doing with it," Jesse said, crouching down and setting the papers on the ground. "And then I'm wiping *my* memory clean," he added, pulling a sheet from the pile and crumpling it up. He tossed it in the pit, set it on fire, then picked up another sheet.

Nathaniel crouched beside him and started helping.

"What was the book you pulled out of your briefcase?" Jesse asked, tossing a couple of sticks on the growing flames when the sea breeze sent embers of burning paper into the air.

Nathaniel chuckled. "Your missus pulled it out of her backpack when I boarded that bathtub posing as a boat and said I just might get that raise if I'm the one giving it to you."

"Be glad you didn't show up here sooner," Jesse drawled, "or you really would have had an interesting ride across the reach. So the book's a field guide?"

Nathaniel crumpled the last sheet of paper and tossed it on the fire. "No, it's a guide to beekeeping." He stood up and wiped his hands on his borrowed sweatshirt as he looked out at the cruiser bobbing on its mooring, then flashed Jesse a grin. "So can I drive on the way back?"

EIGHTEEN

❦

Jesse stood with his hands on his hips and scowled up at Paul, who was methodically disassembling three long, sweaty, and obviously wasted days of work. "Let me go ahead and take the chainsaw to it," Jesse called up to him, "and we'll just start fresh. I bought twice as much lumber as Ray said I should need for this very reason."

"But we can reuse this lumber," Paul said without looking down. "And it'll only take me a minute"— *because it's already falling apart on its own*, Jesse was pretty sure he heard the boy add in a muttered whisper. "You could work on the mast if you want," Paul added out loud.

Another Mainer—this one only *sixteen*—giving him busywork, Jesse realized as he walked to Cadi's old skiff and scowled down at it. For the love of God, he'd built four major cargo berths in the last six years; how in hell hard could it be to build a treehouse? "You had plans for those berths," he muttered to himself, "and a small army of engineers. And I don't remember you touching any tools." He picked up the tall cedar sapling he and Paul had cut down and dragged through the woods behind the ATV—that he was supposed to peel the bark off of with something called an adze, which he'd bought off Ray two days ago. "It would have been nice if it came with instructions," he added.

"What's that?" Paul called down.

"I was just saying it would be nice to have a set of plans."

He saw Paul shift his stance in the large, gnarly old oak and look down at him. "I suggested that to Mrs. Sinclair yesterday, sort of hinting that she could help us draw up some, seeing how she's getting your whole house laid out from just drawings in a sketchpad. But she laughed and tapped my forehead and said we need to see the treehouse in our minds. She said they're organic structures, and the tree we pick should tell us what it's going to look like."

Jesse was pretty sure it wasn't supposed to look like two blind drunks had built it. "And when you built the one with your dad?" he asked.

He saw the boy shrug. "We used scrap wood to build a small cabin on the ground, then used the excavator to hoist it onto beams we'd run between three ash trees." He shot Jesse a grin. "One of the trees snapped in a Nor'easter that winter, and we never saw the treehouse again until the snow melted and we found what was left of it clear over in Fender Cove."

Jesse scanned the shoreline surrounding the small, crescent-shaped gravel beach, then squinted up at Paul again. "Maybe we picked the wrong tree. What about that big bad boy over there?" he asked, pointing toward the other end of the cove. "It doesn't have half as many gnarly branches as this one, but there's another good oak beside it we could run a couple of beams to." He glanced toward the point of land protecting the small cove from the choppy reach. "I don't think we could get your dad's larger barge in here with the excavator on it, but I'm pretty sure Jason Dean's barge could get in during high tide," he added, looking up again. "And his pylon-driver might be tall enough to hoist a small cabin up on the beams if we don't set them too high."

Paul was shaking his head before Jesse even finished. "Dad said he checked all the trees along the beach when he off-loaded the lumber with you, and he told me this was the best one," he said, patting the thick trunk beside him.

This from a man who'd set *his* treehouse on a rotten tree. Was there a reason Little Miss Leave Me Alone couldn't at least have helped them pick which damn tree they should use before banning him from the lower bluff until his house was all laid out?

Did she honestly believe he didn't leave his nice warm bed—and her—every morning before she even opened her sexy baby blues to run down to the bluff and peek?

"I got a couple of buddies who couldn't find jobs this

summer that I bet would come help us," Paul said. "They're not losers or lazy or anything," he rushed on when Jesse realized the boy thought he was scowling up at him instead of squinting. "It's just that their parents wouldn't let them work during school because they wanted them to make good grades to get into college, so all the summer jobs for anyone our age were already taken."

"Your father doesn't strike me as a man who wouldn't care what you got for grades," Jesse said. "So how come he let you work during school?"

Paul slashed him a broad grin. "Because I'm already a genius." The boy changed his stance and drove the claw end of his hammer into a board and pried on a nail. "I've gotten straight A's since grammar school."

"I tell you what," Jesse said, making the boy stop prying to look at him. "You decide you'd rather wear a suit than drive an excavator, you come see me the moment you get your college diploma."

"Now what has Nathaniel done?" a deep, familiar voice said on a chuckle, making Jesse spin around to see Ben and Sam emerging from the woods. "To have you already hiring his replacement," Ben continued as they strode onto the beach.

"What in hell are you two doing here?" Jesse narrowed his eyes at them. "No, *why* are you here? I told you last night I'd see you tomorrow at Jen's bon voyage party."

Ben sobered. Sam didn't have to, because he already looked . . . hell, he looked angry enough to make Jesse stay rooted in place.

"We've been calling your cell phone since six this morning," Sam growled.

"My antenna's down," Jesse said calmly. But then he stiffened. "What's wrong? Is it the kids? Did something happen?" he asked, only to realize too late neither man would be here if anything had happened to Hank or Rose.

Ben stopped in front of him. "The party's been called off."

"Why?"

"Because it's hard to wish someone bon voyage when they've already left," Sam said.

"What? Why would Jennifer leave early?"

"I'm guessing it was Mike's idea," Ben added tightly, his features also turning deadly, "to make sure we couldn't stop them from leaving *together*."

Okay, none of this was making sense. "What's going on?" Jesse whispered. He looked behind him, then backed up and plopped down on a large rock. "I thought Jen and Mike didn't . . . They act like two wrestlers circling each other every time we have a family gathering. Hell, Jen emailed me when I was in Europe a few weeks ago and said *my nephew* was a chest-beating jerk—and she wasn't referring to Hank."

Ben walked over and collapsed on a nearby rock, then scrubbed his face with both hands. "That would be about the same time," he said, sounding as haggard as Sam looked, "that Mike started threatening to torch her sloop."

"But when he finally realized he couldn't talk her out of going," Sam interjected as he sat down on another rock, "we think he started talking Jen into taking him with her instead."

Well, shit; now they had *two* young people to worry about. Jesse shot to his feet. "When did they leave? They couldn't have made it out of the Gulf of Maine yet. I've got her course charts on my laptop. Come on, my cruiser can catch them."

Ben leaned forward and grabbed Jesse's wrist before he even took a step and yanked him back down on the rock. "It's a damn big Gulf, and knowing Mike, he had Jen set a course to Nova Scotia to throw us off."

"Did you call the coast guard?"

"And tell them what?" Sam asked. "That two consenting adults have set sail on the best-equipped, fastest sloop on the planet, but could you search 35,000 square miles of open water for their worried families, anyway? Oh, and when you find them, could you please drag their sneaky asses home so we can lock them in their rooms until they're *thirty*?"

"Ah . . . Mr. Sinclair?" Paul asked from about ten yards away. "Seeing how you have company, I can come back tomorrow to work on the treehouse." He glanced toward the company under discussion, then back at Jesse. "Or I can spend the afternoon taking it down by myself."

"No," Jesse said with a shake of his head. "I don't want you up in that tree if no one's here, in case you fall." He hesitated. "If I let you take the ATV back to camp, can you figure out how to turn on the cell phone antenna? I'm pretty sure it's just a matter of flipping two switches. There are instructions on the inside of the panel door," he added, remembering from when the installers had given him a run-through of how everything worked.

"Oh, sure, no problem," Paul said, backing away. "Do you want me to swing by the bluff and tell Mrs. Sinclair you've got company?"

Jesse sensed more than saw Ben and Sam perk up. "No, I'll tell her. Thanks. I'll call you later and let you know when to come out again," he added, causing Paul to give a wave over his shoulder as he jogged to the ATV parked up on the knoll.

"Yes," Sam said dryly, "we were hoping to meet the *little missus*."

"You know the little missus we're talking about," Ben added. "The one the harbormaster said we could have ridden out to the island with if we hadn't missed her by just an hour?"

"How *did* you get here?" Jesse asked instead of answering.

"Mr. Hatch was kind enough to point us toward an enterprising young man who happened to have the keys to his father's lobster boat," Sam said, a hint of a grin making him look a little less haggard.

Ben snorted. "The little snot charged us fifty bucks a head. In case you can't add," he said, glaring at Jesse, "that's two hundred bucks to go *three miles* because you want *privacy*."

Jesse sat up straight. "Wait, Emma and Willa are here? What about Hank and Rose?"

"We left the kids with Shelby in Keelstone," Sam told him—Shelby being Willa's sister.

And also Jen's mom. Hell, she must be worried sick.

"No, Shelby's surprisingly calm," Sam said, making Jesse realize he'd spoken out loud. "She was already mentally geared up for Jennifer leaving, but I think she feels even better about it knowing Mike's with her."

"Great help that he'll be," Ben muttered. "The first

time Willa took us sailing on the *RoseWind*, we had to fish Mike out of the Gulf. And the second and *last* time he went, he got his hand caught in a slapping sail line and busted three fingers."

"He was fifteen," Sam said with a chuckle. "And he fell overboard when Jen pulled off her sweatshirt. He's almost nineteen now; I'm sure your boy's figured out how to keep his hormones from running roughshod over his brain."

"Like you did when you sailed to Maine with Willa, *Daddy*?" Ben growled. "I swear if those two come back a year from now with a baby, I'm claiming all the proceeds from our bet for giving Bram his first great-*great*-grandchild."

"Come on," Jesse said with a chuckle, standing up and heading up the beach. "I want to see Willa and Emma."

"We're going to have to find them first," Sam said, following.

Jesse stopped and turned. "What do you mean? Didn't you leave them at my campsite?"

"No, we all came down that nice, smooth gravel path that stopped at a narrow ravine and turned into a goat trail. And when we reached a fork in the trail a few minutes later, the women went left looking for you and we went right."

Jesse felt the hairs on his neck stir and looked at Ben. "Did you happen to tell Emma I'm over Pamela?"

"No. Why?"

"And did Emma and Willa hear Oren Hatch mention my little missus?"

"Well, yeah," Sam said. "Why?"

Jesse bolted for the woods at a dead run. "Because the last thing I need right now is for them to welcome *Pamela* to the family!"

Cadi couldn't believe the progress she'd made since she'd found Jeff Acton and his cute little bulldozer building the gravel path from the landing to the bluff three days ago. Even though she hadn't dared steal him for more than a day, Jeff had not only managed to cut down the trees and move all the boulders from inside the house, the genius man had wielded his chainsaw like a carving knife and helped her build a crude but solid frame of the second floor from the trees. It had also been his idea for them to sneak over to Jesse's lumber pile down at the cove and steal enough boards to let her actually maneuver around the upstairs.

Heck, they'd even built a narrow catwalk connecting it to the top of the cliff.

Cadi straightened from stripping branches off the sapling she intended to use to show the final height of the roofline when she heard a deep, drawn-out growl and looked over to see her pet slinking along the bottom of the cliff toward a thick stand of bushes. She scrambled to her feet and scanned the woods at the other end of the house, listening as well as looking for movement. Trusting Wigs' eyes and ears more than her own, Cadi took off, zigzagging through the tape as fast and as quietly as she could, then broke into an all-out sprint and caught hold of a small tree to swing around the tight corner onto the trail. Honest to God, if Jesse was trying to get a peek at his house, she was—

Cadi nearly ripped her arm out of its socket using her grip on the tree to stop herself from slamming into the two women. They all three gasped in surprise, each of the strangers shooting to opposite sides of the trail and Cadi dropping to her knees to avoid colliding with the one that had shot left.

"Are you okay?" the woman asked, grabbing Cadi's arm to help her up.

"I'm sorry, we didn't hear you coming," the other woman said, grabbing Cadi's other arm. "Are you hurt?"

"No. No, I'm fine." Cadi took a step back once they let her go and bent to brush the forest litter off her knees to disguise the fact she was shaking. God, she'd nearly plowed over a visibly pregnant woman. "Are you lost? Or kayakers out exploring the islands?" she asked, straightening and wiping her hands on her thighs. "I'm sorry, but this one is private. There's some smaller islands just to the north and at least two that I know of to the south that I think are owned by the state."

Cadi smiled sheepishly to hide her discomfort over the fact that the two women were just staring at her— slightly slack-jawed—as their gazes traveled from her hair to her face to her body and back to her face again. "I think they're part of an unofficial kayak trail system," she added when they just kept staring. "I heard it goes all the way up to the state park in Cobscook Bay."

"My God," one of the women said softly, "you're beautiful."

"Ex- . . . excuse me?"

"You must be Pamela," the other woman said, her sudden hug-attack making Cadi's attempt to correct her come out as a squeak. "I've been dying to meet you for months now. Oh, I'm sorry," she said, leaning away with a laugh but not letting her go. "I'm Emma, Ben's wife. Holy smokes, no wonder Jesse has been keeping you hidden in New York. You're positively gorgeous." She finally stepped back, only to tug on Cadi's sleeve. "And look at you, out here on his island all dressed in mud boots and fleece, looking just like a true Maine girl."

And still before Cadi could correct her, the pregnant woman launched a hug-attack of her own. "Welcome to the family, Pamela! Oh, I know the men said we should probably ignore the harbormaster referring to you as Jesse's *little missus*," she rushed on, leaning away. "But the very fact Jesse even brought you to his precious island means it's only a matter of time, don't you think?" She gave Cadi one last squeeze, then stepped back and shook her head, lowering her voice to a conspirator's whisper. "Because we all know he's building a house for his future family. I had a feeling you might be the one when Sam told me Jesse actually brought you to Rosebriar last March to help him host a business dinner."

"And bringing you *here* only confirms it," Emma seconded.

All Cadi could do was mutely stare at them, feeling more dumb than a chipmunk and otter and ferret *combined* as she prayed to God she had enough of a tan to hide the fact that all her blood had rushed to her belly in response to the punch it had just taken.

Jesse had a girlfriend in New York? One that these women felt he was involved with seriously enough to *marry*?

"You did too hurt yourself when you fell," Willa said, taking hold of Cadi's sleeve. "Let's find a rock or log for you to sit on before you collapse."

Emma slipped an arm around Cadi as she let the two of them lead her toward the bluff. The women suddenly stopped when they reached the clearing, their concern she was going to faint evaporating on stereo gasps of surprise. "What *is* this?" Emma whispered.

"Oh my God, it's his house!" Willa cried, abandoning Cadi to rush forward.

Emma chose to drag Cadi along as the woman followed her sister-in-law, although she was thoughtful enough to keep her arm around her. "This is Jesse's house? Why on earth would he build down here instead of up on the hill?"

"Cadi!" Jesse shouted, making Emma turn them both in time to see Jesse charge into the clearing followed by two men.

"Cadi?" Emma echoed, dropping her arm and allowing Cadi to step away. "You're not Pamela?"

"What!" Willa cried, rushing back to them. "You're not *Pamela*? We thought she was Pamela!" she shouted at Jesse just as he reached Cadi.

He tried to grasp her shoulders. "I can explain."

"You touch me and you're a dead man," Cadi whispered tightly, pushing his hand away as she took several more steps back. She turned and smiled at the horrified women. "I'm sorry for not immediately correcting you, but I seem to have developed the bad habit of playing along when I'm mistaken for someone I'm not. My name is Cadi Glace, and I live in a tiny town up the coast, not New York. I'm just the architect's assistant," she said, ignoring the muttered curse behind her as she gestured at the full-scale—and damn perfect, if she did say so herself—model of Jesse's home. "Mr. Kerr hired me to come out to the island and tape off the rooms so Mr. Sinclair could get a feel of the layout and overall size of the structure. So if you'll excuse me," she went on calmly as she walked past the corner stake and started along the wall of the cliff, "I'll just call it a day and head back to the mainland and let you all enjoy your visit."

Cadi stopped when she reached her tent and picked her sketchbook up off the folding table, made sure her smile was still firmly in place, then turned and looked down the length of the house at Jesse, who was standing with his arms folded over his chest, staring at her. "I'll leave this here so you can show everyone around your home," she said, waving the sketchbook. She tossed it back on the table, picked up her backpack, then looked toward the bushes where Wiggles had disappeared. "I'll come back and get my stuff tom—in a day or two," she said as she started walking back along the cliff toward the path, figuring she'd have Paul sneak her over here tonight to get her cat.

"You even think about touching that runabout," Jesse said when she was halfway to him, "and the sheriff will be waiting for you at the town pier."

"Fine with me," she said without breaking stride— even though she could barely see where she was walking.

Damn, two minutes more was all she needed, and then she could burst into tears. "I'd much prefer spending the night in jail than on this island."

"I love you," he said—and not in a whisper, either—just as she angled past him, making Cadi stumble several steps before coming to a halt.

She stared up at the cliff to keep her tears from spilling free, not even daring to blink.

"I love you," he repeated when a full minute went by and she didn't respond.

"Trust me, Ms. Glace," a male voice said into the silence from somewhere behind her when another minute passed. "He's never uttered those words to a woman before."

"If you know him at all," another male added, "you'd know how hard that was for him to say."

"And I didn't mean it when I welcomed *Pamela* to the family," Willa chimed in. "I was just being polite because I thought we were stuck with you—her. Stuck with *her*. But if Jesse says he loves you, then we love you, too."

"Please give him a chance," Emma softly petitioned. "He really is a good man."

Still staring up at the cliff, still unable to respond because she was still barely holding it together, Cadi heard movement behind her that seemed to be traveling toward the path as it slowly faded away.

"I adore you," a warm, familiar, heart-shivering voice said into the growing silence. "I desire you. I admire you. I am in awe of you."

Two warm, steady, so very masculine hands gently clasped her shoulders, and Cadi finally let her tears spill free by dropping her head and turning into his warm and so very safe embrace. "Did I mention I love you?" he whispered into her hair. "And that I can't imagine ever living without you? That I would do anything for you? *Be* anything for you?" He kissed the top of her head. "Will you be six years old again with me, Cadi?"

She slowly shook her head without looking up, only to feel his chest stop moving in and out. "But I will be sixteen again with you." She tilted her head back when that chest expanded in a rush. And although she still couldn't see very well, she could definitely tell the dark, Atlantic-blue eyes looking down at her also appeared a little misty. "Sixteen-year-olds can have sex, can't they? Because I really like having sex with you."

"Will you have babies with me?"

She gave a little nod while still staring up at him. "A whole passel of them."

He lifted a hand and cupped her head back to his chest with a heavy sigh. "You're going to dismantle the office at Rosebriar, aren't you?"

She nodded.

"And you're going to make me build a treehouse there, too."

Cadi nodded again, even though he hadn't posed it as a question.

"And I suppose I'm going to have to buy a motorhome."

"A really big one," she agreed.

"You do know it's going to take us a month of Sundays to find Wiggles every time we leave Rosebriar to come here."

"We'll just send our big old scruffy dog to sniff her out. I love you."

Even though the chest she was pressed against stopped moving again, the heart inside it definitely started beating harder. "Excuse me, what was that? There at the end?"

She looked up and beamed him a huge smile. "I said thank you. If you hadn't kicked me off my comfortable couch, I never would have come up with the plan to find Mr. Right." She melted into him. "Hundred Acre might not be Glacier National Park, but I definitely got to experience camping firsthand. Honest to God," she mumbled, "it's beyond me why anyone *wants* to sleep in a tent."

"With their cat," he added, giving her a squeeze. "So will you give me a chance to prove that we're Mr. and Mrs. *Right Now*? That you don't have to travel around getting *more* confident or *more* sophisticated and *more* worldly?" He rested his chin on the top of her head. "Because I really don't want to wait two years to get started on that passel of kids, because I'd really like to still be young enough to stay one step ahead of them as teenagers."

"But we're starting out at sixteen, remember?"

"Yeah, but I'm going to age two years to their one, assuming I don't die of dehydration from sweating bullets every time you cross the reach alone."

She patted his chest without lifting her head. "I'll save up my errands and hitch a ride with you on the one day a week you go to work at your office on the mainland."

Another squeeze and another really, really heavy sigh. "Why am I not—"

"They're here! We spotted the *Spitfire* northeast of the island about six miles out!" came a winded shout from the woods, making Cadi step away when Jesse dropped his arms and turned. "Come on," Ben shouted as he charged into the clearing and gestured at them to follow. "We need your cruiser to go get them!" he called over his shoulder as he ran back up the path.

"Right behind you, brother!" Jesse shouted as he shot after him. He slid to a stop and ran back, snagged Cadi's hand, and shot off again.

"Who's in the sloop?" she asked as she went from standing still to the speed of sound in one second flat.

"Remember the bon voyage party I've been trying to talk you into going to tomorrow? Her. Jen. She's sailing past the island."

"Your . . . brother . . . said . . . *they*," Cadi huffed and puffed while trying to remember where that stupid button was to kick on her jet engine before she fell flat on her face.

"Ben's son Mike is with her. They snuck off this morning before anyone could stop them. Long story. Just run!"

"Slowing . . . you . . . down. Promise . . . to . . . wait . . . with—"

Oh, to heck with it. Cadi jerked free and simply stopped. "I'll wait with the women," she managed to get out in one breath, waving him on as she bent at the waist to suck in gulps of air as he muttered something and shot off again. Good God, she'd probably just burned off the last four pounds of the ten she'd gained building his models—having burned the first six rebuilding the house at full-scale!

She straightened and started walking, only to break into a smile when she'd swear she heard the forest whispering, *Welcome home, Cadi girl. Are you ready for a truly exciting adventure?* just like it had the very first time she'd visited Hundred Acre looking at building sites.

And even though it sounded like the same deep, definitely old, masculine voice as the one back in February, for some reason this time it was eerily familiar—its cadence much like Jesse's, only mixed with the hint of a . . . Texan twang.

Jesse exited the camper on the pretense he needed to go make sure the runabout's dock lines were secure, when what he really needed was five minutes of quiet. His camper was bursting at the seams with people. And Einstein.

He headed down the road to the beach, wondering what Mike had been thinking to bring a ferret on a year-long voyage around the world. Einstein had been so happy to reach solid ground, the little bugger had spent the entire afternoon running all over the north end of Hundred Acre kissing trees and finding mud holes to roll in. Eventually caught, bathed and blown dry, and with his belly now full of kibble—and likely more tuckered out from his morning spent on a sloop surrounded by nothing but ocean than from running through the forest—Einstein had zeroed in on the brand-new human in the group and claimed Cadi's lap as the perfect place for a nap.

Yeah, well, it was a good thing she liked furry little creatures, because Jesse was afraid they'd just gotten themselves a yearlong babysitting job. He stepped onto the floating dock with a chuckle, wondering what Wiggles the ghost cat was going to think of that. Hell, he hoped cats and ferrets weren't mortal enemies. But then he sighed, figuring it would take *two* months of Sundays of searching Rosebriar to find both sneaky buggers every time they wanted to pack up and come to Maine. Jesse stopped in the middle of the dock and decided he better start shopping for a puppy.

He looked down at the runabout and grinned, realizing that when Cadi and Willa had shot over to the mainland to pick up Jen's mother—Shelby had left Hank and Rose and Emma's faithful shepherd, Beaker, in their ex-housekeeper and her new husband's capable hands—the women had apparently made a quick trip to the grocery store. Because when they'd landed on Hundred Acre, the three Sinclair brothers had been pressed into service lugging their purchases up the road to the camper: half a case of Moscato, two six-packs of Moxie, three packages—each—of E.L. Fudge and Oreo cookies, and enough cold meat and cheese to feed a small army. All of which Cadi had probably put on the account she'd confessed to opening in his name in hopes of stretching her dwindling reserve of cash.

He looked out at the forty-three-foot *Spitfire* quietly sitting at anchor next to his cruiser. Jen's voyage was still on, apparently, and Mike was still going with her. In fact, they probably would have been closing in on Cape Cod right about now if they hadn't had to detour to Hundred Acre to drop off Einstein. And although they were only kids in everyone's hearts, Jesse could see everyone's minds had finally realized that two adults had stepped onto the beach this afternoon and calmly but firmly agreed to spend the night, but that they would be gone on the morning tide.

Hence his camper bursting at the seams with people— more than a few of whom were making short work of the wine, his Aberfeldy, and the case of beer Ben had found in the outside storage cubby of the camper. Only Willa wasn't drinking, although she was already on her third bottle of Moxie. Jesse chuckled, remembering seeing Ben refilling Mike's and Jen's glasses of wine. He just didn't know if it was because Ben figured that if Mike was old enough to take on the world he should be old enough to drink, or if he was hoping the boy would be too hungover in the morning to leave.

Jesse slipped his hands in his jacket pockets and turned and stared at the rise above the beach, feeling a wave of contentment wash over him at the sight of light blazing out all the camper windows. Everyone he loved— with the exception of Hank and Rose—was here, on his not-so-private and apparently not all that remote sanctuary, including the woman of his dreams. And whether Miss Glace knew it or not, he intended to—

Jesse stilled in the act of pulling out his cell phone when he caught the sound of words whispering down from the high ridge.

"You did good, boy," a deep, familiar voice said. "I couldn't have done better if I'd picked her myself. Rose says for you to just keep on letting Cadi win your little *discussions*, you hear, and you can have what we did— what we still *do*. Well, except the one about where your

house should be going. I still say it belongs up on that—
Ow! Okay. Okay, woman."

Jesse grinned when he heard the same familiar sigh
that used to echo through Rosebriar on a daily basis
before Grammy Rose's death eight years ago.

"The house is perfect," Bram muttered. "And it belongs right where it is. Now, about that treehouse . . ."

"I've got it covered," Jesse said out loud, holding up
his hand. "Ben and Sam don't know it yet, but they're
going to work on it with me over the summer."

"And my grand—*our* grandbabies? You going to be
working on them this summer?"

"Starting day after tomorrow," Jesse said with a laugh,
pulling his other hand out of his pocket and waggling his
cell phone in the air. "So if you and Grammy will excuse
me? I need to make sure I win this last *discussion*."

"Have a good life, Jesse." That familiar voice gruffly
rolled down the ridge, causing Jesse to still again.

"Hey, you're not leaving for *good*?"

"We'll be right here, Baby Bear," a cherished female
voice whispered, making Jesse close his eyes at his grandmother's pet name for him. "Go on, make the call," she
continued. "I'm on your side on this one—*this* time."

Jesse snapped open his eyes when he felt an unusually
warm, soft gust of wind whoosh by him, making him
turn to see the *Spitfire* slowly swing on its anchor line,
and he grinned again when he realized Mike and Jen
wouldn't exactly be sailing out on the morning tide . . .
alone.

"Okay, then, that takes care of that worry," he said in

relief as he looked down and tapped an icon on his phone. "Now let's see if I'm a really confident or really desperate rascal. I need you to call Regina," Jesse said without preamble when Nathaniel mumbled a gruff hello, "and tell her to be in Bangor with a full crew by noon tomorrow."

There was a loud, cut-off groan—his assistant apparently not covering the phone in time—then a heavy sigh. "And the flight plan she'll need to file while waiting for you to arrive?" he managed to drawl despite still being half asleep.

"I'm leaving the destination up to you."

"I'm going? On the *Boeing*," Nathaniel all but shouted, suddenly wide awake. "Wait—*where* am I going? I didn't hear about any trouble brewing anywhere."

Well, damn; he supposed mentoring a young executive should include teaching him to have a life *outside* the office. But the kid was taking a commercial flight back.

"Pack warm," was all Jesse said. "And I also need you to find a minister and swing by and pick him up on your way to the airport."

"Excuse me? Did you say minister? What denomination?"

"It doesn't matter, so long as he or she is licensed to marry people."

There was a long pause, then a chuckle. "Licensed in what state? No, you said the Boeing, so make that country."

"I'm thinking Alaska this time of year. Just find a glacier we can actually stand on. Oh, and see if you can't scare up a small colony of penguins for the ceremony, and I'll make sure there's an extra zero on your bonus check this year."

What sounded like feet hitting the floor came over the line. "Consider it done, boss."

Jesse ended the call and headed down the dock with a snort. Hell, he wouldn't be surprised to find half a dozen penguins from the Bronx Zoo arguing over window seats when he and Cadi boarded the Boeing in Bangor tomorrow.

Keep reading for an excerpt from

CHARMED BY HIS LOVE

A Spellbound Falls novel

❧

Available from Jove Books

Peg rounded a curve in the peninsula's winding lane and gasped in surprise when she spotted the strange man striding across the parking lot with Jacob thrown over his shoulder. Even from this distance she could see the sheer terror in her son's eyes as Isabel skipped backward in front of them, trying to get the man to stop. Peg started running even as she sized up her adversary: tall, athletic build, short dark hair. Yeah, well, instead of traumatizing defenseless little children, Claude the mad scientist was about to find himself on the receiving end of a healthy dose of fear.

"I swear I'll kick you if you don't put him down, mister," Peg heard Isabel threaten. "He wasn't hurting your stupid machine none. He's just a baby!" And then the six-year-old actually did kick out when the guy didn't stop, only to stumble backward as he merely sidestepped around her. "Charlotte! Peter!" Isabel screamed as she scrambled in front of him again. "Come help me save Jacob from the scary man!"

Alarmed that the guy would go after her daughter when she saw him hesitate, Peg didn't even stop to think and lunged onto his back. "Put him down!" she shouted, wrapping her arm around the bastard's neck as she tried to pull Jacob off his shoulder with her other hand. "Or I swear I'll rip out your eyes!"

The guy gave his own shout of surprise and suddenly dropped like a stone when Peter slammed into his right knee. "You leave my brother alone, you scary bastard!" Peter shouted as he rolled out of the way, dragging Jacob with him.

Peg reared up to avoid Charlotte's foot swinging toward the guy's ribs, although she didn't dare loosen her grip or take her weight off him, fearing he'd lash out at her children. He suddenly curled into the fetal position with a grunt when Peter landed on him beside her.

"Get away from him!" she screamed over her shouting children, trying to push them off when they all started pummeling him. "Run to the—" Peg gave a startled yelp when an arm came around her waist and suddenly lifted her away.

"Sweet Zeus," Mac muttered, dragging her up against his chest as he took several steps back. "You will calm down, Peg, and control your children," he quietly commanded even as he tightened his grip against her struggles.

"Ohmigod, Jacob, come here!" she cried, holding out

her arms. Jacob and Isabel threw themselves at her, actually making Mac step back when he didn't let her go. "You're okay, Jacob. You're safe now," she whispered, squeezing both trembling children. "You're a brave girl, Isabel, and a good sister."

Charlotte called out, and Peg saw the girl pull away from Mac's father just as he also released Peter. Both children ran to her, giving the bastard rising to his hands and knees a wide berth. Peg took a shuddering breath, trying to get her emotions under control. "You can let me go," she told Mac over the pounding in her chest. Holy hell, she couldn't believe they'd all just attacked the giant!

Mac hesitated, then relaxed his hold, letting her slip free to protectively hug all four of her children. "Mind telling me what incited this little riot?" he asked the man who was now standing and wiping his bleeding cheek with the back of his hand.

The guy gestured toward the lower parking lot. "I was taking the boy to find his parents, because I caught him inside my excavator not five minutes after I'd just pulled him off it and told him to go play someplace else." He shrugged. "I figured his mother or father could explain how dangerous earth-moving equipment is, since he didn't seem to want to listen to me." He suddenly stiffened, his gaze darting from Jacob to Peter and then to Peg. "They're twins." His eyes narrowed on the boys again. "Identical."

Pushing her children behind her, Peg stepped toward him. "I don't care if they're sextuplets and were *driving* your excavator or stupid submarine." She pointed an unsteady finger at him. "You have no business manhandling my kids. And if you ever touch one of them again, I swear to God I'll—"

"Take it easy, mama bear," Mac said, dragging her back against him again. "He was only concerned for Jacob's safety. As well as yours, apparently," Mac said quietly next to her ear. "Did you not notice he didn't defend himself when you and your children were attacking him? Duncan's intentions were good."

Peg stilled, a feeling of dread clenching her stomach. "D-Duncan?" she whispered, craning to look at Mac. "He . . . he's not Claude, the scientist?" She lifted her hands to cover her face. "Ohmigod, I thought he was the guy who scolded Jacob for climbing on the submarine yesterday."

She peeked through her fingers at the man she and her kids had just attacked, horror washing through her when she saw the blood on his cheek and scratches on his neck. "Ohmigod, I'm *sorry*," she cried, jerking away from Mac and rushing to her children. Even though he was over half as tall as she was, Peg picked up Jacob and set him on her hip as she herded the others ahead of her, wanting to flee the scene of their crime before she burst into tears. "C-come on, guys," she whispered roughly, her heart pounding so hard it hurt. "Let's go to the van."

Mac's father plucked Jacob out of her arms and settled him against his chest, giving the boy a warm smile as he smoothed down his hair. "That was quite a battle you waged, young Mr. Thompson," Titus Oceanus said jovially, shooting Peg a wink as he took over herding her children away when Mac pulled her to a stop. "I'll have to remember to call on you young people if I ever find myself in a scary situation," Titus continued, his voice trailing off as he redirected them toward the main lodge.

Damn. Why couldn't Mac let her slink away like the humiliated idiot she was?

"It will be easier to face him now rather than later," Mac said, giving her trembling hand a squeeze as he led her back to the scene of her crime. "Duncan's a good man, Peg, and you're going to be seeing a lot of him in the next couple of years."

Wonderful. How pleasant for the *both* of them.

"Duncan," Mac said as he stopped in front of the battered and bleeding giant. "This beautiful, protective mama bear is Peg Thompson."

God, she wished he'd quit calling her that.

"She's not only Olivia's good friend, but Peg is in charge of keeping the chaos to a minimum here at Inglenook." He chuckled. "That is, when she's not creating it. Peg, this is Duncan MacKeage. First thing Monday morning, he and his crew are going to start building a road up the mountain to the site of our new resort."

MacKeage. MacKeage. Why did that name sound familiar to her?

All Peg could do was stare at the hand her victim was holding out to her, feeling her cheeks fill with heat when she saw the blood on it. Which he obviously only just noticed, since he suddenly wiped his hand on his pants, then held it out again.

Peg finally found the nerve to reach out, saw his blood on *her* hand, and immediately tucked both her hands behind her back. "I'm sorry," she whispered, unable to lift her gaze above the second button on his shirt—which she noticed was missing. "We . . . I thought you were the man who scared Jacob yesterday. He had nightmares all night and I barely got him back here today."

He dropped his hand to his side. "I'm the one who needs to apologize, Mrs. Thompson, as I believe you're correct that I shouldn't have touched your son." She saw him shift his weight to one leg and noticed the dirt on his pants and small tear on one knee. "I assumed he was the boy I'd just told to get off the excavator. And having a large family of young cousins, I thought nothing of lugging him off in search of his mother or father." He held out his hand again. "So I guess I deserved that thrashing."

Damn. She was going to have to touch him or risk looking petty. Mac nudged her with his elbow. After wiping her fingers on her pants, Peg finally reached out, and then watched her hand disappear when Duncan Mac-Keage gently folded his long, calloused fingers around it.

Oh yeah; she had been a raving lunatic to attack this giant of a man. Not that she wouldn't do it again if she thought her kids were being threatened.

Okay, maybe she *was* a protective mama bear.

It seemed he had no intention of giving back her hand until she said something. But what? *Nice to meet you? I look forward to bumping into you again? Have we met before? Because I'm sure I know someone named Mac-Keage.*

Damn. She should at least look him in the eye when she apologized—again.

But Peg figured the first three times hadn't counted, since she'd mostly been sorry that she'd made a complete fool of herself trying to gouge out his eyes with her *bare* hands. But looking any higher than that missing shirt button was beyond her. "I'm sorry!" she cried, jerking her hand from his and bolting for the main lodge, her face blistering with shame when she heard Mac's heavy sigh.

Duncan stood leaning against the wall of Inglenook's crowded dining hall, shifting his weight off his wrenched knee as he took another sip of the foulest kick-in-the-ass ale he'd ever had the misfortune to taste, even as he wondered if Mac was trying to impress his guests by serving the rotgut or was making sure they never darkened his doorstep again. He did have to admit the ancient mead certainly took some of the sting out of the claw marks on his neck, although it did nothing to soothe his dented pride at being blindsided by a mere slip of a woman and her kids.

Hell, if Mac and Titus hadn't intervened, he'd probably still be getting pummeled.

Duncan slid his gaze to the bridesmaid sitting at one of the side tables with her four perfectly behaved children, and watched another poor chump looking for a dance walk away empty-handed. Peg Thompson appeared to be a study of innate grace, quiet poise, and an understated beauty of wavy blond hair framing a delicate face and dark blue eyes—which was one hell of a disguise, he'd discovered this morning. He couldn't remember the last time a woman had left her mark on him, much less taken him by surprise, which perversely made him wonder what the hellcat was like in bed.

She was a local woman and a widow, raising her four children single-handedly for the last three years, Mac had told Duncan just before leaving him standing in the parking lot bleeding all over his good shirt. After, that is, Mac had subtly explained that he also felt quite protective of his wife's friend. A warning Duncan didn't take lightly, considering Maximilian Oceanus had the power to move mountains, create inland seas, and alter the very fabric of life for anyone foolish enough to piss him off.

But having been raised with the magic, Duncan wasn't inclined to let the powerful wizard intimidate him overly much. He was a MacKeage, after all, born into a clan of twelfth-century highland warriors brought to modern-day Maine by a bumbling and now—thank God—powerless old drùidh.

And since his father, Callum, was one of the original five displaced warriors, not only had Duncan been raised to respect the magic, he'd been taught from birth not to fear it, either. In fact, the sons and daughters and now the grandchildren of the original MacKeage and MacBain time-travelers had learned to use the magic to their advantage even while discovering many of them had some rather unique gifts of their own.

Hell, his cousin, Winter, was an actual drùidh married to Matt Gregor, also known as Cùram de Gairn, who was one of the most powerful magic-makers ever to exist. And Robbie MacBain, another cousin whose father had also come from twelfth-century Scotland, was Guardian of their clans and could actually travel through time at will. In fact, all his MacKeage and MacBain and Gregor cousins, whose numbers were increasing exponentially with each passing year, had varying degrees of magical powers. For some it might only be the ability to light a candle with their finger, whereas others could heal, control the power of mountains, and even shape-shift.

Duncan had spent the last thirty-five years wondering what his particular gift was. Not that he was in any hurry to find out, having several childhood scars from when more than one cousin's attempts to work the magic had backfired.

That's why what had happened here last week wasn't the least bit of a mystery to the clans, just an unpleasant shock to realize that Maximilian Oceanus had decided to make his home in Maine when the wizard had started rearranging the mountains and lakes to satisfy his desire to be near salt water and the woman he loved.

Duncan sure as hell wasn't complaining, since he was benefiting financially. Mac was building his bride a fancy resort up on one of the mountains he'd moved and had hired MacKeage Construction to do a little earth-moving of its own by building the road and prepping the resort site. Duncan figured the project would keep his fifteen-man crew and machinery working for at least two years.

And in this economy, that was *true* magic.

Spellbound Falls and Turtleback Station would certainly reap the rewards of Mac's epic stunt, since there wasn't much else around to bolster people's standard of living. Not only would the resort keep the locals employed, but stores and restaurants and artisan shops would soon follow the influx of tourists.

It would be much like what the MacKeage family business, TarStone Mountain Ski Resort, had done for Pine

Creek, which was another small town about a hundred miles south as the crow flies. Only it was too bad Mac hadn't parted a few more mountains to make a direct route from Pine Creek to Spellbound, so Duncan wouldn't have to build a temporary camp for his crew to stay at through the week. As it was now, they had to drive halfway to Bangor before turning north and west again, making it a three-hour trip.

Then again, maybe Mac didn't want a direct route, since the clans had recently learned the wizard was actually allergic to the energy the drùidhs he commanded gave off. And that had everyone wondering why Mac had decided to live so close to Matt and Winter Gregor, who were two of the most powerful drùidhs on earth.

Apparently the wizard's love for Olivia was greater than his desire to breathe.

Not that Duncan really cared why Mac was here; only that the money in his reputed bottomless satchel was green.

"Have ye recovered from your trouncing this morning, MacKeage?" Kenzie Gregor asked. He looked toward the Thompson family sitting quietly at their table and chuckled. "I can see why ye were so soundly defeated, as together the five of them must outweigh you by at least two stone."

Wonderful; help a man rebuild his home after it was nearly destroyed by a demonic coastal storm, and the guy felt the need to get in a shot of his own. But then, Kenzie was an eleventh-century highlander who'd only arrived in this time a few years ago, so Duncan figured the warrior didn't know better than to poke fun at a MacKeage.

Kenzie might have his drùidh brother Matt to back him up, but the sheer number of MacKeages was usually enough to keep even good-natured ribbing to a minimum.

"If you're needing a lesson on defending yourself," William Killkenny said as he walked up, a large tankard of mead in the ninth-century Irishman's fist, "we could go find a clearing in the woods. I have my sword in the truck, and I'm more than willing to show another one of you moderns the art of proper fighting." He looked toward the Thompson table, then back at Duncan and shook his head. "It pains me to see a man defeated by a wee slip of a woman and a few bairns."

"I think Duncan is probably more in need of dance lessons," Trace Huntsman said, joining the group. "Have I taught you nothing of modern warfare, Killkenny?" Trace slapped Duncan on the shoulder even as he eyed William, making Duncan shift his weight back onto his wrenched knee. "Our friend here knows the only way he's going to defeat the Thompson army is to lure their leader over to his side. And women today prefer a little wooing to feeling the flat of a sword on their backsides."

William arched a brow. "Then someone should have explained that to his cousin, don't ye think? Hamish kidnapped Susan Wakely right out of Kenzie's dooryard in broad daylight, and rumor has it he wouldn't let the woman leave the mountain cabin he took her to until she agreed to marry him."

Trace gave Duncan a slow grin. "So I guess it's true that you first-generation MacKeages inherited many of your fathers' bad habits?" He shook his head. "You do know you're giving us moderns a bad reputation with women, don't you?" He nodded toward the Thompson table. "Maybe you should go ask her to dance and show these two throwbacks a better way to win the battle of the sexes."

"And let her trounce me twice in one day?" Duncan gestured in Peg's direction. "I believe that's bachelor number five walking away now, looking more shell-shocked than I was this morning."

"Sweet Christ," William muttered. "The woman just refused to dance with a fourteenth-century king of Prussia."

"Who in hell are all these people?" Duncan asked, looking around Inglenook's crowded dining hall.

"Friends of Titus, mostly," William said, "who aren't about to incur old man Oceanus' wrath by not showing up to his only son's wedding."

"I can't believe he dared to put time-travelers in the same room with modern locals," Trace said, also glancing around.

"And serve liquor," Duncan added, just before taking another sip of mead—because he really needed another good kick-in-the-ass. His knee was throbbing, the scratches on his neck were burning under his collar, and social gatherings weren't exactly his idea of a good time. But like most everyone else here today—the small party from Midnight Bay plaguing him now likely the only exception—Duncan wasn't about to insult the younger Oceanus, either, considering Mac was his meal ticket for the next two years.

"Uh-oh, your target is on the move," William said, his gaze following Peg Thompson and her ambushing children as they headed for the buffet table. He nudged Duncan. "Now's your chance to show us how it's done, MacKeage. Go strike up a conversation with the lass."

"Maybe you could offer to let her children sit in your earth-moving machine," Kenzie suggested. "That would show her ye don't have any hard feelings."

"Kids and heavy equipment are a dangerous mix," Duncan growled, glaring at the three of them. "Don't you gentlemen have wives and a girlfriend you should be pestering?" He elbowed William. "Isn't that Maddy dancing with the king of Prussia?"

"Oh, Christ," William muttered, striding off to go reclaim his woman.

Kenzie also rushed off with a muttered curse when he saw his wife, Eve, start to breastfeed their young infant son under a blanket thrown over her shoulder.

Trace Huntsman, however, didn't appear to be in any hurry to leave. "If it's any consolation," Trace said, "Peg Thompson was more rattled by this morning's attack than you were. Maddy and Eve and my girlfriend, Fiona, were there when Peg came to Olivia's cottage. Fiona told me it took the four of them over twenty minutes to calm her down." He shot Duncan a grin. "The women all promised Peg they would have done the exact same thing if they'd caught a stranger manhandling their child. Can I ask what you were thinking?"

"I wasn't thinking," Duncan said. "I manhandle dozens of children every time my family gets together. Everyone looks out for everyone's kids, making sure the little heathens don't kill themselves or each other. Hell, that's the definition of *clan*."

Duncan tugged his collar away from his neck as he eyed the widow Thompson leading her gaggle of children back to their table, each trying to reach it without spilling their plates of food. He sighed, figuring he probably better apologize to her again, seeing how she owned the only working gravel pit in the area.

Just as soon as Mac had hired him to do the resort's site work, Duncan had started calling around to find the closest gravel pit to Spellbound Falls. He would eventually dig his own pit farther up the mountain, but he needed immediate access to gravel to start building the road. Duncan had been relieved to discover that the Thompson pit was just a mile from where the resort road would start, and that it had a horseback of good bank run gravel. Only he'd also learned Bill Thompson had been killed in a construction accident three years ago.

Which is why a feather could have knocked him over this morning as he'd stood beside his truck in the parking lot changing his shirt, when he'd finally put two and two together and realized he'd just pissed off the person he wanted to buy gravel from. Assuming she'd even sell to him now. And then even if she did, he'd likely be paying an arm and a leg for every last rock and grain of sand.

"Which branch of the military were you in?" Trace asked.

Duncan looked down at himself in surprise. "Funny; I could have sworn I left my uniform in Iraq."

Trace chuckled. "You forgot to leave that guarded look with it." He shrugged. "It's common knowledge that every MacKeage and MacBain serves a stint in the military." He suddenly frowned. "Only I've never heard it said that any of the women in your families have served."

"And they won't as long as Greylen MacKeage and Michael MacBain are still lairds of our clans," Duncan said with a grin. "It'll take a few more generations before we let our women deliberately put themselves in harm's way."

Trace shook his head. "You really are all throwbacks. You must have a hell of a time finding wives. Or is that why some of you resort to kidnapping?"

Duncan decided he liked Trace Huntsman. "There's no 'resorting' to it; we're merely continuing a family tradition that actually seems to work more often than it backfires. And besides, it beats the hell out of wasting time dating a woman for two or three years once we've found the right one."

"You don't think the woman might like to make sure *you're* the right one before she finds herself walking down the aisle, wondering how she got there?"

Duncan shifted his weight off his knee with a shrug. "Not according to my father. Dad claims time is the enemy when it comes to courting; that if a man takes too long wooing a woman, then he might as well hand her his manhood on a platter."

Trace eyed him suspiciously. "Are you serious?"

"Tell me, Huntsman; how's courting Fiona been working for you?"

"We're not talking about me," he growled. "We're talking about you MacKeages and your habit of scaring women into marrying you."

"I did notice you managed to get an engagement ring on her finger," Duncan pressed on. "So when's the wedding?"

Trace relaxed back on his hips and folded his arms over his chest with a heavy sigh. "You don't happen to have an available cabin in Pine Creek, do you?"

Duncan slapped Trace on the back and started them toward the refreshment table. "Considering Fiona is Matt Gregor's baby sister, I think you might want to look for a cabin a little farther away. Hell, everyone within twenty miles of Pine Creek heard Matt's roar when he learned she was openly living with you without benefit of marriage."

Trace stopped in front of the large bowl of dark ale and glared at Duncan. "A fact that has brought us full circle back to women being warriors. The only reason I'm still alive is because Fiona puts the fear of God into her brothers if they so much as frown at me." He looked at Peg Thompson, then back at Duncan—specifically at the scratch on his cheek. "Trust me; the strong-arm approach won't work on any woman who can handle children. Not if a man values his hide."

Duncan refilled his tankard. "Which is exactly why I'm still a bachelor," he said, just before gulping down his third kick-in-the-ass like a true highlander.

From *New York Times* bestselling author
Janet Chapman

The Highlander
Next Door

A Spellbound Falls Romance

———

Legend has it love is carried on the rising mists of Spellbound Falls, and not even time-traveling highlanders are immune to its magic...

Birch Callahan has seen the trouble men can cause. After witnessing her mother's four marriages, Birch now runs a women's shelter and doesn't want a man in her life. But there's something about her neighbor, Niall MacKeage. Birch can't figure out how the cop can be so big and gruff and yet so insightful and compassionate—and sexy. Or how she's falling for a man who acts like someone from the twelfth century.

Niall knows that Birch is attracted to him, even if she seems to distrust all men. Yet he also knows she has a secret—something that drives her to place herself in harm's way for the women of her shelter. Niall would gladly rush to Birch's side to protect her from harm, but with their secrets standing between them, he'll have to reveal his own truth if he wants to keep her...

janetchapman.com
facebook.com/LoveAlwaysBooks
penguin.com

M1677T0515

From *New York Times* bestselling author
Janet Chapman

For the Love of Magic

A Spellbound Falls Romance

After forty years of marriage, Rana Oceanus has done the unthinkable and run away from her mighty, magical husband. Not that she ran very far, having purchased a house in Spellbound Falls right on the shore of the Bottomless Sea, where she intends to prepare for the scariest battle of her life. The only flaw in her plan, however, is that she is still very much in love with Titus...

Shocked and deeply shaken that his wife really has left him—though he still can't fathom why—Titus sets out to win her back. But when grand gestures of his esteem don't seem to further his cause, he conjures up some of his original courtship magic. His plan backfires when Titus discovers that dealing with demons is far less threatening than the little secret his very mortal wife has been keeping from him...

janetchapman.com
facebook.com/LoveAlwaysBooks
penguin.com